ANDRE NORTON
& LYN McCONCHIE
the KEY of the KEPLIAN

ASPECT

WARNER BOOKS

A Time Warner Company

WARNER BOOKS EDITION

Cover design by Don Puckey
Cover illustration by Kevin Johnson

Aspect is a trademark of Warner Books, Inc.

Warner Books, Inc.
1271 Avenue of the Americas
New York, NY 10020

Ⓦ A Time Warner Company

Printed in the United States of America

First Printing: July, 1995

10 9 8 7 6 5 4 3 2 1

STALLION OF LIGHT

◆ ◆ ◆

Eleeri bent her concentration on the pendant. Around it grew a soft glow, a blue-green that brightened by the minute. Without thinking, she reached out and gently drew the Keplians into the mind-link. The pendant flared with a blaze of light so great that her eyes shut involuntarily. She opened her eyes to stare in wonder.

Before them stood her pendant made flesh, a great black stallion. No true horse as Eleeri knew: this was the spirit of horses. Intelligence shone from the blazing sapphire eyes, pride in the crest of his upthrust neck. Power flowed in every sinew, power of strength and of the Light.

. Runes flared blue on either side of a gap in the trail. The stallion cantered through and turned to watch them.

Tharna watched the stallion nervously. *Stallions often kill colts that are not their own get. I fear him.*

But before either adult could move, Tharna's foal followed the great beast . . .

◆

"[Witch World is] one of fantasy's most beloved and enduring creations."
—*Rave Reviews*

To those who ensured this book in some way.

To Greg Hills, who persuaded me to begin writing as an amateur.

To Steve Pasechnick of Strange Plasma, who purchased my first professional story.

To my agent, Susan James of Curtis Brown Ltd., whose acceptance of me as a client strengthened my belief in my work.

And to my friend and collaborator Andre Norton. Your books were the first in the genre I ever read. They opened new Worlds and still do. May you live and write them forever—less is unacceptable!

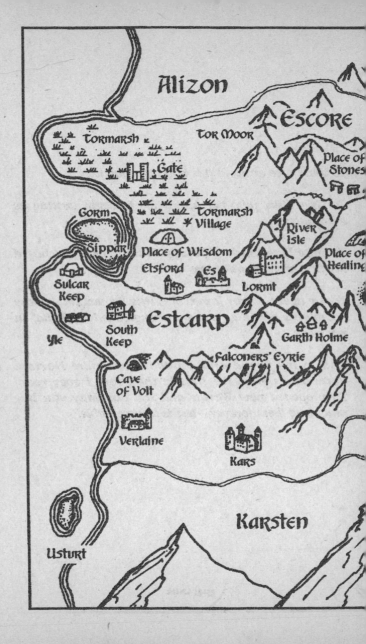

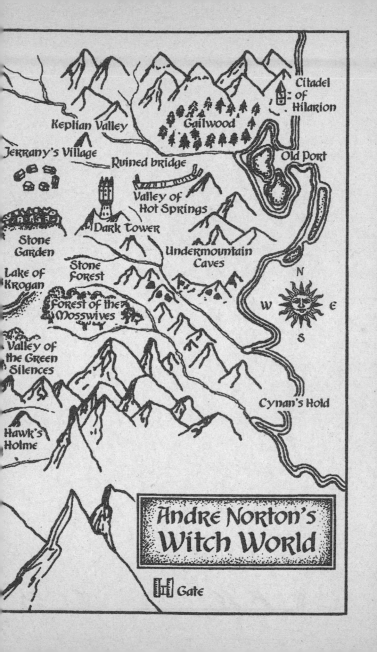

1

The old man was dying. Once, she had thought he would live forever. Now she was older and knew that all things died in their time. This was his. His eyes met hers calmly and she knew then that he would tell her what to do.

He studied her as she crouched beside him. She was too thin for beauty but in his eyes she was not only beautiful, she was beloved: the daughter of his son's daughter and his only living descendant. The coming of another race had been hard on his people. Too many had died from diseases they had never known as free-rangers. Others had taken as starving coyotes to the firewater offered all too often.

Disease had slain his son, ill fortune the boy's daughter and her man, leaving this one alone. Other blood had mingled with that of the Nemunuh over the generations: his own mother had been half Navajo, the daughter of a white man by his Indian wife. His eyes watched the girl. Eleeri he had named her, from the ancient tongue used only by those of power. There were few of those nowadays; in too many lines the gift had faltered and died. But in the child it had come again, flowering into the true horse-gift and into ties with other life.

The girl watched him, sorrow in the huge gray eyes. Her long black hair hung past her thin shoulder and she brushed the shining strands back with an impatient hand. As her hand lifted, powerful tendons stood out in the hollow of a wrist. The slenderness was a disguise; here was one who was all wire and whipcord. Long, long ago, women had been warriors and accepted so by the Nemunuh. Far Traveler had trained his great-granddaughter well. In these degenerate days none of the young men could match her in bow or knife skill. Nor could any, man or woman, match her with horse or hunt. He smiled up at her, then spoke, his voice weak but clear.

"I named you Eleeri. Now you must prove my naming."

The child was puzzled. That her name meant "Walker by Strange Roads" she had always known. But what road was she to walk? The old man smiled at the wrinkled brow.

"Go into the high hills, find there the beginning of the road of the gone-before ones. That you shall walk, leaving fear behind you. Walk as a warrior. As the last of my line shall you go forth with all I can give you." A jerk of his head indicated a small heap in the darkened corner of the room. "At sunhigh let you go with the light, and Ka-dih bless you." He sighed softly. "Would that you could ride, but I sold the last horse. Nor can you wait too long. The woman who calls on us will come today. You must be well gone before she arrives."

Eleeri shivered. She must indeed. It had been only her great-grandfather who had saved her six years ago. She remembered the brutalities of her aunt and uncle. Her father had not disdained the Indian blood of the bride he had taken, but his sister and the rancher she had wed had been far otherwise. When Far Traveler died, by white man's law she would fall back into their hands, being not quite sixteen. If there was a way to flee, she would take it.

A road of the gone-before ones? Her heart leaped. Many were the stories of those ancient people; even in the school she attended the truth was known. Some of it, at least. She had read there of the Anasazi, the books reinforcing the old tales Far Traveler had first heard from his mother. But that there was a road she had never known.

Black eyes twinkled in her great-grandfather's seamed face. A face like a map of the hills and gullies of his land. Brown as the dust, yet alive as the land itself.

"Bring me my parfleche." She brought the tanned deerskin war bag and waited. From it he drew out a piece of white deerskin tanned and scraped to perfect suppleness. He spread it on the bed and she gazed down. His hand lifted, wavering a little.

"Here . . ." his fingers touched, "here is our land. Follow the stream high into the hills. Upon the hillside, there is first the white stump of a great tree struck by lightning." Eleeri nodded; she had seen that. "Farther up, there are the marks of a place where the hills fell long ago. Quartz seams the rocks above." She nodded again. That, too, she had seen in her hunting. "Leave the stream and follow the map where it shows here." Once again his fingers rested on the skin. He paused to breathe deeply and in the silence they both heard and recognized the sound that came to their ears.

Far Traveler cursed. "She comes, the meddling one. You must leave me and go."

"I will not leave you to die alone." She hurried to the

door and peered out. Many miles down the road, the small red car labored to climb the steep grade. Eleeri seized a key from the hook and ran into the yard. Swiftly she locked the gate into the yard, before running back to her great-grandfather.

"She may think we are out if we keep silent."

The old man chuckled. "That one is like the pack rat; always she pries into every corner. No locked gate will keep her from us long. You know their customs. Once she sees me, she will have you out of here and where you cannot escape. You must run, my child. Run so fast and so far she cannot ever find you again. Only the road will hide you now."

Eleeri set her face. "I will not leave you to die alone."

"I do not plan to die alone," came the low words. "Fetch to me my bow, my knife. Bring the war paint I prepared."

Eleeri ran, to return with the items. Squatting on her heels, she watched as her kinsman rose from his bed. By the sweat on his forehead, she could tell it was a terrible effort, but she did not speak. He had lived as a warrior; it was fitting he should die as one. She watched as he stripped to breechclout and slowly donned his ceremonial buckskins. Arming himself, painted face set, the old man marched to the doorway. Fierce black eyes gazed up at the sun. On the road below, the red car was closer.

He began to chant then, softly. The death song of his race. He finished the first part of the song and turned to her. A hand gestured, then another song lifted into the clear air. Blessings on a warrior about to ride forth. The Blessing of Ka-dih and of the tribe. Then he turned again to look up into the mountains. The chant rose louder as he listed his deeds, prayed that he might be acceptable as a warrior. His song ended on a last wild cry and then his face changed. His hands lifted in greeting and he took a step forward.

As Eleeri gasped, light seemed to flow about him. She felt as if great winds beat about the house, then she cried out as Far Traveler crumpled slowly. Around her, warmth flowed, welcoming a warrior home, comforting her who was left behind. She bowed her head quietly. It was well. Her kin whom she had loved with all her heart was gone on his final journey. It was for her now to take her own road—the road that had been his last gift to her. The red car was nearing the final bend below her. In ten minutes or so it would be at the locked gate. Eleeri remembered her uncle's hate, the beatings, the scorn for a quarter-Indian. She would die before she was returned to that. She set her teeth and with a burst of strength those who did not know her would have found hard to believe, lifted her kinsman and carried him into the house. Swiftly she laid him out on the bed, bow and knife at the ready.

Outside, the car was silenced as it reached the gate. A voice called as the gate was rattled. Eleeri seized the pack and other items laid out waiting. She had no time to look them over. She must trust that her great-grandfather had known what she would need. She stooped to kiss the withered cheek, adding the map to her possessions as she did so. Outside, the voice called again, more urgently. The girl smiled bitterly. Far Traveler had been right about that one. She would not leave without something.

Silently the girl drifted to the back door and opened it. Never settle for one exit, her great-grandfather had always said. And better if the other is hidden. A wicked smile lit Eleeri's face for a moment. She could hear the rattling of the gate as it was climbed, then the voice again, louder, nearer. The front door, too, was locked; that would slow the pack rat. She slipped around the edge of the house using the tumbledown outbuildings as cover. A section of fence lifted aside once two iron pegs were removed. Quietly she replaced it, ramming the pegs home again. That would puzzle the white-eyes. The voice rose urgently, followed soon after by the sounds of a breaking window.

Screams followed, interspersed by cries of Eleeri's name. Feet ran to and fro, the repetitions of the girl's name become almost frantic. Eleeri was sorry for the distress; she supposed the woman meant well. But she would not allow herself to be returned to a home where she was despised. If only Far Traveler had not insisted on helping her work about the house the previous day. Not only had he aided her, he had also been in a shed several hours doing something with the door shut against her. She guessed now that he had felt his death close, and it must have been the pack she carried that he was preparing. The social worker came only once a week. Up until then they had managed to hide Far Traveler's growing weakness from the woman.

They had hoped that his strength would last another few weeks, just until her sixteenth birthday. Then she might have been permitted to live on the few remaining acres in the house the old man had built. She grinned fiercely. Her aunt and uncle would find little of benefit remaining. The land that had once belonged to the Two Feathers family was sold long ago. The personal possessions, the tiny house, and a few acres of waterless land were all that remained. Eleeri could have made a living there. She could hunt, break horses, keep alive a tiny vegetable garden, and thus survive. But to an outsider the inheritance was worthless.

She peered around a tree, eyes searching the yard below her. The figure of the woman emerged, running clumsily from building to building. Eleeri nodded to herself. It would be hours before searchers could arrive. She knew they would come. The social worker was not one to let her go in peace.

She shouldered her pack and checked her weapons. The map hung limply over her belt, ready to hand, as she leaned into the long climb. She moved with a slow confidence. She must not wind herself in the climb. If she was followed, she might have to use all her strength to escape. Better that she did not waste too soon what strength she had. According to the map there was far to go and all of it through rough country. If they had a helicopter out looking, it would be her skill that saved her, not her strength or speed.

Below, the red car was fleeing down the mountain road. The woman who drove it was equally determined. The child must have taken to the hills. She must be found, taken to a place of safety. Her superior had been a fool to allow the girl to live with that old man. She might have known this would happen. Furthermore, typical man, her supervisor was away from the office when things occurred. She bit her lip thoughtfully: it did leave her in charge. He wouldn't be back for almost a week, and she would have the girl back by then. No matter what he said, the child was under sixteen, and her aunt had always said they would take her back. She ignored the report on file that described the treatment meted out to Eleeri under the guardianship of that same family six years earlier.

So the girl had been punished a time or two. Children needed a firm hand. She drove faster, eager to reach her office and call out those who would find the girl for her. It would take some time, but she was sure she could convince those in authority that the child was in danger. She could lay it on thick: A young girl lost in the mountains, mad with grief. A real suicide risk. If they didn't find her, it might not look good in the papers. She never looked into her own mind, never knew that she had hated a young girl and an old man for their pride, for the dislike they showed when they faced her intrusions.

There had been something in the poise of the girl that had sent a shiver down the social worker's spine. In a land where the deaths of settlers were still remembered, she had not been the right woman to work where she did. Her family remembered even as Eleeri's uncle remembered and recounted the massacre of kin. The woman despised those under her care. That she was despised in turn infuriated her. She would find the girl, give her to a decent civilized family. They'd tame the child.

Far above her now, the "child" climbed beside the stream. Behind her the ancient weathered stump of the tree showed clear in the bright sun. Ahead she could glimpse the scars of the slide that had occurred some one hundred years earlier. They overlay others. For some reason this part of the cliff always slid every century or so. Eleeri gazed up as she neared the base of it. She was still wearing the clothes she had donned on rising. They were her oldest and almost in rags, as she had intended to clean out the rusty iron guttering. She could *spare* them, and she should rest for a while, too.

She dropped her pack well up the stream, returning toward the landslide to climb higher. Soon she was at the top, surveying the fragile crumbling rock at her feet. She smiled a little. Far Traveler had always said that a trick was worth miles to the pursued. Some time later a long rumbling roar of sound echoed around the nearby hills. A scrap of shirt showed at the edge of the new mounds of scree. If they dug, they would find more scraps deeper in. She had placed them there before she started the slide. From then on she took to the stream itself. Let them try to track in the water; she knew a place she could emerge without leaving scent easily found. She hurried now; the water was freezing.

Farther along her trail, she rested and ate some of the food Far Traveler had provided in the pack. As she did so, she explored the pack's contents with interest. Clothing, a complete case of stainless steel needles in all sizes, thread, fish hooks, the list appeared endless. But then the pack was no mere rucksack, but one of the large, framed type which could carry a hundred pounds weight of supplies at need—and if the wearer could bear the weight. It appeared to be empty now, and she lifted it to begin the repacking. That was odd, there was still weight. She delved, turning the pack inside out to find that under a layer of cloth, there was a leather belt finely carved with a line of running horses. It bore a bone buckle, engraved with tiny prancing horses, their eyes inlaid in jet. The weight as she held it up explained the still heavy pack which might now be light enough to be truly empty. Fascinated, she turned the belt over, examining the back.

Ah! It was laced with a long sinew. She pulled that out partway and peered inside the overlapping edges. Then she sat back. How long had Far Traveler planned her escape, had he always feared his life would be ended too soon for her safety? Within the belt lay treasure. Gold, melted and cast into thin disks from the pinches of gold dust he had panned for years from this stream. It had never been worth the work to others. A week's hard labor would produce less than a fifth of one of these disks. A man could work in a better job for far better wages any day. Yet for years her great-grandfather must have toiled to gather the yellow grains and melt them into this.

She lifted the pack but still it felt a fraction too heavy to her balancing hands. She dug under the cloth lining again to come up with a small doeskin pouch. Opening it she spilled the contents onto a palm. Purple fire caught sunlight, blue and softer amber glowing among the color. Kadih, but the old man must have been gathering this for long. Amethyst was found in the hills hereabouts, but the pieces were usually flawed. These were not. They were small, but of the finest, clearest color she had ever seen. Even as a semiprecious stone they were worth much money.

She studied the stones that added blue hues. They had to be sapphires. But where had Far Traveler found those? There were none of that stone in her mountains. Not that there were many here—she counted five—but they appeared to be fine stones as well. She also found amber: two pieces carrying burdens within them. Seeds of some plant she had never seen before.

She picked one out curiously. Her fingers seemed to transmit warmth to the amber, and to her surprise, it glowed. She put it down again. Perhaps her great-grandfather had known more than he had said about the road she was to follow. She had a feeling that the amethyst stones were for trade—the gold, too—but the amber might have another purpose. Idly she placed a piece of it in her pocket, then, moved by something, she placed the second piece in a pocket on the other side of her jeans. She carefully repacked her belongings and stood up. By now the woman from social services must have reached the township. The hunt would soon be raised.

In that Eleeri was only partly correct. The law there was reluctant to become involved. It was several hours before they agreed to send out searchers, and by then it was close to darkness. The hunt was held up until morning, and Eleeri gained time. Time she used well, moving along the trails at a steady stride as she kept one eye on the map. She kept moving until dusk on that second day, then made a quick camp. Carefully she rolled a half-buried stone aside and lit her fire within the hollow. She ate, drank, and studied her tiny camp. The gathered fire-wood would do until dawn. The rocks behind her would reflect the fire's heat to where she lay, and the plaited grass screen would help to keep the heat in and the drafts out.

She rose at first light to eat, and drink hot tea. Then she rolled the stone back into place, hiding the ashes of her fire. She rubbed the underside of the rock with pungent leaves before she did so. That should baffle any trailing noses.

She trotted down to the trickle of water, carrying her pack. Once there, she stripped and washed. Then she packed her jeans and other clothing, taking out instead her deerskin shirt and pants. She put on the carved belt with its secrets, tucked the pouch into the front, and added the knife in its fringed sheath to the belt. Her bow and quiver were hung within easy reach on the pack corner.

She looked at the map long and hard. From here on she would be in strange country. In her hunting she had ranged far, but never in this particular direction. She must now rely on the map and her good sense. Setting her shoulders, she began to follow a faint deer trail. It went in the right direction and would make for easier walking— for a while, at least. She moved steadily on as the sun rose. At midmorning she halted to drink a little and rest a few minutes. Then she was moving on again. By noon she was deep into unknown mountains on a trail that skirted a drop far down to canyons below. She wondered what the woman from social services was doing now.

Then she turned her mind resolutely. To allow fear of pursuit to overcome one was folly, so Far Traveler had always said. It weakened the pursued, strengthened the pursuer. She was child to this land; it would not give her up lightly. She was warrior; she would not surrender easily. Far down her back trail, men dug frantically in a fresh slide. It would take them all day to be sure no child's body lay under the weight of rocks and cold earth. But the feeling she had been tricked strengthened the rage and determination of the pursuer. The woman drove back down the road, cold fury in her eyes. She had been promised a helicopter the next morning.

Another night, another camp, and Eleeri slept soundly, but by dawn she was gone, following the map. She was nearing her destination if she had not misread, and her heart was torn. To leave her own land, her own place, never to stand beside Far Traveler again . . . she shrugged that last away. No matter if she stayed or went, her kinsman and her home were gone.

She pushed on through the day. By now she guessed that those who hunted her would have found the slide to be a trick. That would please nobody—to be made a fool of by a young girl. Still, what matter, if it had bought her another day?

It was almost noon when she heard the first sounds of helicopter blades above her. At once she ducked into a crevice. As she stretched along it, her doeskins blended into the dry brown earth. She remained motionless as the helicopter swooped overhead. Nor did she turn her face upward—Far Traveler had warned her against that.

Long ago he had fought in the white man's war. Planes then had been able to see the shade of an upturned face. They would fly low to encourage movement. She stayed facedown and silent. The sound beat away to the east and she moved then, running lightly along the trail into the cover of brush ahead. From then on, she moved with caution, one ear open always to the sky. Twice more the helicopter swept overhead as it searched. She cursed it savagely. Why were they hunting her in this direction? What had led them to think she would be in this part of the mountains?

Eleeri had no way of knowing that the woman had enlisted the aid of a rancher with dogs. It had taken long enough, but finally they had struck her trail where she had left the stream. Now they followed, the copter ranging ahead. Twice where it could, the machine had landed, airlifting man and dogs over a rougher time-consuming area of the trail.

They were closing in on her, Eleeri thought. Somehow they were moving faster than she could. She halted in cover to stare at the map once more. There! She was to take the right-hand fork of a path that led from a certain rock. If the rock was still standing, if the path still existed. By now she was certain that the map was old, very, very old. The land had changed over the years. She could only press on and pray it had not changed more than she could recognize.

At least the rock was there. She halted to peer at it. Yes, she was sure this was the one. It had the vague outline of a hawk. There was no longer any sign of a path, but if she went to the right, there was footing through a patch of upraised rock spikes. She prayed she was on the correct path.

By now the baying of dogs carried to her ears. The copter was overhead more often, so that she could only advance in short rushes where there was cover as the aircraft swung away. But the depression she followed brought her to the next sign, a cave mouth she passed quickly. She halted for a moment in shadow to listen. The dogs must be a scant hour behind her now. Far less as the crow flew, but with the mountains as they were, only a crow could travel directly. Dark was closing in and the watcher overhead was departing.

She gazed at her map in despair. There were still some miles to go. She sank to the ground, her shoulders aching, her legs leaden. She was hungry. She must rest, eat, and hope for a miracle. She ate and drank swiftly and lay down wrapped in the soft hand-woven blanket that had been in the pack.

For a couple of hours she slept heavily, then something caused her to wake with a start. She sat up to gaze about her. Bright as the last days had been, the nights had clouded over with each dusk. Now above her the stars shone out.

For a moment she bowed her head. The gods were kind to their daughter. Now she had light for her feet: the moonlight would make a path she could follow. She must go more slowly, the shadows could be treacherous, but she could walk—and walk she would. She gathered her pack onto still-weary shoulders. Slowly she trudged down the smoother way that lay before her. This way, or so the map claimed. If she could put enough distance between her and those who followed, she might reach sanctuary before they could take her. She had no idea what she would find at the end of the road. Only that Far Traveler had been certain that, once there, she could not be followed.

She walked the moon down, then rested until faint light began to glow in the sky. Then she stood and walked again, more swiftly now, pushing herself, feeling the strength drain from her body. It no longer mattered. She would reach sanctuary and rest, or she would be taken. Either way, her growing exhaustion was of no account. She set her teeth and thrust herself onward grimly.

The water bottle at her belt was all but empty. She kept herself to small sips. She brought out the map one last time—yes, here. She had almost reached the place. She stood in slumped weariness as she stared at the trail ahead. Her eyes teared. That—*that* was her sanctuary?

Ahead, the path narrowed to nothing at the edge of a cliff. Two great rocks stood sentinel before the drop. Across them another had fallen, like the lintel of a doorway to thin air.

A trickle of water ran over the cliff face where she stood. As one in a dream, she rinsed her water bottle, drank, and refilled it, hooking it back to her belt. A fatalism possessed her. It was ended, she had beaten them all to reach her sanctuary—and for what? For a place to die? Far below she could hear the roaring of the river. Then from behind a ridge the copter swooped. She could see a triumphant face staring out at her as it swung past.

Warrior fury rose to possess her now. Once her people had been the rulers of the land. The Nemunuh, the enemy people. Was she now to be taken like a rat in a trap—she, daughter of the people, child of a line who had tamed the horse and ridden all the plain? Far Traveler would not have sent her here to die. This was a thing of medicine, a path of power. She would trust the power. She rose and stretched almost casually; then like a sprinter she hurtled forward, pack bouncing. Within the hovering machine, triumph turned to horror. The Social Services woman shrieked wildly.

"Stop her, stop her!"

Eleeri reached the rock guardians and, still running with all her fading strength, plunged through. A flash of chill, a flare of light, and she was still running, but on green, ankle-high grass. She halted, stared wildly about her, and then her legs gave way and she sprawled onto soft turf. Behind her was nothing: no rocks, and mountains only far into the distance. The air was sweet with bird song and the scent of growing things.

Silently she bowed her head. She had been right to trust. Here she would rest, and later she would travel toward the mountains. With a deep feeling of contentedness, she laid out her food and unhooked her water bottle. Silently, as she feasted, she thanked the gone-before ones for their mercy, and for their road.

Above the mountains the helicopter had turned for town again. In it the woman from Social Services was busy with her excuses. She'd been right, the girl *was* suicidal, it had been correct to pursue her. No doubt they would find the body when the river chose to deliver it downstream. If not, well, it wasn't important. There were other files, other people to be seen to.

The man who rode with her was silent. He knew what he'd seen. He also knew better than to speak of it. But in his mind and to the end of his time he retained the memory of a green land, only a brief flash, but it would keep him wondering as long as his life lasted. There had been something about the place, something that had called him. Still, he would say nothing. If the child *had* escaped, what was it to him? Good luck to her.

2

A bird was singing loudly somewhere close by as Eleeri sat up. Her eyes were busy about this new land. Legend had it that there was no going back, that no one who walked the road of the gone-before ones ever returned. She shrugged. She could get killed just as easily back there as here. At least here there was no welfare and her aunt and uncle couldn't reach her. She'd be careful, though. There might be worse things than those that had sent her running. She folded her blanket, putting everything but some food back in the pack tidily. Then she began to walk as she ate.

The mountains drew her as they loomed in the distance. By her calculation it was some twenty miles before she would strike the foothills. She'd skirt them and continue east; there was something in that direction which seemed to draw her. She tramped cheerfully, eyes and ears alert. The land appeared deserted. It was strange: so fertile, so rich, yet without people or homes. She scanned the grass.

Perhaps this area was like the plains her kind had roamed once. Perhaps there were other tribes here who would challenge her.

She rested and ate at sunhigh, then moved on. Slowly out of the heat haze, buildings began to appear. They were a little off to her right and she veered away, moving more slowly. She could hear no sounds. Workers usually made noise, but here there was only silence. She circled cautiously, in no hurry; this was all unknown territory—wise to be watchful. As she moved in toward the clump of buildings, however, she could see that they must be abandoned. Here and there a roof had fallen in; signs of fire showed. Finally she allowed her feet to drift up to where the main door had once kept out all intruders.

She slipped inside like a shadow, eyes flickering about. Her skin crawled. Something bad had happened here, and that not so very long ago. The wood still smelled of fire. She touched it, studying the black smudge that fouled her fingertips. She rubbed them together and sniffed. Whatever had happened here had occurred within the last year.

A wind shift brought a ranker scent to her twitching nostrils. She knew that one. It was the stink of meat close to bones. She shivered and moved quietly in that direction. Better to know what it was she faced here.

Her nose led her toward stairs that hung fire-blackened from stone supports. She padded upward, careful to test each step. Here was *not* the place to break bones.

In the largest room above she found the source of the stench and bit back a cry of horror. They'd been a family once. Now they were just bones clothed with rags of flesh, tatters of once-good clothing. From the way they lay and what she could see of clothing and bones, there'd been parents and three small children. Even for the children there'd been no mercy from whomever had struck here.

Now that she was face-to-face with the remains, she could better estimate the age of the destruction. Perhaps six months, more than four or five for sure. Was this an everyday occurrence here, or was the land at war? Eleeri padded lightly from room to room. In each she found death or signs that invaders had searched. This may have been a prosperous place once. She'd found enough signs to know that the occupants had been decently dressed, well housed, with several servants and a dozen workers.

By then her hunt had taken her through the outbuildings as well. All had died, servants with masters; but there were no animal bones. Nor could she find, on casual search, any signs of valuables. The place had been thoroughly looted, and from the signs she suspected it had been before the bodies had cooled.

She was eager now to be on her way. It might go ill for her to be found by those who had done this. Pack bouncing, she trotted briskly away from the roofless hold. She traveled far into dusk, halting only when it was too dark to see. She made no fire; a cold camp was better than an attack in the night.

By daylight she was on her way again. The land was changing as she walked. At first there were only isolated clumps of brush, but gradually they merged into large areas that clothed the flanks of the hills before her. Large trees formed outcrops, islands in the brush and grass. Eleeri felt more comfortable with cover available.

At midday she ducked into a patch of trees and found a small stream. Here she washed, lit her fire using dry wood, and settled to eat. Once the meal was ended, she checked her supplies. Plenty of tea, powdered milk, and salt remained, but most of the solid food was gone. She must find a place she could camp for a longer period and hunt. Meat must be dried or smoked, greens gathered, and a horse found.

She sighed for want of a horse; all her life there'd been horses. All but the period with her aunt and uncle, when they'd refused to allow her one. A horse, a horse, her kingdom for a horse. She giggled softly at the words. She didn't have a realm, but if she did, she might well give it up for a really good horse.

A week later she was still skirting the mountains, but they had turned in a curve to the east, so it was now in that direction she traveled. Several times more she had found homesteads and searched. The results left her wary indeed. No two places had been destroyed at the same time. It meant that either war swept often over this land or there were some exceptionally efficient and unpleasant bandit bands out here somewhere.

From the evidence in one of the homes she knew that the attackers had played the same games with women as that sort did in the world she had left. If she fell into their hands with not even a common language to plead in, events would be probably lethal. She reached up a hand to touch her bow. She would not be taken easily. Those who tried would pay.

By now she was well east and, from the strong breeze, she knew she was traveling toward a sea. She crested a small hill to face that wind. It blew salt air in her nostrils, a promise of fish, driftwood fires, and salt to replenish her small supply. All these were hers in another day. She stood, staring out over the gray waters, wondering who sailed them and in what sort of ships. She had always been self-sufficient, but always before she had had her parents or her great-grandfather to fall back on. Now she was alone, and while it did not frighten her, she wished for company. A horse, Eleeri thought wistfully for the hundredth time. A horse would be wonderful.

She laughed to herself. She was gaining an insight into her ancestors. This must have been how they had once felt, with all the plains spread before them and no way to travel from water source to water source except by foot. Here there was water enough. But she moved so slowly it was as if she were an ant crawling across the face of the land. With a horse she could travel more swiftly, hunt more easily, run from danger faster. She could talk to the horse, care for it, revel in the company of a friend.

She looked ahead thoughtfully. Farther on the mountains seemed to close in towards the shore. They could prevent her continuing North-East. Yet that was the way she was drawn. She shrugged. She would travel in her preferred direction so long as she was able. She did not wish to take to the higher mountains above the foothills she now traversed. Those mountain heights had a strange look to them. The land there looked almost as if it had been wrung out and dried that way.

She had continued to follow the seashore and was not surprised to see a river flowing into the salt water ahead. Rivers, of their nature, flowed seaward. Her head jerked up. People, of their nature, settled in such places. She slunk through cover and turned to follow upriver. Maybe here in this isolated place she might find those still living? She headed deeper into the mountains with every step. It contented her. Of plains blood she might be, but she was mountain-born. Here was her natural home.

A day later she stood on the riverbank, ears alert, eyes watchful. At her feet hoofprints traveled before her, three horses carrying heavy loads, but not so heavy as to indicate double-riding. So, three men, all large and probably strong. There were no signs that others had come this way in a long time. This trio were either rovers or traders traveling to some settlement they knew upriver. But somehow she had the feeling they had not ridden this way to trade. She swung pack to shoulder, trotting swiftly but with ears alert for alien sounds. They came, a confused shouting followed by a man's scream. A horse whinnied as Eleeri broke into a run. She halted within the edge of cover, staring at the scene below.

There was a hollow here, like a sort of shallow dish. Within it were the walls of a small hold and a tiny patch of growing grain. Berry bushes showed bright fruit in a line along one side of the walls. A flowering vine climbed another. But part of the sheltering wall was broken down. Smoke had stained the roof. The violence had reached here, too, but perhaps the people had returned to guide their home into a second, weaker flowering.

Below her a man lay sprawled. Beside him a scruffy pony grazed unconcerned. Her gaze swept on to where one man battled two more. Swords flashed in the weak sunlight and even as she watched, the man on foot staggered and fell.

Both horses had overridden him in the last attack. Now the attackers swung their mounts into a turn less than a hundred yards from where Eleeri watched. She could see their faces, alight with bloodlust and cruelty. Beyond them the man reeled to his feet again, blood streaming down his face and from an arm which hung limp. She watched as he tried valiantly to raise his sword again.

Ka-dih, a warrior fights before me. Eleeri acted without thinking. Her people had always esteemed courage above most other abilities. She reached for a dried stick and broke it with a loud crack that echoed in the trees.

Both horsemen reacted. They split, each spinning in a different direction to face the danger. Experienced, the girl noted. But the only weapons seemed to be swords. There was no sign of guns or even bows. She smiled dangerously, rustling the bushes about her in a quick line. Let them believe she ran in fear.

Like any predator, they reacted to a prey who ran from them, sending the horses in pursuit. They aimed ahead, believing they could cut off the fugitive. But Eleeri had not continued to run. Instead she had doubled back and cut to one side. The horsemen charged into the brush several yards in front of her. Her bow sang a soft death song and both men fell with screams. The first landed limp and motionless, the second thrashed, trying to get to his feet again and failing. He was hard hit but not yet dead.

The girl sprang forward, knife in hand, to be diverted back into cover as the horsemen's previous quarry reeled into view. With a shout he leaped and swung his sword, and the surviving bandit lay still. Now the swordsman peered about and it was with difficulty that Eleeri repressed a gasp as she saw his face clearly for the first time. He looked very like Far Traveler. He was old, wrinkled with age and living, his eyes were gray even as hers, and his gray hair had once been black, or so she thought. Her eyes narrowed as he swayed, then his sword fell from shaking hands.

Before she could move, he simply collapsed. Well, he would come to no harm lying there for a few minutes. Better to secure the horses before they went too far. She shed the pack and ran quickly to cut off their departure. She leaped lightly into a saddle and sent the horse trotting toward the others. With them secured, she could look about her. She beamed at her loot: three horses and all their gear, packs, bedrolls, saddlebags that bulged, weapons, possibly even food. She swung her chosen mount back to where the swordsman had fallen.

Dropping quickly from her horse, she studied the man. It had probably been loss of blood that made him faint. The wounds were not of themselves serious. She bound up his head and tore the shirt seam. Under the torn shirt were the remnants of once-powerful muscles. *Hough!* This one had been a warrior. Remembering the scene which had brought her into the fight, she amended that. He was *still* a warrior. But not a young man anymore. He'd done better, despite his age, than the bandits had expected. One against three and he'd killed one man before they began to get the better of him. She nodded: the dead man's gear and mount would now belong to this swordsman. It was warrior right. She now had twice as much; she'd be content with that.

She looked down, wondering how she was to get the man to shelter. Perhaps a travois? Knife in hand, she moved swiftly, and soon he was back at the gate of the ruined building. Eleeri unhooked the pony and exerted all her strength to drag the stretcher in through the door. Once inside, she allowed herself to rest for a few minutes, then rifled the bandits' packs quickly. She laid out bedding and rolled the man onto it. It was filthy and probably verminous, but it would provide warmth. That was more important than a few fleas and a smell.

Both the man's wounds had stopped bleeding by now. She bathed them in water heated over her small fire, then dusted on antibiotic powder. From what she had always heard, more people in primitive societies died from infection than almost anything else. She checked the packs for food. Dried meat with a foul taste, moldy cheese, stale water. Gods, if she hadn't killed them, their food probably would have. She scraped the mold from the cheese and made soup from her own supplies. This she fed spoonful by spoonful to her half-conscious prize.

He sagged back when she finished feeding him, already asleep again as she rose. The horses should be cared for. Then she could explore while the light lasted. Moving about the beasts, stroking, talking, she allowed herself to relax. With that came the tears. She had wondered what it would be like to kill; now she knew. It felt . . . She paused to consider her own emotions. She hadn't killed to survive. She could have walked on and left the old man to die. She'd chosen instead to fight.

She felt no guilt; the attackers had been killers, torturing and baiting a man old enough to be their father's father. Then why was she crying? She had done right, she felt no great guilt at her deeds. She decided that it was only a relief of tension. She'd been wound so tightly for so many weeks now that it was relief just to relax and be a girl. Tears didn't mean weakness here and now, she decided. Just as long as no one knew or saw.

She wiped her eyes and, with the horses roughly stabled, returned to the main house. This one was different from the others she had seen. It was bare, for one thing. No rotting tapestries, no clothes in chests—no bones, either. Perhaps being so far from the other places, so isolated up in these hills, the people had had time to flee whatever threatened. It was clear where the old man had been sleeping. The one upstairs room with an intact roof showed signs of habitation. For a good long time, too, she guessed. She drifted outside and peered at the berry bushes. She found a container and picked until it was full. Then she tasted one. It was tart but refreshing, bursting juicily under her tongue.

She ate a handful, putting the rest aside for later. She dropped more blankets over the sleeping form by the fire. Her fingers touched his forehead. No fever as yet. Good. She banked the fire carefully, leaving a large log to burn slowly, and placing other branches nearby to feed the fire as it burned down.

Then she slipped outside with her blanket. She'd sleep in the stable. A pile of loose hay was by a door and into that she burrowed, folded blanket beneath her. It was always possible that there were more bandits around. She had no intention of being wrapped in a hampering blanket if they appeared. Hay piled on top of her would provide warmth and concealment. The blanket beneath would keep off the chill of the stone floor.

She slept lightly, but nothing disturbed the night. Waking at dawn as usual, she slipped back to the house. Her charge must have woken at least once during the night. The berry-filled pot had emptied. She picked it up and walked outside. She drifted about the bushes, enjoying the sunshine before returning with a filled container.

Old eyes surveyed her as she entered. He spoke, a slow series of words ending on a rising inflexion that seemed to signify a question.

Eleeri shook her head and spoke in turn. "I don't speak that language. But I'll learn if you teach me." She waited.

The old man looked surprised and spoke again. Eleeri could tell it was not the same tongue as before, but it was still one she did not know. Again she shook her head. A third try, and a third shake of her head. He lay peering at her in bafflement. Then his hands began to move. He reached out for the pot and tapped it, slowly speaking a word. The girl grinned, repeating it carefully. He corrected her pronunciation and moved on.

A week later she had the rudiments of a vocabulary in two languages. By then her new friend was working beside her a short time each day. Twice Eleeri had gone hunting so that now meat dried in the smoke from the hearth.

She learned of the land gradually as her vocabulary grew. Once Karsten had been rich, thinly populated but at peace. But then invaders came and persuaded the ruler to attack some section of his people. A Horning the Ruler had called it, thrice horned to death and destruction.

Cynan, he told her, had been old even then. A neighbor had escaped to warn, and old or not, Cynan had rallied his kin to gather all they had and flee. In Estcarp, those who survived the pursuit had scattered. Grieving for those slain, the old warrior had slipped back across the mountains to hunt a different prey. His hunts had exacted a high blood-price for his dead.

He had gone back then to seek out other fugitives and with them he had traveled again to Estcarp, where distant relatives held their lands. But it was not his land or his home, and he had fretted. He had almost determined to go back when . . . Eleeri was unsure of her understanding at this point. Cynan appeared to be saying that witches had changed the mountains to trap the Karsten army. She shivered. In school they had taught her that superstition was an enemy. But when she looked at these mountains, she feared this was no superstition.

Weeks passed and became months as she stayed with the old man. Winter would be on them soon, and she must increase the food store. Grain now filled one bin, hay the loft above the ancient stable. Smoked and dried meat hung in a larder with apples and other fruit and berries put by for the snows.

From a clay deposit by the river, Eleeri had made dishes fire-baked. To those she had added cooking pots and water containers. Well-washed bedding and hay-stuffed mattresses provided comfort, and the three bandit horses were sleek with good living. Their gear shone, supple with her care, and all three would come at a call to nuzzle her affectionately.

Cynan had noticed that right from the first the beasts had trusted the girl. She might know nothing of witchcraft, but there was power there of some sort. She was the best rider he had ever seen, but beyond that the horses obeyed her in strange ways. She spoke to them, and her requests were granted as if the words were understood.

He and the girl sat by the fire one night. It had snowed for the first time that season and the air beyond the fire's warmth was chill.

"Eleeri, be careful who you approach in this land. The memory of what was done to us lies heavily on Karsten still."

The girl raised eyebrows. "What has that to do with me?"

"Your looks," the old man said bluntly. "You may be no witch, you say you have no power, but you look like one of the race. Gray eyes, black hair." He ticked the points off on his fingers. "Your cheekbones are high and your chin more pointed than blunt. You are slender, as we tend to be." He nodded. "I know you are not of our blood, but from the outside and to one who may have only heard a description, you appear to be of Estcarp. Be very wary. Karsten blames the witches for what happened to their land."

Eleeri snorted. "Oh," she said sarcastically. "It was their duke who went crazy and ordered a massacre. As far as I can see, all the witches did was defend their land and their people."

Her friend sighed. "I know that. But after the turning of the Mountains, I think few were left in this land who were sane. The army died almost to a man in that turning. Women bereaved do not reason, they simply hate. With most of the leaders dead and our duke slain, those left turned often to violence to settle their needs. Those who escaped turned to kill in reply. It became a cycle from which Karsten has never broken."

"Tell me more of the Horning. Why would a ruler murder his own people?" Eleeri questioned.

The old man sighed. "It's a long story, but I will tell you what I can briefly," he said. "Karsten has always been a divided land in some ways. It was my people, the Witch People of Estcarp, who held a portion of it for long years before others came. But we are slow to breed, with long lives."

"Is one the reason for the other?"

"No. It is the witch gift. The women who have it leave home and family as small children. The witches school them to the use of power."

"Are power and gift the same, then?"

"No, my dear, but one is born from the other. The gift you have. That is the ability, the talent. But power is gathered to it over long years of work and learning. Power exists in many things also and may be tapped by one who has the gift. It is like to, say, your gift to handle horses. If you had never used it, the gift would still be there, dormant. But each time you used it, learned what you could do, it grew."

Eleeri reflected. That made sense to her. She returned to the Horning. What had divided the people?

"Our people settled here in Karsten. The capital, Kars, grew on an excellent port where the Sulcar come. They are a race of sailors. Their women and children travel with them on all but the dangerous trips which explore unknown lands. Then others came. They took much of the land we had not used. For very many generations we lived side by side in peace."

"But what changed it?"

Cynan sighed softly. "Nothing stays the same forever. I think perhaps there were some who had always been jealous of the witch gift. When the Kolder came, they used power of another kind to turn the duke against us. Their power could not break us; because of our touch of the gift, our people could stand against it. To rule Karsten and the other lands they coveted, they must be rid of all with our gift. Thus they set the duke to run mad. We were thrice horned as outlaws. The hands of all were against us and no matter what might be done to us, there was to be no accounting."

Eleeri shivered. With license like that she could well imagine some of what would have been done. Cynan touched her shoulder in understanding. "It was all a long time ago. Other things came of it all. Some were good to balance evil."

She looked her question.

"If some of Karsten feared and resented us, others were our friends. In the days when we died for being what we were, some of Karsten stood beside us. They hid us, risked their lives and all they had to keep us safe and smuggle us away over-mountain to Estcarp. None of us forget that not all were greedy for what we had.

"Nor was that all." He smiled gently at her. "You are not the first to enter these lands through a gate. Long before you came Simon Tregarth. He wed a woman of the gift and much power."

"But I thought the witches had to stay virgin."

"So they do; that is why our people grow less. It is also why the witches cast out Simon's wife from their midst. Yet, perhaps because Simon was not of our race, his wife retained her gift."

Eleeri flung back her head, laughing. "I bet that annoyed them."

"It did in truth. Still Simon wed Jaelithe his witch lady. Then came an event almost unheard of among us. At one birth she bore three children, two boys and a girl."

"Triplets!"

"Just so. But all of that is a long story, too. Suffice it to say the girl had the gift. The witches had her away to their place of learning, but her brothers rescued her. They fled to the mountains. There to the east there is a very ancient land over-mountain, Escore. There even now they live and fight against evil."

"What evil?"

The old man sighed. "Am I to tell you the whole history of all the lands? Generations ago, Escore was our land, in part. We shared it with many creatures, and other races, too. But adepts rose. They learned great power, and with it came evil. Some turned to the darkness to aid them. Others battled them to save the land and those who inhabited it. Still others chose to withdraw, either through gates they created or into their own strongholds. Eventually my people fled Escore. There were others who chose to remain."

His mind wandered back. Both to the tales of his boyhood and those later stories he had heard. "There was another race. Like us but tied more strongly to the land. They chose to stay. They are led by the Lady of the Green Silences: Duhaun, Morquant, and other names she uses in the old tales. She is one of great gifts and power. Now she or one of her line rules the Valley of the Green Silences, where good strives always against the evil many adepts unleashed."

"You said other creatures and races? Do you mean that

there's more than one? What are they like?" Eleeri was leaning forward in her interest.

"There are Gray Ones, or so the word comes. They are not men but have affinities with wolves. They fight with teeth and talons, not swords, nonetheless they are formidable fighters and intelligent to some extent."

"Who else?"

"Keplians and Renthans. The Renthans are both beautiful and intelligent. Often they act as mounts for those of the valley. They fight always for the Light." He sighed. "I know little of the other, the Keplians. They look like black horses in many ways. They may come to one who has lost his mount, appearing tame to the eyes. But if you mount, then they bear you away to be devoured by evil. The adepts who turned to darkness often used them as mounts. It is said that despite their beauty, the only good Keplian is a dead Keplian."

"But what about Karsten here?" Eleeri queried. "As I came toward this place, I found keep after keep which had been destroyed. None of that was old. I'd say most of it had been done within the past year."

"When it looked as if we'd lose, the witches turned the mountains," Cynan said slowly. "They used the power to wring them out into new shapes. The current duke and all his army were within the mountain trails. I suspect very few could have escaped. After that, others tried to become duke. Each time they must fight against those who reject them. For more than thirty years now the people of this land have looted and been looted in their turn. Here and there men have gathered families and sufficient fighters to make some sort of peace in their lands. But those places are few. Even Kars is lawless, so I hear."

Eleeri was bewildered. "How can people live like that? The land will end up with no one, surely."

"In many places it has. How many living did you see as you crossed the land?'

"No one."

"You see. To the north and east the land is empty. It is to the west and south, along the seacoast where traders still come, that people are to be found."

"Traders?"

"The Sulcar ships sometimes touch port. They come armed and wary, but they do come now and again."

The girl nodded, remembering all he had told her of that race of seafarers. "What about the Falconers you spoke of? Are any of them still around?"

Cynan sighed softly. "That I know not. They left the mountains before the turning. They took service in many places and with many people. I think they would live yet as a people; they are strong fighters and proud." His eyes met hers. "But never mind others. What do you plan? You will not stay here beyond the snows. I feel your restlessness even now. You could travel over-mountain to Estcarp. I could give you places where you would be welcome in my name."

Eleeri blinked. "Are there still trails?" Then she snorted at her own stupidity. "Of course there must be; otherwise you wouldn't have been able to get back. How does the land lie there?"

She watched as he drew a burned stick from the fire and drew on the stone floor. "I see," she finally said. "If I return along the mountain edge to the west and cross north, then I'll be in Estcarp." She laid a slim finger on the blank portion. "What land lies here?"

Cynan was silent for a long time. When he finally answered, she was conscious of a rising desire. There was something in the name of Escore as he said it, something which drew her even as the east had originally drawn her here to this secluded valley. She studied the map silently before she spoke.

"Our river—if I followed that, I would arrive in time in this land?"

"So I think, but I do not know for certain."

Eleeri stood and walked to her bedding. She hauled firewood, banking the fire for the night as she thought. The pull, the feeling of rightness grew stronger. She settled into her bedding and allowed her body to relax.

From his bed the old man watched her face. Just before sleep claimed them, he spoke again. "You've decided, haven't you?"

"Yes. When spring comes, I will go to Escore. Will you come with me?"

"No. I was born here in this hold. I came back to die here. But if you meet any who knew me where you go, tell them I still live."

"I will." She drifted into sleep then. A destination determined. Escore . . . she would go to Escore.

3

The winter was both a time of friendship and a time of hardship for Eleeri. Cynan taught her all the scraps of languages he had picked up over a long busy life. To that knowledge he added warnings, hints, and beliefs about the places of the Old Ones, their natures, and beginnings. His mother had possessed some small gifts, so that the girl's increasing abilities failed to distress him as they might have another. The girl herself barely noticed that her gift was growing, stretching as she used it. She had always had the horse gift; it was a part of her.

But in the clear air of this new land, things were changing. Before she had been able to handle the wildest mare, soothe the most savage stallion. Foals had run to her for comfort. By the time she'd reached seven or eight, Far Traveler had been using her to start the training process for the horses he accepted. Beasts trained by her seemed to be calmer, more intelligent and sensible. Eleeri had loved the work but hated it when each four-footed friend left again. She knew that all too many owners would treat them as cheap machines.

She loved horses, the feel of hard muscle sliding under her hands as she groomed. The rough strands of mane, the scents and the sounds. But she loved most of all the feeling of communion she had with them, their trust and returned affection. Over that winter she did not regard it as odd that this communication deepened. It had been rare for her to keep a horse past the few weeks necessary to explain their new duties to humans. With these three she had spent much time and many months. Of course they had responded. But Cynan, watching, knew that it was far more. There were times when it was as if the minds of girl and horse mingled so that beast and rider were one.

He deliberately moved onto that subject one night. "Eleeri, the power often comes as it will and not as you will it." She glanced up, but said nothing. "You say that in your own land none have great power, only small gifts that tend to lessen with each generation." The girl nodded. "Then think on this. Here it is not so. It may be that here the gift you have grows. I do not believe it is so small as you think, and such gifts untrained can be dangerous. If you come upon anyone who can, let them teach you."

"Look, I don't think I have the power you do. But"— she looked up and smiled, a smile of affection for the old warrior—"I promise I'll get teaching if I can find a willing teacher. And"—she held up a hand before he spoke— "I'll make sure this one is of the Light before I begin to learn, okay?"

"Okay."

Cynan returned to the shirt he was mending and Eleeri to the deerskin trousers she was making. Over the autumn she had hunted well, and not a hide or fur had been wasted. The quiet isolation of winter was a time for using these. She planned to leave Cynan a complete set of the deerskin garments along with a fur cloak. She knew that nowadays his old bones ached in the cold. She also planned to make a pair of special knee-high moccasins for him. The hide under the foot was to be triple-layered and the moccasins would be fur-lined. That would keep his feet warm and dry when he must go into the snow to tend the beasts next winter.

She glanced at him from the corner of her eye. It would not be easy to leave. But he would be furious if she stayed. He would know it was to look after him, and his pride would be cut to the heart. She understood the pride of a warrior. She would not wound the old man by counting him as less than he was. He had come back to this place which had once been his, to die. They both knew it. Here in a tiny graveyard higher into the hills lay the bodies of his wife and last child. The bodies of his parents, and his siblings. The hold had been the refuge for his bloodline for so long, the years faded to dust.

Her mind wandered to his words. She wasn't sure . . . perhaps her gift *was* growing stronger. But why should she have any great gift at all? It was true that there had been medicine men and women of ability in Far Traveler's line. Too many times she had been forced to bite down on hot words as her schools decried those gifts, calling them native superstition. Something snagged on her thoughts and she dimly recalled the teasing that her grandfather had given his wife. Yes . . . she concentrated, and the memories grew a little clearer.

They had been around the table: her mother Wind Talker, her father, and his parents. It was on one of her grandparents' rare visits to Eleeri's home. Her grandfather had been speaking of Cornish superstitions and their use.

" . . . a method of control in many cases."

"Then you don't think there was ever anything more?" That had been her mother.

"Not to denigrate your beliefs, my dear, but no, I don't. I think that it was usually a way to handle large numbers of people. To persuade them into suitable actions. For instance, in New Zealand a tapu may be placed on shellfish to allow the numbers to recover after a bad season. The people believe they will be cursed if they touch them until the tapu is lifted. In this way their elders control them and the food supply."

He had suddenly chuckled. "If I believed all the old talk, I'd never have married your mother-in-law."

His son moaned. "Not that old tale again, Dad."

But Wind Talker was interested. "Is there some story?"

John Polworth leaned back, coffee cup in hand. "Story, that's all it is, but it does show the power of superstition. Your mother was a Ree before I wed her. The old folks said that was an uncanny line. Reckoned that a long time ago the women had been priestesses of another faith and that it was bad luck to wed them. Jane's great-grandmother was Jessie Ree. They said she could call storms or calm them if they came. Lot of rubbish, but my folks didn't want me to wed Jane."

Wind Talker leaned forward. "But you married her despite this."

"I did indeed, my dear. I'll have no truck with such nonsense, and so I told them. Jane Ree is the one I want and that was my last word on the subject." He drank from his cup and set it down again with a decisive thump.

His wife smiled at them. "It certainly was his last word. But his parents never quite accepted me until John said we were leaving. He'd had the offer of a good job across the water, and maybe the people there would care less about superstition and more about the fact he loved me and I was a good wife. So we came and we've never re-gretted it."

Eleeri sat, remembering the feeling of warmth and love that had surrounded her then. In later years she had heard other reasons for the hasty departure of the Polworths from Cornwall to their new country. A war had been com-ing, and John Polworth had no time for war. It didn't fit into his plans, to die fighting in a country far from his own, for a cause he was not sure he believed in. So he'd married Jane swiftly and accepted the promised job in America. By the time war touched the United States also he was in a reserved occupation. She might have scorned him as a coward. But Jane knew it had not been that alone. He would have been no use as a fighter and he knew it.

She wondered if he had ever regretted his decisions. He had loved his wife, that had not been in doubt. He had ap-peared happy in his work and country, too. But did he ever wish to be back on his rock and seagirt land? She shrugged. Perhaps he'd had a wish when he knew in that last few seconds that he and Jane were about to die.

It was strange that both her parents and grandparents had died in accidents. It had been the year following that night around the table. A vacation, a crashed plane—and among the dead, the names of her grandparents.

Her parents had been killed in a car crash the year after that, when she was nine. For a whole six months she had lived—derided, despised, and humiliated—with the Tay-lors, her aunt and uncle. Finally she had fought back with a smuggled letter to Far Traveler. But before he could come, her uncle had caught her releasing a horse he was breaking. She could not have helped herself; the animal's weary pain and confusion had cried out to her beyond re-fusal. But it had happened before. He was a man of quick and brutal temper and she was the despised Indian. He had beaten her far more savagely than he had intended, but it had saved her in the end. Far Traveler had come that afternoon.

Her relatives had made the mistake of refusing to allow him entrance. But with the rise of Indian rights and consciousness this had been more foolish than they had realized. Her great-grandfather had gone to find a man he knew. This one had spoken to others, and Far Traveler had returned with support. She had been brought out and, partly from the pain of her beating, partly with the knowledge that this might be a way out, had fainted within the circle of adults. Action had been swift after that.

She had been discussed, questioned, and refiled. Far Traveler had accepted her into his home, and certain friends had stood surety that she would be cared for. She might even have believed herself to have been safe, beyond the malice of a man steeped in hatred of her race, but for that last glimpse of him as she was taken away. He had watched, eyes bright with hatred. A long measuring look said that one day he would have his chance to pay her back for this humiliation. She had known that once Far Traveler died there would be no refuge. The Taylors would take her back, aided by social services people who would believe it was best for her.

She guessed that the years after that only distilled Taylor's hatred. That in the time before she reached sixteen he would be able to build a cage of lies that would entrap her, perhaps forever. She had made her choices, and freedom beyond hope had been the result. Maybe Ka-dih, Comanche god of warriors, had watched over her.

She now bent to her work again. Maybe the blending of the two bloodlines had each strengthened the gift. She knew her people had often had the horse gift, but hers was stronger by far than usual. She shrugged again. It was hers; the how no longer mattered.

Across the fire Cynan watched her, unnoticed. Firelight glinted on the high cheekbones, the aquiline planes of her face. The gray of her eyes turned to black in the shadows and the black of her hair to night. She looked to be slight with the long fine boning typical of his own race, but he had seen the strength under that deceptive appearance. The girl was a warrior. He'd spent much time teaching her sword drill, but even he could teach her nothing she did not already know with bow and knife. She moved with apparent slowness, the smooth motion deceiving the eye. In reality she was swift, fast-reflexed, and controlled.

From things she had let slip it would seem that her kinsman had trained her almost half of her life. You'd have thought the man had known where she would go, what choices she would make. Cynan smiled to himself. In all probability it had only been an old man's memories. The girl had been taught as Far Traveler had been in his own distant youth. In teaching the child, he had unconsciously returned to the days when life was simpler for his people. But in so doing, he had given her an excellent education for the world she now found herself in. Maybe the gods had had a hand in it after all.

His eyes touched her with affection. She was a good child, kind and generous. He must persuade her to leave as soon as the path was clear. If she stayed too long after that, she would discover his secret. It had been only her aid that had brought him through *this* winter. If she realized this, she might choose to stay. He would rather that she left believing him to be alive behind her. And so he would be, through the spring, the summer, and into the autumn. But he could feel the knowledge deep inside himself. As the year faded into the death season, so would he.

Before first snows he would be gone. He smiled; it was time.

But he would not have her here mourning over his body. He'd seen the pain the death of her kinsman still caused her. Let her ride out knowing she'd left him well prepared for next winter. As the last days of next autumn faded into the land, he would seek out the graves of his loved ones. There he would lie down and pass to join their spirits. He would not have the child there to grieve when it happened. Nor would he have her live the next winter alone in a deserted hold.

His mind wandered. The horses: he needed none of them; she must take the three. He wished to give her a leave-taking gift, too.

He rose quietly and strode up the ancient stone stairs. He'd given almost everything of value to his far kin before he returned here. One thing yet remained. He pressed a stone in the wall, caught at the edge as it swung out. Within was a tiny casket carved of a glowing golden wood. Fingers fumbled at the catch, then the lid rose to release a sweet scent and a soft flare of light. He chuckled softly. Of all the things he could have kept, it had been this one. It would weigh nothing; she had enough weight to carry. But that she would love this he knew; it was right for her. Perhaps Another had a hand in this, too.

He replaced the stone and returned to his mending. When the time came, he would be ready. In the meantime, it would be well if the child also learned to write at least one language in this world that was new to her. He rose again to fetch what he needed.

"What are you up to now?" Eleeri asked him. "You haven't sat still for a minute this evening."

Cynan looked at her thoughtfully. "There are several things I know which may help you in days to come. Two I could teach you while winter keeps us inside this hold: one is reading in the tongue of Estcorp; the other is signing."

Eleeri jerked upright, her eyes suddenly alert. "Your people have a sign language?"

Cynan smiled. "I see yours do also. Ours developed only with the need to fight. Oh, hunters had always held some signs in use. But when we rode to war and as scouts, the language developed greatly. You learn well and quickly. If your people also had such a language, I think you would have no trouble learning ours."

"Then I will, and I'd like to try reading as well. My great-grandfather always said that one should learn if any were willing to teach, that knowledge was never wasted."

"He was a wise man," Cynan commented. "Come, sit beside me and I will show you the signs. After that . . . I have only one book, but you will learn well enough with that to read."

The winter moved on slowly, and at last the thaw started. With many months to study, Eleeri could now sign in the simple language of hunting and war as well as any born to this variation. She could also read, albeit with some stumbling over unfamiliar words.

By now she was more than ready to ride. Furs and skins had all been made into stout clothing. Saddles and horse gear were mended and oiled. She would use the horses in turn to hunt, as yet they were unfit for a long trail.

Water trickled down the stones of the hold, dripped miserably from the roof, gathering in deep sticky mud in doorways. Eleeri heaved a sigh. She hated that, but it would all pass when the weather warmed further.

It did so, and to her surprise, Cynan insisted on coming out to ride once the land had dried.

"The mud has gone and my bones no longer ache so

much." He smiled at her. "Besides, there is something I would show you." He refused to say more, leading her deep into the hills as her sturdy pony obediently followed the tail of Cynan's mount. They rounded the bend to find themselves in a small cup of flat land. Most of it was taken up by . . .

"The place of the Old Ones you told me about?"

"Even so, my child." He dismounted laboriously. "Sit here on the grass and listen." He waited until Eleeri was settled comfortably. "My people worship Gunnora. She is the Lady of fruit, grain, and fertility. Lady of love and laughter. In her name we celebrate the change of a girl into womanhood. The amber pieces you showed me are of great worth. They contain seeds and could be sold as amulets of her symbol. I think they did not come to you by accident. Guard them well. Do not show them to others, but if you can, pray to Gunnora at need."

Eleeri considered that. It sounded as if this Gunnora was the same as the Corn Woman, goddess to many Indian tribes. She would feel no sense of wrong in praying to Corn Woman under another name.

"I can do that, and I'll cherish the amber. What else?"

"In Escore and on your journey there will be danger. Not only from beasts and man, but also from creatures of evil. They could imperil more than your body. I would ask of those who built this place if they will grant you guards."

The girl blinked. Was he going to ask for ghost guard dogs or magic swords?

Cynan saw her confusion. "You have seen me place the small pebbles I carry about the doors. Those are guards, in a way. While they lie in any entrance, nothing which is of the Dark can enter. Men who are wicked, that is another thing," he added as both remembered the bandits.

"Is this Gunnora's shrine, then?"

He shrugged. "For all the time my family has lived here, we have prayed to her. The Old Ones built this place, but if it was Hers when it was laid down, we do not know."

Eleeri studied it. It was simple, of a spare elegant design. Merely a pavement laid out in a star made from many hues of marble. Around the edge on each star point stood a tall white pillar. Yet it breathed a tremendous feeling of peace. Of a harbor safely attained. She was drawn again, rising without hesitation to approach the edge.

"What do I do?"

"Think about your need to be guarded from evil. Then step forward to stand in the star center if you can."

She obeyed. At first it was difficult. Cynan had told her of many creatures who fought against the Light. But she'd seen none. It was hard to create them in her mind, along with a request for protection against them. It became easier the longer she tried.

Holding them in her mind's eye, she walked forward.

Behind her, walls of mist lifted between the pillars so that she vanished from Cynan's sight. He relaxed. That which dwelled here had accepted her as Daughter to the Light. It might refuse her request, but she was safe.

Within the mist walls, Eleeri stepped to the star center. There she bowed her head in a polite acknowledgment. Warmth gathered around her. So, there was something here. She would ask for help.

She did so, to receive in turn a wordless question. How much would she value this favor? After that it seemed that her mind would burst, as into it flowed a montage of evils. She saw Gray Ones run mad, killing, rending with tooth and talon all who crossed their paths. She saw odd-looking small creatures covered with a long coarse hair like roots, who burrowed to bring a slow smothering death to those who fell into their traps. Pools of evil showed as blighted blotches on the land. Into them she saw those unguarded stray and be consumed, body and soul together.

She shuddered. "What do you want?" Fear grew as the images all but overwhelmed her.

You! Slay Cynan and I will give you power over anything you desire.

"NO!" Eleeri stepped back in anger. "You're supposed to be Light."

He is dying.

"His life is his own."

There was the sensation of being gathered into strong, loving arms.

Well said, child. The guards you ask shall be given. Before her a figure grew: a woman taller than Eleeri, with shimmering hair. It flowed golden down the straight back of the figure, caressing the woman's green gown, tendrils straying outward. Without volition Eleeri knelt. Her hands were caught in long fingers as she was lifted up again. Then Eleeri's hands were turned over. Into them the woman dropped four small smooth stones.

"Cynan will show you how they may be used. Good fortune ride with you, Eleeri of another people." She began to fade as the girl fumbled with the pouch about her throat.

"Wait, oh, please wait."

The woman's shape firmed again. "What is it, child?"

"A gift for a gift." Purple and blue fire flashed in Eleeri's hands. She held out the gems left to her by Far Traveler. Somehow it seemed right that she should offer them. The woman stooped. The green and gold seemed to deepen as she took into her hands the bright pebbles. Mist swirled, brightening in the woman's colors as she faded once more.

"A gift for a gift indeed, child. You who bear my guards also bear my symbols. Call on me with them in darkest times. I shall not forget you. Light bless your path." She was gone, and Eleeri felt almost bereft. Slowly, cradling her four stones, she walked from the pavement.

Cynan was waiting. He said nothing, seeing the stones and the strange look on the girl's face. Silently he led her back to the patient ponies. That night he taught her the stones' warding. He found it interesting how swiftly she learned. It had been a matter for gossip once. Did those who came through gates have a gift given by the passage? Or were only those with the gift drawn to gates? It was said that Simon Tregarth had had little of the power in his own land, but a far greater portion in this. Could it be that beyond the gates the power was damped, to bloom more powerfully once the gate was passed? A thought to consider over long nights.

It took a week for Eleeri to learn all Cynan could teach her of the four stones. By then she, too, was beginning to wonder about her power. Always she could remember her horse-gift. There had never been a time she did not possess that. But since her arrival in Karsten, it seemed the gift was growing, and expanding into other areas. Cynan had shared his own questions, so that she, too, suspected many in her own world might have latent abilities. Still she did not wish to hold power. From what her friend said, it made of one too good a target. Still, the four ward stones had replaced the gems in the pouch at her throat. She suspected they would be weapons to her hand once she began her travels again.

But before that she had something she wished to do.

Many things, in fact. She must hunt the yearling buck, culling out the smaller and weaker. They would be meat for Cynan. The old man had been trying to hide his growing weakness. He talked of her departure as soon as the last of the mountain snows were gone and the trails well dried. She knew why well enough, but it was his choice. If she was not there when he finally died, she could remember him as he had been to her: a strong friend and a teacher.

She hunted well. Then, closer to leave-taking, she made up her mind. The next day she would ride to the graves of his kin. She would scythe the grass short above the graves, place flowers. In her hunting she had found a brightly flowering bush with sweet-scented blooms. Now she raised one carefully. Back at the graves she gathered stone to stack along the earth that bordered where Cynan might wish to lie. She replanted the bright shrub in a mound of earth and leaf mold, next door to the grave of his wife. If he chose to lie there, it would be a fine marker for him who would have no other.

A month later, they rode down to the sea. There they gathered as much of the salt as they could scrape from the rocks. One by one they filled rock hollows above the reach of the waves. Over the next week the water would evaporate, leaving more of the priceless crystals.

With the coming of the warmth again, Cynan was stronger. His muscles moved more smoothly, but the knowledge of his death was still there. Each season from now on would be his last for him. Still, he often forgot as he hunted with the child, raced her along the beach, horses pounding through the sand.

Spring began to shift into early summer. His larder was filled with meat both dried and smoked. His bins were full of fruit and nuts, and the gathered greens the hills provided. At last he spoke.

"The trails are dry. It is time you left."

Eleeri nodded. "Next week."

"No." His head shook firmly. "That you said last week and the week before. Let you spend tomorrow with me, the next day preparing. Ride out the day after that. It is time." His hand stretched out to touch hers. "Child, child, to all things there comes a time. This is yours—to go. It is mine also, that you know but we will not speak of it." He eyed her sternly and nodded as he saw accceptance. It was well. He stood and yawned. "I'm for my bed, and you, too, youngling. In the morning I will show you I can yet run you into exhaustion."

She made a small jeering noise and headed for her own bedding. "I'll sleep eagerly to see that."

All the next day they spent together. They talked, strolling about the upper rooms of the hold as he told her of how it had been. They picked berries, sweet and sunwarmed, laughing like children together. They waded at the river's edge, spearing small fish. These were a wonderful evening meal spiced only with the sea salt and herbs from the hill's bounty.

The following day they readied the horses. Eleeri would have left him the strongest, quietest beast, but Cynan refused.

"I have no need of a horse. I never needed one before they came, I do not require one when they can leave with you. Sell two of them, trade one for supplies, I care not. But they are of no use to me." His real reason was unspoken but understood by both.

The girl said no more. Quietly she filled her pack with articles she might need. The stirrups she bound high on the two beasts she would not ride. Her chosen mount was a sturdy dun, black of mane and tail, with legs dappled high in that same shade. A good horse in hills, surefooted and sensible, with hues that allowed him to fade into the landscape.

She studied the other two. Both were more showy, one chestnut, the other gray. Both wore polished mended gear and should fetch good prices if she chose to sell. Finally she ran out of things to do and returned inside. There she blinked in surprise. From somewhere Cynan had found a large cloth. This had been placed over the huge old table. Somehow he had moved that toward the fireplace and decorated it with branches and berries. Candles spread puddles of light across the feast that lay there.

Within the doorway Cynan bowed ceremoniously. "Be welcome to my house, Eleeri, Daughter of the House of Far Traveler. Feast with me before you take your road again." He took her hand, drawing it through his arm as he conducted her to a seat.

She ate with determined appetite, laughing at his jests and storing all this in her mind. When they were done he stood.

"Long ago I had a thing made. It was to have gone to a daughter of my House. Her gift was friendship with beasts, and I deemed this which I had made to be right for her name day. But the turning came and she rode out to fight." For a moment his eyes held ancient pain. "She never returned, nor could they bring her body back to me. She lies somewhere in these hills, holding still her watch against the enemy. Now I would give this gift to you, if you do not count it unlucky." From under a leaf he produced the small gleaming casket and handed it to Eleeri.

The girl gasped. "It's so beautiful."

Cynan laughed. "The casket is not the gift, girl, that lies within. Open it and see."

He watched as she gently lifted the carved lid. Her eyes lit with wonder as she twined fingers in the cord to lift the pendant free. It dangled from her hand, carved from some black stone with bright ruby eyes inset in the tiny arrogant head. A loop of silver was attached to a lock of flowing mane and through that the plaited cord Eleeri twisted in her fingers. It was a horse, and yet not quite a horse: there was something in the stance that betrayed intelligence. The eyes seemed to hold a life of their own and to look boldly up at her.

"Cynan, it's wonderful. Where did it come from?"

"From these hills. I say that I had it made, but that is not correct. I had the loop attached, the cord plaited, the casket carved. The beast itself I found. Before the hills turned, there was a place of the Old Ones near here, perhaps an hour's ride away. After my wife died, I went there often for the peace and comfort it brought me. One day I found that. I took it up and it seemed as if it was a gift of the Old Ones. I thanked them for it. Promised that she who would wear it was one of some power and would cherish it with respect." He smiled. "I swear that it grew warm then in my hand. I took that as a sign it was truly right I should take it. Now it comes to you."

Her hand closed around it tightly. "It's the best present I've ever had. I'll never part with it, Cynan, and I'll always remember you when I see it." She placed the cord about her neck and shifted the tiny horse to hang in front. "Now—I have something for you, too."

She trotted away to return with a bundle clutched in her arms. "Here, shirt and breeches of deerskin and a fur cloak. You know how you feel the cold. And look, I made you moccasins to keep your feet warm. They have fur lining and triple soles." She giggled. "Go and try them on. I want to be sure I got the sizes right."

Cynan came down the stairs several minutes later. In the firelight she could almost believe him a warrior of the Nemunuh. His face broke into a happy grin as he advanced across the floor. He turned slowly.

"You have no need to worry. They fit well and they are warmer than any clothing I have had for more years than I would wish to number." He straightened. "I will wear them to bid you farewell tomorrow. For now let us sleep; it is best to take the road early. That way you waste none of the day."

It may have been a gift of the gods . . . they slept well and soundly that last night. Both had feared a wakeful night knowing this was good-bye. But their sleep was swift and their dreams kind. At first light both woke. Together they ate and drank in silence. Then Eleeri brought the horses and mounted. Beside her Cynan was dressed in the clothing she had made for him. She leaned down to take his hand.

"I will always remember you." Her vision was blurred by tears. "I love you." Her hand lifted. "For the feast you gave me, fair thanks. For the welcome of your gate, gratitude. To the ruler of this hold, all good fortune, and bright sun in the days to come."

Cynan moved forward and as she leaned down, he reached up to hug her hard. "Ride in strength, warrior. May your weapons never fail and may Ka-dih bring you at last to a place befitting his daughter." He slapped the pony firmly on its hindquarters and it started down the trail. As long as the road lay straight, Eleeri turned to watch him. At the bend, she lifted her hand and heard his final call echoing after her.

"Farewell, child. My love go with you."

She rode on, tear-blinded, knowing she would never see or hear him again. Ahead lay an unknown future. Thus far she had prospered. What would her tomorrows bring?

4

$\mathcal{S}$he rode steadily while daylight lasted. By now she had learned minor spells, and with them she set up a secure camp. Gunnora was very similar to one prayed to by the Nemunuh, and Eleeri felt at home with the amber amulets and the lady. Holding her amber, she marched from corner to corner of her small encampment invoking the protection of Gunnora. The Place of the Old Ones might have vanished in the turning, but she now had her four pebbles from the ruins, a valued gift. In the half-light they glowed a soft comforting blue and she placed them with care.

To this routine she kept as the days moved past her. It may have been the amber, or the pebbles, she did not know. But she saw nothing more dangerous, as she journeyed upriver, than the occasional beast at its hunting. These she always bespoke in friendship. The only event of note was the appearance of a magnificent female falcon. The hawk was clearly hungry and Eleeri caught a brief mind-picture of a nest full of squawking babies. She grinned in sympathy, sending friendship and tossing up a plump rabbit previously transfixed by one of her arrows. The female snatched it out of midair with a sharp cry.

As she flew with her gift, a feather fell from her. Long, sharply marked in black and white. A prize. Eleeri dropped from her pony to gather it in. Tucking it into her headband and mounting her pony again, she sat straighter. There might be no eagles in this land she had found, but a hawk's feather was good medicine, the more so since it appeared to have been a gift. She would wear it with pride, remembering her people.

Days slipped into weeks as she moved through the mountains. Often she was forced to backtrack when the trail she followed became blocked or simply vanished. But there was a growing sense that drew her always to the northwest.

It was as if she were wanted there, as if a calling grew louder as she traveled. She laughed softly at her fancies, but she held her course. It fitted with the small amount Cynan had been able to tell her of an ancient land new-found by his kin. She hunted as she went, sharing often with those of the wild. She saw a hunting falcon several times and each time Eleeri offered food. It was found acceptable, and while the birds would not come near her, she was clearly to be counted friend.

At last the river shallowed, narrowing even though the land was flatter. The girl began to scout farther from it across the broadening plains. It was on one of those side trips that she saw the village. She allowed the horses to graze while she studied it, lying flat atop a hill. Not a village, really, more one of those holds like Cynan's. It seemed to consist of a main fortified building surrounded by other, smaller homes. Probably, if danger threatened, everyone retreated to the main protection. She'd be cautious. According to Cynan, they should be friendly, but it paid to be careful.

She called her beasts and swung into the saddle. Picking her way down the hillside, she allowed her mount to pace toward the gates. There was a considerable amount of noise coming from a fenced area behind one of the larger buildings. Over the babble of voices she heard the sudden blast of a furious horse, a whistle that rose in violent challenge. She made no attempt to resist that call, but kneed her pony around the building, there to halt in outraged fury.

Within a high-fenced corral a mare fought her captors. She was black as night, with a coat that gleamed in the sunlight. Behind her struggled a newborn foal, he, too, black, under the slime of birth. He fought to rise, but was as yet too weak to make his slender legs obey him. He fell again with a tiny squeal and the mare went crazy at the sound. Forgetting anything but the distress she witnessed, Eleeri raced her horses forward, almost trampling spectators.

Her voice rang out like a bell, "What happens here? What do you do?"

A dozen voices answered her. "A Keplian, lady. Gerae caught one of their mares."

"Why treat her so?" She noticed that the ropes holding the mare from her foal had slackened as those who held her stopped to listen.

"Why? But lady—she's a *Keplian!*" the man before her spluttered. He seemed to think that was explanation enough. Eleeri did not.

"I don't care what you name her. Is that any way to treat a beast? What evil has she ever done you?" She eyed the man who hauled hardest on the ropes. "Do you claim this mare attacked you? Did she slay kin of yours, threaten your child? For what reason does she pay, and her foal with her?"

The man fell back at the sight of her anger. "She's just a Keplian. We kill them where we find them. They're evil." He straightened proudly. "Yes, they're of the Dark."

Eleeri was watching as the mare used the slackened rope to reach her foal with a comforting nose. "I see nothing evil here, just a mare who tries to protect her baby." From the confused babble behind her she heard a short conversation.

" . . . away from the hold."

" . . . gone to the valley. He'll not return for days."

"Then what do we do? This may be a woman of the power."

The girl hid a triumphant grin. Their lord seemed to have gone away for some time. Already this bunch looked disposed to fear her, at least a little. She sent a mental command to her mount, and allowed her back to straighten slowly. Horse and rider seemed to loom now in a martial pose, awing those who gathered about her on foot. Slowly—portentously—she removed an amulet from her shirt pocket.

She dropped lightly from her horse, walking over to where the handlers still kept a strain on the ropes. Lightly she touched the foal on his wet nose. The amber brushed the small muzzle and glowed softly.

She held the amulet high. "Gunnora has spoken: There is no evil in this one. He has harmed none and must be freed."

From the back of the crowd a man thrust his way. He was burly of build, with blond hair that glinted in the sun. He scowled viciously.

"The foal is too young to have done aught. But he will grow to be evil. All Keplians are followers of the Dark. Here we kill those who are of the Dark. Where do you come from, lady, that you do not know that?"

Eleeri returned question for question. "Where do *you* come from, man, that you would torture a dam and her newborn foal? Who told you they are evil, when Gunnora herself says the foal at least is innocent?"

His voice overtopped hers in a sudden roar. "Innocent? The Dark ones slaughtered my family when I was a child. A year since my brother was murdered by their kind while on a mission for those in the Valley of the Green Silences. Must we stand here while this woman seeks to take from us our lawful prey?" He moved forward.

"Are you so hot to kill that you ignore payment?" Eleeri asked softly.

The forward movement halted. "Payment?"

"Aye. Gunnora says that the foal is innocent. If she does not say the mare is clearly evil, will you release both to me in return for weregild?"

He blinked thoughtfully, diverted for this moment as he considered. "What do you offer, lady?"

Good, she was back to being a "lady" again. "I cannot offer you the worth of a family slain, a brother dead, but I can offer two for two." She waved a hand at the saddled, bridled horses that followed her.

A singularly nasty smirk spread over his face and he nodded. "Done, lady." Nor did he seem to care any longer whether Gunnora adjudged the mare. He held out his hand for the reins and both horses went to him at Eleeri's order.

"Now, lady. You get that pair out of here before sunset. You have one day. After that they're fair prey again."

"I will need to buy food, fill my water bags."

"No. You get nothing here. *We* do not traffic with the

Dark. Take your 'friends' and get out before we stone you." He moved forward, with the savagery in his eyes deepening. She could see that he was delighted with his bargain but would attack her as well if he felt safe enough. His eyes had already begun to rest covetously on her saddlebags and plump bedroll. Her hand flicked to her bow, stringing an arrow before he could close on her.

"Stand back, man. I have bargained fairly and will have that for which I have paid." She called a sharp order to the men who still held the mare. "Release her." They hesitated, and she moved the arrow to center on the man who stood staring. "Release her, *now!*"

He called a reluctant command and the bonds fell away. With a swift heave of her body, the mare freed herself and leaped to her foal. With a sinking heart, the girl saw that the smirk was back. What now?

"All right, now let's see you convince that devil from the Dark to leave. The foal can't walk." He chuckled viciously. "The mare'll kill you if you go near it now she's free."

Eleeri nodded, but her heart lifted. He'd misjudged. "Maybe, and maybe I'll kill *you* if you don't leave now. You are a stupid, cruel, ignorant man. If all in this village are of your kind, I will be glad to leave. Now get away from here before I lose my temper." Her eyes flamed with rage and the man retreated. With a final sneer, he slouched around the corner, leaving a small group to stand watching. One approached cautiously.

"Lady, if Gunnora judges these, then it is not for us to naysay her. But truly their kind follows the ways of the Dark. We cannot trade with you for anything obvious. Gerae will know and make our lives hard for us. But if there is anything small we could provide?"

Her mouth suddenly watered. Her supply of salt was

running low. If she had that, she could continue to feed herself easily by the hunt.

"Salt—will you trade as much salt as you can spare?" He nodded and vanished hastily along with others. They returned bearing small hide bags containing not only salt but ground flour and some kind of sweetener. From the bandits she had killed she had taken small coins in silver and copper. These she proffered with a quiet comment.

"Of Karsten but nonetheless valuable. Those who owned them have no more use—for anything, even hunting those not of their kind."

She could see that idea sink in. The word was even whispered in a soft hissing. "A spy—she has been spying in Karsten."

She handed over the coinage, watching faces. They seemed to be happy with their bargain but not so delighted that she had overpaid.

"Are there other villages to the north?" She would find out what she could while they were well disposed.

"No, lady." A hand rose to point. "That way is the forest of the Mosswomen." A finger swung then to the northeast. "That way are the mountains again. Between those there is the river. Gerae will pursue you; best you leave the Keplians and go. Then he will kill them and leave you alone."

"If he follows me," Eleeri said in a hard-edged voice, "it will not be a stranger to you who dies. Thank you for your trading." The man who had spoken for them nodded.

"Go in peace, lady. But beware of those beasts who are not truly beasts. The mare will kill if she has the chance, and so will Gerae. You are between the mountains and sea with no place to hide if you take them." He turned away, his friends following, fingering their bounty in the Karsten coins. Eleeri turned back to the Keplians. The foal had managed to gain its feet, but looking closer, the girl could see why Gerae had been so amused. At some stage it had been struck brutally across the hocks. The small animal's hind legs were swollen and bruised. There was no way it could walk any distance, and even as she watched, it sank back to the dusty ground with a forlorn whicker. The mare eyed her, standing protectively over the baby. Eleeri felt a surge of anger at the people who could treat a tiny foal so cruelly, and before she had thought, she was moving closer, crooning gently.

The mare stamped warningly, and Eleeri reached out with her gift. To her surprise, she felt the tiny jet horse under her shirt give out a flare of warmth. Her fingers touched it. Strange . . . it was warmer than its contact with her skin warranted. She allowed it to fall before her throat and saw that the mare's eyes were fixed on it, wide with interest. She began to talk softly, explaining. The mare appeared to listen. Now she was trying to urge the foal to his feet once again. The baby tried and failed.

"Mare, we must leave here. That man will come back and kill your foal soon." She reinforced the message with mind-send, becoming interested in the strength and clarity of mind-pictures from the mare.

"If I lifted him onto my horse, I could walk and we could travel away from here. If you will let me help him."

From the mare she received a blast of distrust. Slowly she reached out to stroke the baby. As she did so, she allowed her mind to broadcast admiration. How beautiful he was, how strong and sturdy. How brave. It would indeed be a terrible thing to see him die. She would risk more even than she already had to prevent this. Her mind drifted to other horses she had known, and to her surprise she felt a gush of contempt from the mother, a feeling of indignation. They were *not* horses; how some human had felt about those others was nothing to her.

Eleeri smiled, sending acceptance. But whether they were horse or not, that man would return to kill. Did the mare still wish to be here when he did? She did not. Then she must allow the girl to aid her foal or remain with him to see him die. Pictures of the mare fighting came in reply.

In return, the girl sent pictures of the mare dying, shot through with arrows and spears. Then her foal, bound, slaughtered, discarded, and dead.

Capitulation. The mare would graciously permit the human to help her. Moving with a slow smooth motion, Eleeri lifted the small beast and placed him comfortably on the bedroll-padded saddle. Taking the reins, she walked to the gate and opened it. The mare paced after.

They passed through and departed from the village. Hating eyes watched them go.

Gerae decided he would not follow too soon, or too obviously; his word had been given before too many. He would wait this day and the next. The moon was nearing full. Tomorrow as soon as the moon rose he would be on their trail. Then let the witch see if she could put him off with bribes and clever words.

His mind dwelled on her slender form, the arrogance of her voice. It would be pleasure indeed to teach her that he was not to be so despised. He spent his day making plans and preparing for a journey. It had been kind of her to give him the horses that would help him to take her.

Eleeri had learned well the lessons of war Far Traveler had taught her. He had passed along many wise sayings and warrior maxims. One might be translated as "Believe there will always be pursuit and act accordingly." She believed, and to the mare's indignation was acting accordingly.

They had struck the branch of the river within an hour's fast walking. There Eleeri led her small party into the water to travel upstream for another couple of hours. At the beginning of a long stretch of shallow water she allowed a few scattered hoofprints to show.

Then she turned them about and they waded back downstream. Where the river forked, she took the fork to the far side and continued to wade. She suspected that Gerae would follow as soon as he could escape the eyes of his neighbors. This wouldn't make it so easy for him, particularly if he sneaked off after dark.

She mind-sent this to the mare and received a feeling of amused agreement. Something about the response caught Eleeri's attention. There had been a note of intelligence in the sending. The amusement had been more sophisticated than the simple emotion of an animal. She spoke again, sending as she did so.

"May I be favored with a name I can use for you and the small one?"

Distrust!

"It doesn't have to be your own, just something I can use. Humans feel awkward when there is no name."

Amusement again, consideration. Then *I am Tharna. My son is Hylan.*

Eleeri halted her footsteps before she realized. That had not been the mind-send of a beast. It had been the clear concise sending of an intelligent mind.

The mare's mind sent wicked laughter. *Humans! They say we wear beast shape, therefore we are beasts, and stupid. True, the males of our kind are often not as bright, but we are more than mere animals, shape or no shape.* The mare found with surprise of her own that the human was pleased with this. *Why does this information delight you?*

Eleeri tried to explain and gave it up, simply sending her emotion in a rush of feeling. Increased anger at the treatment of mare and foal, friendship that could be deeper with an intelligent mind, admiration of the pair— of the mare's courage, of the foal's beauty. It was that last which melted the receiver a little.

My son is a fine colt. I marvel, human, that you appreciate him. Yet I suppose even a dull human can see his beauty.

Eleeri assured her she could. She glanced at the slender legs as they hung over the bedroll and a thought occurred.

"That man will pursue us all, I am sure of it. Do you know much of this land? Is there a place where you might be safe?"

If he follows us alone, there are few places. There is nothing to divert him from our trail. Nor would my kind become involved. They would see no reason to do so. I see no chance of being free of him unless he is killed.

Eleeri walked on in silence, considering. If Gerae wouldn't stop following, then he would just have to be dealt with. She'd seen his eyes on her and her possessions. If he could kill all of them, he would have a good horse, its gear, and everything else in her saddlebags. It might even be that the thought of loot pulled him more strongly than the death of the Keplians.

There'd been something else in his last look. If he took her unaware, she, too, might be a long time dying. He hadn't scrupled to torture a foal. Out here where no one would know her ending, he was unlikely to have scruples about her, either.

To take her mind from the thought, she began to question Tharna. "What do you know of the Dark?"

The mare's skin shivered in response. *There is a tower on the lands my people graze. For long and long it was empty. Half-ruined. Then one came. The Keplian stallions answer his demands. They have become still more cruel. We have always been enemies to others who share the lands. We kill them where we can, as they kill us. Now the tower lord demands we do not do this.*

"How does he enforce that?"

He can lay on us a compulsion. At first he did so often. The stallions were used to bring humans to him.

"How did they bring humans?"

Tharna snorted in apparent amusement. *Humans love horses. Are my kind not far more beautiful? We appear tame. When we appear willing to be ridden, humans will risk much for that favor. Once on our backs, they are caught. Unable to dismount. They may thus be borne to the tower.* She whisked her tail in disgust. *I do not approve. That is, I did not. Now I think it would be well if humans were all taken to this tower lord. They are his kind. Let him use them.*

"What *does* he do with them?"

I know not. Only that they go in and do not come out again. Eleeri was left to consider that in silence. Her mind then returned to the worry of Gerae. The mare, too, believed he would follow them. He might even be able to obtain help from others if he lied with sufficient conviction.

Her eyes went to Hylan. His legs were badly bruised, and she was no trained vet. It would be at least a week before the injuries healed sufficiently for the foal to do his share of the walking. On the other hand, Gerae already had two good horses, thanks to her bargain. He could ride both into exhaustion to catch her—*if* he could find them at all. With luck he was floundering about on a riverbank many miles from here. She regretted giving up the horses she had cared for and loved. Gerae might ill treat them in an effort to catch up. But if she kept to her tactics of muddling trails, he would spend more time watching the ground and riding slowly. That would spare innocent beasts as well as possibly gaining her and the Keplians time and miles on him.

Tharna agreed. Not that the Keplian cared for horses, or for humans, but the safety of Hylan was everything to her. If this man could be kept from her foal, she would agree to any idea which might work. She, too, understood the danger; with her colt unable to walk, she must reluctantly depend on the human to keep him safe. It galled her. But at least the human spoke to her fairly, treating her as a Keplian and not as one of the stupid beasts they rode.

Two days passed as they continued to follow the river road. At intervals they halted for the colt to nurse. At night they took it in turns to watch, half a night each. Both had the feeling that behind them Gerae followed.

They were right. Worse still, he was not alone but had successfully convinced two others to join him. Thus far they had been spectacularly unsuccessful in their hunt. They had chased the trail upriver, found the deliberate hoofmarks, and wasted more than a day following farther upriver as they scanned the banks. Then, fearing they had missed where their quarry had left the water, they had backtracked very slowly. They had then ridden on into the beginning of the mountains.

"She wouldn't come here, Gerae. It's to my mind they've gone on down the other fork."

"Why would they do that?"

His companion snorted angrily. "I reckon they won't take that foal into the mountains. It won't be able to walk yet, not for days. No, they'll stick to the plain. Hope to lead us into some Keplian trap. If we split up, we can check the bank on both sides at once. That'll cut down tracking time."

It did, but by the time they struck Eleeri's tracks again, she and the Keplians were skirting the mountain spur. They kept within the foothills. As long as they traveled at a walk, the foal was no great burden to the horse. At first the mare's bruises and lash marks had pained her greatly, but with the passage of days they healed slowly. The girl's obvious concern for her, the offering of herbs to help her heal, surprised the mare. She was not used to a human who liked her. That Eleeri honestly did, and that the emotions of that liking and would-be friendship were coloring her every mind-send, were gradually winning the mare over.

They had spoken little as they marched. Now Tharna found herself wanting to talk, to discover why this human was so different from those others she had known.

She hovered over her foal. Hylan was improving with each day that passed. Soon he would be able to walk part of the trail instead of being carried the whole time. The human's interaction with the foal had also surprised her. Hylan clearly trusted the girl and Tharna wasn't sure she approved that. But the human had helped the colt's injured legs, rubbing on the juice of mixed herbs to ease the pain. She laughed with him, stroked and patted him with affection. Lifted him with such care at each resting place. The mare watched her colt as he trusted, and slowly she, too, began to trust.

Behind them the pursuit had quickened. The three had met others, who had loaned them spare horses in their supposed pursuit of killers in exchange for their own leg-weary mounts. The trade enabled the trio to press the trail hard.

Days slipped by. The colt spent more and more of his time walking on his own legs now, strengthening with the love and care showered on him. Tharna felt strange as she watched the human throw gentle arms about him. She felt the overflow of love as Eleeri stroked her son. Without consciously deciding to do so, she had steered their trail around the Keplian lands. Thus far they had met none of her own kind.

She feared their reaction if they did. How would they see her wanderings with this human. Worse still, how would they view the friendship between a Keplian foal and human? She could guess at that one. She had no desire to see her son slaughtered as a traitor. As they walked, she began for the first time to question her allegiances. She wanted to talk over her thoughts but feared to speak. This could still be some trick of a cunning and clever race. Perhaps the girl had fooled her. Time would doubtless show, if she made no foolish moves herself. She paced on, following the lead horse.

Unknown to Eleeri, they had been seen. Valley scouts had spotted them as they skirted the mountains, and watched the direction of their travel. They had not been close enough to see more than a girl with three horses, but they mentioned it to the next travelers they met. These were Gerae and his men, well astray to the northwest. With that information they rode hard to intersect Eleeri's path.

Do you believe we have left those behind? Tharna queried as they slowed for the trailing colt.

The girl sighed. "I fear not. Indeed I had ill dreams last night, dreams of pain and death, of evil that swooped to drink blood." She quickened her feet as Hylan caught up. "I think we need to rest for several days soon. Hylan grows stronger, but all this walking is still too much for him. He needs time to grow in peace, but where do we find such a place?" As they followed the path to the east, they had climbed around the foothills. High up as they were, all were able to see that far ahead there lay a river, glinting brightly in the sunlight.

"Perhaps there in the mountains beyond the river we can find a place to be safe. For Hylan to grow."

The mare said nothing, plodding on. That direction seemed as good as any other to her. Only let the foal be safe. To ensure that, she would travel with a human, traverse her whole land, deal with demons and powers. Anything, as long as her beloved son survived.

She was young, Hylan her first foal. The coupling that had bred him had been, for her, a shocking experience. She had been overawed by the larger, older stallion. She had rebelled, but a bitten shoulder and several powerful kicks had subdued her. It was nature, but she was not eager to repeat the experience. At the moment she did not miss the company of her own kind.

That night as they camped, Hylan was better. Previous halts had seen him sore and leg-weary. But now, as the days passed, he was adjusting to trail life and his legs healed slowly.

This camp, for the first time he bounced as they halted. Eleeri went to him, running her hands gently down the slender legs. She massaged, stretching each leg in turn with a hand under Hylan's fetlock. He made small nickering sounds of pleasure, enjoying the attention. Released, he galloped in a wide circle, bucking as he flew past. Eleeri laughed, turning to Tharna to share the moment.

"He's improving. Soon he'll be outrunning you."

I would give my life to have it so, the mare sent soberly.

"Yes." Eleeri's mind turned back to their conversation

of previous days. "Tharna, why *are* humans so afraid of your people?"

The mare was silent. Then she tossed her head. *Perhaps because we have never allied with the Light. Many stallions deliberately chose the Dark, so that we are all accounted evil. Shamans, others who seek aid to ride into darkness, all come to us. All humans know of us is that we carry them away, never to be seen again. Or that those of the Dark use us as mounts.

Once as a foal I saw a human taken to the tower. It was just after the lord had come there. The man fought well. He cried aloud, calling on powers and struggling to leap from the stallion's back. He failed. Her hoof kicked idly at the turf. *I do not approve of this. Let the humans leave us alone, and we should do the same.*

Eleeri agreed with a short nod. The conversation lapsed as they turned to watch the colt again. Hylan had no time for serious discussion. He was too busy enjoying the warm evening.

The next day, across the plain they marched. If they found a ford or bridge, they could cross. If not, they must search. Something told Eleeri that safety might be found in the bordering mountains.

She had come to love the Keplian foal; for Hylan she would fight as ferociously as his dam. She was unsure about the mare, sensing Tharna's own doubts about humans still. But it no longer mattered to her. She loathed the cruelty with which the Keplian had been handled. She would fight before she allowed Tharna to fall into such hands again.

Late that night she, too, wondered how others would act if their small company was spied. Other Keplians, of the true Dark or not, would surely seek to slay them all. She roused early and ate as she saddled the horse again.

There was a feeling at the back of her neck that said to hurry, hurry.

Next morning they moved out, heading directly for the river at a brisk walk. Hylan bounced along, and the sun was warm on their backs. But still Eleeri was uneasy. She felt as if hostile eyes watched. She eyed brush to her right. Was the danger there? Where?

Then from the clump of trees toward their left came wild cries. Eleeri spun to see three riders bearing down on them. In one flashing look she recognized Gerae. So, he'd found them and now he came to count coup, to take his prizes.

Tharna was racing forward to fight, but spears held her off. Her opponents laughed as blood streamed from her wounds. They would ride around her, take the foal. She could only die with the bitter knowledge she had failed him. She shrieked, rising on her hind legs. If it must be so, it must be so. Better to die fighting for her son than to live and see him die before her. She plunged forward.

5

Behind her Eleeri spun her mount, then froze him with a mental command. Her hands moved even faster as bowstring snapped taut and arrow flew. She had always had an eye for bow skill, but the years of Far Traveler's teaching and her own hours of practice had refined this even more. Now she shot, whipped another arrow to bow, and shot again. The men who fronted the frantic mare went down. Neither was dead, not for those fractions of a second before Tharna reached them. After that they were not only dead but bloodily so.

Gerae had seen them fall. He fled—at the fastest speed he could goad his mount to attaining. But arrows fly faster. Tharna had started after him, and as he slid limply from his racing horse, she reached him with teeth and hooves. Not until the body was all but shredded did she desist. Hylan stood by. To a small colt untouched, it was all very exciting, but he was hungry again. He whickered hopefully.

His mother leaped for him, running her muzzle over his body. He was uninjured. She swung her hindquarters to allow him to nurse and stood, deeply contented. The girl approached and Tharna made an ugly sound, a kind of low snarling.

Eleeri looked into her eyes. They blazed a terrible red. She'd never really noticed that before. But now that she thought of it, the mare's eyes had always had a reddish cast. Oh, well, Tharna wasn't a horse; it was probably the Keplian eye color. She moved forward, crooning to the colt. Her mind reached out to her friend as she did so.

Tharna was off guard mentally. For the first time the girl's mind penetrated her surface thoughts. She swayed in shock. Ka-dih, what was this one to whom Eleeri had given friendship? A roiling maelstrom of emotion met her startled mind. Different. Terrifying. She disciplined herself. This was Tharna. They had traveled together, cared for Hylan together, fought to guard one another. This was a Keplian, she reminded herself, not a horse; she must accept Tharna's differences and cherish the friend in her.

As she struggled, the mare stood motionless, waiting, poised like a predator. With a wild effort, Eleeri subdued her fears and walked forward.

"Battle-sister, is Hylan unhurt?"

A vast surprise enveloped her so that she halted. Her emotion? No, it was the mare's emotions she felt. She lifted a slow hand to stroke the mane out of her friend's eyes.

"What is all this surprise, and is Hylan unhurt?"

The mare found mind-voice. *My son is uninjured, thanks to you and your arrows. But—* she faltered, *you still wish to travel with me?*

"How not?"

*You touched my mind truly. I felt it, I felt your shock,

your fear. Others of your kind have done this and always they have then turned against us to kill. Will you now hate me and mine, seek to slay?* She peered down thoughtfully. *Once, when I thought of this, I wondered if reaching our inner minds sent humans mad. Humans hate and fear us as it is. Maybe to know us is to fear us even more.* Her skin shivered.

Eleeri reached out again. This time, knowing what seethed below the surface thought, she was able to control her instinctive fear. Gradually she made sense of the seething power, the blazing emotions, finding they quietened as she did so. It was as if her own lessening of fear soothed the mare's. Using that knowledge, she smoothed out their emotions until both were calm again. She stood thinking as the colt nursed.

"Tharna, it seems to me that we act on each other."

The fine powerful head above her nodded.

Eleeri leaned against a warm shoulder, absently stroking it. "That first contact with your mind was terrible. But when I thrust away fear and returned, it was no longer so frightening. Now, as my mind touches yours without fear, your mind, too, is calm." She deepened the bond slowly and spoke then, asking the question she had thought before.

"Are you of the Dark, battle-sister? I do not think so, but those others did."

The mare shook her head and stamped a hoof, bringing a squeal of indignation from the foal. He hadn't finished yet. His mother should remain still.

*We are not born to the Dark, only to shade and shadow. Some make the choice to join wholly with the Dark, others do not. Long ago when the adepts warred, we were made. Why, we do not know. They made other races, too.

*Many of the stallions turn to the Dark, fewer mares.

Our males are more warlike. The stallions resent humans, I think, for their fears, their hates, and for all that humans seem to have.*

"Would you turn to the Dark?"

The mare lowered her head to Eleeri's shoulder. *Not now, battle-sister. You killed your own to save mine.* A soft nose brushed against a softer cheek. *I have always refused to speak your name. Now I do. Eleeri I name you. Battle-sister you have named me. Do you also name me as friend?*

The girl's hands smoothed the warm hide. "I do so. Neither un-friend nor half-friend are you, but friend. Sister-kin, if you will accept it so, and kin to the small one."

Acceptance and a shy pleasure radiated from the mare. Arms about the muscled neck, Eleeri stood for long minutes, savoring the communion. She loved horses, but they could only fill her loneliness so far. But this, this was fullness. A kin-sister, a friend, one to speak with who could reply. One to care for who cared in return. She pushed herself away and took down the bag where she kept her herbs.

"A good sister would care for your wounds." She brushed on the soothing juices with gentle fingers. Her hands admired the powerful muscles, the sleek hide, the arched and flowing mane and tail.

Under twin pleasures of hand and mind, the mare relaxed, savoring the first deep communion she had ever enjoyed. Friendship wove its way through her being. Only with her mother had she felt this acceptance before. She felt the bitterness drain away, her hatred of humans who condemned what they could not understand. This one was not like that. This one had faced all she found, and accepted.

She felt as if she floated, trusting, serene. Long moments slipped by. She loved this one, battle-sister, friend, kin-kind. The Dark whispered to her—and was rejected. Who had need of such a night when sunlight beckoned? Besides, she knew well that always the Dark betrayed. So many of her kind had been seduced by its wiles, and lived only long enough to regret that seduction. She would not be one; she was shade and shadow, but not the Dark, never the Dark now that she understood the Light.

In perfect accord, the three set out on the last mile to the river. Hylan did not understand what had happened. He only knew that his mother and friend were happy. It was enough.

Do we cross the river or follow it? Tharna queried, scanning the plain doubtfully. In her mind Eleeri saw pictures of the Gray Ones who often roamed this area.

"If this is their place, best we get away. From your mind they're no respecters of either of our kinds."

They trotted hurriedly along the riverbank. No crossing could be seen and the water ran deep and strongly.

"Do you know this area well?"

Tharna shook her head. *I think the river runs far. It comes from the western mountains, and I have heard of a lake somewhere to the west also. The Gray Ones avoid the area; there are ruins there which are un-friend to their kind.*

"Good. Then we'll go that way," Eleeri said practically. "Any place they don't like should be right for us." She headed her mount upriver and the Keplians followed.

Now travel together was delight. They explored each other's ideas and the mare heard much of what a different world could be like. About them the scenery was unchanging.

Eleeri had time to muse upon Tharna's mind-pictures of the Gray Ones and what Cynan had said of them. It was possible Tharna's enmity for the creatures colored her impressions to some extent. Still, Eleeri thought, they did not attract her as any kind of ally. They walked upright in a slouch. The head was narrow, with tooth-filled mouth and small red eyes gleaming from shaggy, dirt-matted gray fur. From Tharna's memories Eleeri knew the brutes to be intelligent. Well, they could speak but rarely did. Their habits were such as to disgust most intelligent beings. They wore no clothes, nor did they carry weapons.

They were fighters if brought to bay, or in the grip of battle-madness. Otherwise they preferred to fight only when the odds were strongly in their favor. Like much of the Dark, they feared to cross running water. Until blood-mad, they would hold back from that.

Since they were nearing Gray One territory, Eleeri kept her bow ready now. Beside her the mare, too, was thinking. The way she and the human seemed to agree interested her oddly. The Keplians had no real legends of origin. There were only vague beliefs that they had been created by adepts during the ancient wars. Some had believed horses to have been the basis for that creation. They had been slain if they voiced that belief, though. No stallion would endure the idea. Yet it felt so comfortable to walk beside this human. So peaceful.

She watched the plodding pony. What would it feel like to bear a human like that? Not with saddle and bridle, but bare of back, feeling every shift and sway of the human's body? She thrust the idea away, concentrating on Eleeri's enjoyment of the day instead. She could read some of that. The river flowing by in crystal ripples, the stones' gray hues, the brown of river earth showing in patches where stones had shifted. Shrubs and often large clumps of trees provided shade and shelter for many bright birds.

For the first time Tharna found beauty pointed out to her, a mutual delight.

Their thoughts flowed together more casually now as they found pleasure in each other's company. Hylan, too, seemed to be gaining in intelligence. The mare wondered about that. Could it be that such communion allowed him to find potential denied to others of his sex? Stallions mated and fought—that was their destiny. But was it? She followed the horse as her mind grappled with new ideas. She was certain that no one of her kind had ever been friend and sister-kin to a human before. Or if they had, it was time out of mind ago. No legends existed of this. No human had ever been moved to accept a Keplian as friend; always before they had fled or given battle when minds touched.

But this one had done more. And it was as if Eleeri's acceptance of Tharna had opened new doors within the mare. As if—as if it were *right* that they be friends. The Great Ones of old had designed Keplians. Had it been for this, to walk as their friends? The human—no, *Eleeri*— admired her friend's beauty and strength. She spoke with pride that Tharna could outspeed the horse. There was love and friendship in her mind whenever she turned to Tharna or Hylan. Was this how it had once been intended to be?

The mare did not know, but she knew that this idea pleased her. Her kind lived in isolation even among themselves. A mare would fight savagely for her foal, but only as long as he suckled. After that, he was ignored. Would she cease to love Hylan once he grew?

She shivered her skin, to chase away the idea as she would a fly. Never. She would love her son as long as they both lived. Her head came up and, feeling the sunlight on her back, she leaped, twisting into the air. It felt good to unkink powerful muscles. She thrust up again and with a baby squeal of excitement Hylan followed suit.

Eleeri looked back and laughed as the Keplians bucked and bounced in the clear air. With their friendship assured, it was wonderful how Tharna had become almost a different being. The colt, too, was growing, in mind abilities as well as size.

Race you to the river!

They had drifted away as the water curved slowly to their right. Now hooves pounded as horse and rider, with the Keplian mare before them, thundered toward the line of trees again. Hylan fell back, baby legs unable to keep up with even a horse as yet. His indignant cry was lost in the drum roll of hooves. They halted at the river and drank while Eleeri puttered along the bank watching the current.

"Does a stream run from this to the lake?"

As I remember, it does, Tharna responded.

"Well, we'll stay this side of the river until we reach it. The stream should be shallower and so should the river, once we've passed the lake. We may be able to find a ford then."

The Keplian stared out across the water. It was true they could not risk crossing yet. Hylan was too weak to risk him in such a current. But the river was slackening; if it continued to do so, they might be able to risk a crossing soon. She would be happy to be out of the Gray Ones' territory. More than one Keplian foal had fallen to their teeth, even mares weakened by birthing or accident. She sent agreement and wandered on along the water's edge.

Hylan arrived then and she licked him lovingly. He was so strong, so beautiful. Altogether a marvelous son—there had never been such a one, so wise and so clever. She followed the water and Hylan trailed his mother as Eleeri remounted. Their pace was slow. Not that the land was so rough, but large thickets of brush were now appearing along the riverbank. Rather than force passage, the friends were detouring around these, and each took them farther from the river until they found a path back.

The brush was a nuisance, the girl thought. But it was beautiful. The leaves were a light and silvery green. Berries grew in bird-appreciated profusion, and many species feasted merrily. She leaned down to pluck handfuls for herself after checking with Tharna. The ripe globes burst sweetly in her mouth. They had the smallest touch of tartness to their taste, just enough to quench thirst as well as hunger. She ate as they traveled, and when the bushes began to thin out, she dismounted. To the surprise of the Keplian mare, her friend now dug in the earth by a bush.

What is it that you do?

The girl looked up and grinned. "These berries are wonderful. I don't know where we're going, but I thought it'd be nice to have them when we get there."

As she spoke, she was carefully separating several tiny runners from their mother. She had dug out the turf in which their roots were encased and now she tucked plants and earth securely into a saddlebag. Tharna looked on, eyes wide with interest and amusement. Humans: no wonder the world changed about them. It would never have occurred to a Keplian to do that, even if they could. Yet why not? Would it not be useful to have food where you wished it?

They paced on, following the life-giving water. As Hylan tired, they rested; with the night they slept. Time had no meaning beyond that. Rain drove them to shelter until it passed, then they moved on again. As they waited, Eleeri had chosen sticks. Now as she rode she smoothed the shafts, looking them over carefully and discarding a few. Two of the arrows she had shot at Gerae and his companions had been broken in their fall. The third Tharna had broken in her haste to ensure the man's death. There would be other dangers; best she had a good supply of arrows. She worked as she rode; with Tharna ahead, the horse would merely follow.

Within two more days her quiver was full. She continued to work. It was not hard to do; she could converse with her friends as well. But once an enemy was sighted, there would be no time to make weapons.

Later she believed that something must have warned her. The impulse to make the arrows had been so strong. By the time they were attacked, she had more than three dozen riding in quiver and bedroll. Just after daylight they paused as Tharna mind-sent.

Danger, sister-kin. The scent of Gray Ones comes to me on the breeze. They track us swiftly.

Eleeri sent her mount into a slow trot. "How far ahead is the lake stream, do you think?"

Last time the wind blew from there, it was far yet. But that was a day's travel ago. I think by now it is close, although the smell blows away from us. What should we do?

Eleeri thought quickly. It was the art of a warrior to make such decisions based on little knowledge and yet be correct. She spoke and the Keplians obeyed. Hylan leaped into a canter, running ahead of his dam and her friend. He could mind-send some distance by now, sufficient for them to know what was ahead. With luck, the pursuing pack would see that the adults kept to a steady pace, and assume the foal merely played.

Hylan raced up the shallow rise ahead, scanned the land before him with staring eyes. Down a long slope the lake glinted ahead under the sun. A stream lightly tumbled to it from the lustier river. He sent that and ran on.

The stream could be crossed near its junction with the lake. The water was deep, but the adults would be able to forge passage; it was not that strong a current. He stood there waiting. His family was some way back by now and could not be contacted.

Within the trees the Gray Ones trotted more quickly. Ahead their prey was dawdling. They could come up with them soon, then the feasting. There were more than a dozen of the pursuers. They could overcome any miserable Keplian and human. Their mouths watered. The foal would be the most tender; the mare's despair would spice the dish. They hurried on.

Eleeri had held to the slow trot. It covered ground without tiring them, but kept them ahead. A quick flicker of her eyes to the rear and she saw that those who followed were closer. Still she kept to the pose of unwariness. Tharna crested the rise and as they started down the long slope, both received Hylan's mind-picture.

As one they leaped forward, linked in battle plan. The thunder of hooves spurred the Gray Ones to hot pursuit, but the companions were minutes ahead as they reached Hylan and stream. With flying fingers, Eleeri detached her stirrup leathers, buckling them together and looping them about the foal's belly. Then she thrust her mount forward into the water, Hylan at his side. The support would keep him close, keep his head above the water as they swam.

At the stream Tharna turned at bay. She would hold the Gray Ones while her foal crossed. It looked as if there had once been a ford here, but either the water was higher than usual or it had altered over time. Now the water was deep enough to force Eleeri and her mount to swim, but there was still one advantage left to them. Along the stream banks, thorn bushes grew thickly; only at the ford was there a clear space to the water.

Perhaps in another place the bushes thinned, but the pursuers seemed disinclined to search it out. Tharna stood before the gap, hooves at the ready, teeth bared. Eleeri was pressing her mount as hard as was safe. Even with the thorns protecting her flanks, the mare was in a lot of trouble; those wolf things hadn't looked like pushovers to her. She splashed up the far bank, reached down to release the foal, and swung her horse back to the water. For a brief moment she sat to assess the situation.

Tharna was holding them. Not easily, but the hunt was unwilling to risk her teeth and hooves. Still the sounds were becoming more frenzied. Soon they would work themselves into a killing rage in which even death did not matter to them. If only Eleeri could break them before that occurred.

She heeled the horse downstream, where she could see the Gray Ones better and at an angle to the mare. Good. The bushes were low enough so that from the bank where it rose a little on this side, she could get a shot. She drew her bow, strung an arrow, waited as she breathed in, then loosed.

Before the hunt could react, another arrow was already in the air, then another. Thanks be to Ka-dih for driving her to making these. Crude they might be, but they carried well enough and shot straight over this slight distance. They also killed, as the Gray Ones could now attest. Within minutes four of their number were dead, three more wounded. It was enough for the pack. With yelps and threats, they withdrew. As Tharna swam to join her, Eleeri kept watch.

"What do we do about them? Will they follow?"

The mare snorted to clear her nostrils. *I think it unlikely. We have cost them dear and they like to fight only when the odds favor them. What they may do is alert any of their kind on this side. Best we leave swiftly and hide our trail if we can.*

Eleeri eyed her. Foam spattered sleek black flanks, blood dappled lower chest and one leg.

"What sort of shape are you in if we do have to run for it again?"

If we must, we must. I'll keep up.

The girl snorted in turn. "I'd feel happier if we cleaned you up first. Rest while I do it, then we can move on. Besides, I think Hylan is hungry."

The foal proved that at once as he slid around his mother's hindquarters, settling to nurse. Carefully Eleeri swabbed at the slight wounds marring Tharna's hide. They were shallow, but— a thought occurred to her.

"Tharna, those wolf-people, um—you don't get anything from their bites, do you?"

The mare looked bemused. With that question had come a very odd mind-picture of her turning into a Gray One herself.

What is it you fear?

Eleeri felt a little foolish, but better safe than sorry. "Well, in my world there are tales. That one who is bitten by a being like that will become one each full moon."

The mare felt a painful sensation in her chest. A constriction—her breathing began to choke—then she was making a terrible squealing whinnying sound.

Eleeri leaped forward in despair—it was happening. Oh, gods, there must be something she could do. Tharna pushed her back with a soft nose and stood head hanging down. In high indignation the girl suddenly realized that the mare was laughing. She relaxed. She'd never heard such a sound before, but her own mouth curved into a grin as minds met.

"So it doesn't happen here. I get it."

Oh, sister-kin. It is as well. What a thing it would be if the Gray Ones could increase their numbers in such a way. But no, the only thing that their bites do is kill you if they go deep enough. These are shallow wounds, slashes more than bites. You have cleaned them, so they will not fester. Hylan has rested and drunk; let us go now.

Eleeri mounted and sat a moment surveying the land within eyeshot. The lake was veiled in a faint mist; something told her they should travel away from it. She nudged her mount upstream and studied the river. It was shallower after the loss of the stream water. If it continued to grow shallow, they would be able to cross it with care in a few more miles. The land was beginning to rise again very slowly. Ahead lay more mountains, deeply scored by canyons and ridges. Her heart yearned toward them.

She turned back to her friend. "Is there a direction you'd prefer?"

None. Make a decision for us, battle-sister.

Wordlessly Eleeri looked forward to the mountains. They called; she would answer. Within them it might be that they would find a place to shelter. If nothing else, they would find places to hold off Gray Ones who came hunting. Her mind settled as she kicked the horse forward. It would be the mountains.

The mare and foal fell in behind her as she rode. Unconsciously the girl had mind-sent as emotion touched her. They, too, were drawn by the mountains now. The tiny group trotted forward, leaving the stream and lake behind them. On their right the river tumbled, bright glittering water over black rock rapids.

Soon they would have to cross it before it shifted in the

half circle that would drive them back to the lowlands. They reached the fork by nightfall. Eleeri reached for her stirrup leathers again and called Hylan. Tharna was puzzled.

Why cross now?

"Old saying: cross rivers before you sleep."

The mare looked even more puzzled and the girl sent her a swift succession of mind-pictures. Of rivers that rose in the night and could no longer be forded. Of enemies who struck at a sleeping camp, leaving warriors with their backs to a river and no place to retreat safely. The mare nodded silently; agreement flashed between them. With the foal safely secured, they swam the shallow branch. It was close to dusk and they walked on to look over the other fork. There, too, the water was low.

They hesitated at its brink. To sleep here within the forks was to have a secure camp. Eleeri glanced thoughtfully at the banks and bushes. They could camp in that clump of high brush and be screened from casual view. There were large heaps of old dry wood along the riverside, tossed up by ancient floods. If she prepared a fire, it could be lit if danger threatened. Her suggestion was approved and even Hylan aided in gathering the logs. With that in place as darkness fell, all felt more secure. The wood was old and tinder dry. It would flame at the very breath of fire, and Eleeri's lighter was always nearby.

Great dark masses against the half-lit sky and stars, the mountains loomed. The girl lay looking up at them and wondering what had happened to her over the last year. She glanced down at her watch. It ran on a long-life battery and still worked. She peered closer and smothered a sudden laugh. Today had been her birthday. She was seventeen today.

She drifted off to sleep, still smiling. It had been some

birthday, running from werewolves in the company of a couple of talking horses. This last year had been a lulu. She couldn't wait to find out what the next might hold. It wouldn't be boring. . . . She giggled drowsily and sleep came down like a cloak.

6

The dawn was fine again and the second river fork appeared lower. They crossed with care, trotting up the farther bank.

Into the mountains?

Eleeri still felt the drawing from the bulk that now loomed higher before them. Somewhere within that maze of upthrust crags they would find what she sought.

"Yes, but I see no need to make too great a haste."

They strolled, enjoying the bright sun, the berry bushes, the birds that were different from those of the plains but sang as sweetly. Hylan skipped, bucking and capering from one to the other. He was growing swiftly; soon he could be weaned and independent. Tharna feared that. In her own foalhood she had seen the colts change then. They became duller, more savage, more apt to accept the Dark, to be its tools.

She adored her son, her firstborn, but she had never been quite as the other mares herself. She had questioned, where they accepted. It was strange, traveling with Eleeri; it was as if some of the girl's intelligence was communicated to Hylan. He was more intelligent, more questioning than other colts of his age. He thought more.

They ambled on past tall trees housing squawking red and blue birds. Tharna paused to graze on a succulent patch of grass, her mind still busy. Ahead of her, Eleeri strung her bow and shot quickly. A rabbit dropped. A fat buck. Humans ate meat, Keplians ate grass, Tharna mused. Although those who accepted evil might well be fed on other, less savory foods.

Yet this was her sister-kin; she felt closer to the human than she ever had to her own kind. Hylan loved Eleeri. Keplians were like Gray Ones, Flannan, Thas, Krogran—all races made by adepts. Her mind made a sudden wild leap. Could it be—was it possible—could her kind have been made to accompany humans? Perhaps a human who loved horses greatly, one who wished for an intelligent one to walk beside him as a friend, not as a servant? She grazed absently, mind busy with this concept. In trusting the human who saved Hylan, in becoming her friend, had she unknowingly fulfilled a long-ago destiny? She decided she liked the idea, but she would not share it, not yet.

Into the foothills they moved, wandering along likely trails, investigating dead-ended canyons, and drinking from tiny streams. But always their main course was deeper into the mountains. Now and again they returned to the river, although it was greatly depleted by now, almost a stream itself. Eleeri was restless. It was as if something called her to act, but what she was to do, she did not know.

One morning before dawn, she shuffled off her bedding

and rose to walk. Her feet took her higher, out of the gully and on up the slope above it.

From the north and a little west there came a sudden wrenching pull. At her throat an answering warmth awoke. With a stifled gasp, she leaned forward, opening her shirt. The jet horse pendant swung free, eyes afire in the miniature head. But even as she watched, they changed, no longer points of fire but now the deep blue of sapphires. She blinked. The color remained. Over her settled a conviction that this was a sign. She cupped the pendant in her hand and turned away. The eyes glowed red. Back to the direction that tugged at her—blue eyes again, and now light seemed to emanate from them also.

The girl looked down. Cynan had given her this as a leave-taking. Had he had any idea of what it was he gifted? She thought not. Slowly she allowed the pendant to swing free. Then she spoke in a whisper.

"In that direction must we go to seek the Light?" The pendant flamed, a brightness that made her squeeze her eyelids shut. She opened them cautiously. This was medicine of some kind. From what Tharna had been able to tell her of this land, it was unlikely anything of the Dark could counterfeit that of the Light. Thus the pendant was probably truthful.

She touched the tiny horse with a forefinger, stroked the proud head. "As you say, so shall we do. We travel to the north and west to seek the Light. Guard our journey, bring us safe to the Light." She did not know to whom she spoke, only that she felt them to be half friend at least, or even whole friend. That there was work for her here—that she was sure of. Did not the gods always seek human aid? It was ill to meddle with matters of the gods, but worse still to refuse an asked-for help. She paced slowly back to her bedroll. From the upper slope she had seen a single peak to the northwest. In that direction they would travel at daybreak. She hoped Tharna would not mind.

The mare was suspicious. *How do you know that you were not tricked?*

Eleeri held out the pendant silently. The eyes still shone a rich blue in the sunlight. The color of the light, of life. The mare was silenced. Her son bounced happily. To him it was an adventure. He was more than eager to be on their way, and already he was trotting down the faint trail in the direction Eleeri had pointed out. Girl and mare sent amusement to each other, swinging onto the trail behind him. Before them the peak loomed, but they would not hurry. Thus far they had seen neither Gray Ones nor other creatures of the dark in the hills, but it was as well to be wary. There could yet be dangers not altogether of the Dark.

In these higher hills feeding was thin. The mare must graze longer to find sufficient food. Eleeri found enough small game to feed herself with far less difficulty. She used the time to explore, allowing her mount to graze with the Keplians. On foot she scrambled up and down crags, investigated caves, and thoroughly enjoyed the stretching of muscles grown stiff from riding. Slowly they neared the peak. By now the imperative was strong enough to be felt by all but the pony.

Why does it call to us also? Tharna looked about her. *We wear no pendant; we are of the shadow. This is a thing of the Light.*

Eleeri, who was standing close, put up her arms about the sleek neck, then patted the colt as he pushed her for attention. "The pendant was changed," she said slowly, feeling the rightness of her words as she said them. "Maybe we are being led to a place where you also will be offered a change."

The mare reared back. *And if we do not wish to be other than what we are?*

"Then you shall not be," Eleeri said positively. "It is to my mind that you are offered a gift. It is for you to take it or refuse. I will not allow you to be forced into that which you do not wish. This I swear, sister-kin."

Tharna's agitation subsided. *We travel with you, but if I fear this thing we seek will change us against our wishes or even yours, our roads part. Until then they lie together.* She resumed grazing. Eleeri refrained from pointing out that by that time it might be too late. If it was, it would be too late for her, too, since she would set herself against anything that menaced her friend's wishes. She flung the thought from her with a twist of her shoulders. This seeking was of the light; she knew it. As soon as her friends had finished grazing, they would find the source of the compulsion. It could not be far away now.

After a long weary day of search, she was forced to admit her defeat.

"If this place is anywhere about, I certainly can't see it."

I have heard that such places may be hidden. Your pendant showed you the direction. Should you not wait, eat and rest, then call on its help? Maybe it can aid us again. Tharna was practical. Eleeri sank to the grass and dug busily in her saddlebag. From it she drew cold meat and a bag of rather tired-looking berries. From that the mare understood her advice to be accepted. She grazed, keeping an eye on the girl. If there was anything she could do to help when the time came, she would do so willingly.

Without intent, Eleeri fell asleep. The long day had been tiring, and with her stomach full, sleep came easily. She woke just as dawn flamed the sky. Her pendant slipped naturally into her hand and she gazed at it thoughtfully. Could it help her to find this mysterious place?

The truth was, she wasn't at all sure why she was searching. Only that it had grown to be a driving force. At first it had been a quiet calling. A longing for a place to be free in safety. Later, with her love for the mare and colt, the need for a refuge had become obvious. They must have a place where Hylan could grow in peace, where they could live without fear. But under that there was still the call. As if something inside of her yearned for a home she had never known. It was foolish. She remembered her home with Far Traveler perfectly well. But this was something else. Something silly, Eleeri thought. It wasn't possible to be homesick for a place you'd never lived in. Was it?

She gazed at the land around her, foothills merging into solid higher mountains. The land was rough but not the brutalized mountains of the turning. There the witches of Estcarp had wrung out the mountains like a dishcloth, using their power. Here the land was simply ordinary mountains bordering this land of Escore. Far away over the horizon lay the Valley of Green Silences. There the lady led the fight against those of the Dark. Eleeri would stay away from the valley. It was just possible they'd expect her to join them. To conform. They might even object to Tharna and Hylan.

She shook her head. She and her friends would be better off finding a refuge of their own. She studied the pendant in her hands. Cynan, once he had seen she had the horse gift, had insisted on teaching her spells to go with the amber amulets and pebbles from the place of the Old Ones. She stared down thoughtfully. The pendant had helped her before. Would it aid now? From behind her came a soft whicker of amusement.

No answers without questions, sister-kin. Ask!

Eleeri bent her concentration on the pendant. Around it grew a soft glow, a blue-green that brightened by the minute. Without thinking, she reached out and gently drew the Keplians into mind-link. The pendant flared, giving forth a blaze of light so great that Eleeri's eyes shut involuntarily. About her throat she felt a tugging—harder, harder—then it was gone and she opened her eyes to stare in wonder.

Before them stood her pendant made flesh, a great black stallion. No true horse, Eleeri knew. This was the spirit of horses. Intelligence shone from the sapphire eyes, pride was in the crest of his upthrust neck. Power flamed in every sinew, power both of strength and the Light.

With a leap he was away, and they scrambled to follow. Hoofbeats clattered up the trail and the girl bit back a cry of exasperation. They'd come this way the day before. There was nothing here. She scanned the earth under the hooves of her pony. It was hard-packed, probably an old deer trail. Rock walls rose on either side, as if this had been originally a stream bed. The occasional drifts of small stones within the curves suggested this was so. But the trail was dry now. Perhaps a change of direction, a landslip higher up now diverted any water.

The stallion swung to one side. Here the curve was larger, more of an angle. He stood poised. Then, before them all, runes flamed blue on either side of a gap Eleeri had not noticed before. She gaped at them, recognizing some. Cynan had drawn them for her and taught her to use them along with her pebbles. They were ward signs. Below blazed runes of Light, runes of guard against the Dark. They were reinforced by some she had not been taught. But she could guess them to be of power.

She turned in her saddle to look back along their trail.

This was clever: The entrance was narrow. Any who entered on horseback would have to do so in single file. The trail to this point was also narrow, steeply uphill and winding. Above, it steepened still further. To reach this entrance from uphill or down, those who came would be moving with slow caution because of the trail. They must then thrust through an opening just wide enough for one mount. If a good-sized area lay beyond, they might well have found their refuge. Judging from the rune-guarded entrance, it would take a very powerful creature of the Dark to force its way inside.

The stallion appeared beyond the wards. He turned to watch them.

"This is it. I know it." Eleeri was sure now, but Tharna watched the stallion nervously. "What is it, do you fear him?"

The mare spoke softly. *Stallions often kill colts who are not their own get. I do fear him.*

"He's not Keplian," Eleeri said quietly. "And more than a horse, too, I think. I don't believe he'd harm Hylan, or us, either."

As if the great beast had heard her words, he paced toward them. A regal head lowered to nuzzle the soft nose of the foal. A half-rear, then again the reassuring touch to the foal, and he was away, back through the gap to await their decision. Before either adult could move, Hylan had followed, small neck arched in imitation. The runes flared up as he passed. Tharna eyed them with worry.

What if they will not admit me?

"Then we look somewhere else for refuge."

Eleeri could feel her friend's fear, but before them Hylan waited. Tharna moved toward him, step by slow step. The runes blazed higher as she approached. Slowly they changed; a more silvery hue now shone in them. The girl could feel that it was becoming an effort for her friend to move, as if she waded through deep water. Without thinking, she touched with her mind, reassuring, comforting. With that linkage the effort was gone. Freed, the mare leaped to her son and caressed him with soft nuzzlings.

Eleeri followed, seeing in her turn the runes' light shine higher. The stallion ran on into a widening canyon and they gathered themselves in his wake. Before the far end of the canyon he paused and reared. His commanding whistle rang out, echoing from the cliffs. Again and again he warned without words: they were not to come this far until summoned. Then he was gone. Eleeri ran forward in distress. She had grown to love her pendant, gift of Cynan. Was she now to lose it?

Half-hidden in the lush grass it lay, tiny sapphire eyes winking up at them in the sunlight. With a sigh the girl plucked it from its nest and threaded the cord through the loop again. She felt a little strange with it now, knowing what it could be. Yet surely, if it had not been intended for her to take it up once more, it would not have returned to this form.

She strained her eyes to look down at the end of the canyon forbidden to them. A mist lay there, shot through with warm golden glimmerings. Power smoked from it. She would stay well away until asked; that was not something to meddle with uninvited.

She gazed about the remainder of the canyon. Surely this had been a hold once. In contrast to the outside, here the grass was lush and thick. Fruit trees and berry bushes lined the cliffsides.

Berry bushes! That reminded her. Laughing, Eleeri reached for her saddlebag to extract the tiny saplings she had taken. Then and there she dug out a square of turf in line with those other bushes. Lovingly she placed the saplings to add to the line. Water? She stared about as Hylan lowered his head; she could hear him drinking. She trotted over to see what he had found, to be amazed by the water's container. Hidden by the knee-high grass was a spring welling up. It flowed into a marvelously carved stone basin. Yet it was not this that amazed her. The water appeared to be flowing *uphill* from the spring. She measured with her fingers. It was true.

Oh, well, as long as the water continued to flow, she should leave well enough alone. She reached for her pack and took from it some of the dried meat. She had no time to hunt; the place was of too great an interest to do aught but explore. She wandered along, staring as she walked. If in high summer there was still water and good growth, then this was indeed a suitable place for them to remain. But why had they been called here? Perhaps the answer lay in the golden mist. She'd wait; sooner or later she'd find out. There was no hurry, she reflected, the peace of this place seeping slowly into her bones. She rounded a natural buttress in the cliffs and found herself looking at human habitation. She fell back with a small cry.

Then she grinned. The doors gaped wide, rotting from their hinges, and within she could see the drifts of leaves piled up on stone floors. How long had it taken for the doors to fall away? she wondered. Yet the spring still flowed. She studied the massive stones. They needed no power to seal them; they were sufficient to themselves. Only the wooden doors had failed, and they could be replaced, no doubt.

She walked over to stand before the entrance. Would she be welcome here? She placed a gentle hand on the massive stone doorpost. Runes glowed into life, the now familiar blue. She could not read them, but a comforting warmth stole from them, like a welcoming hand that greeted a beloved visitor. She moved to the doorway and paused, speaking to anything that might hear and accept.

"To the ruler of this place, gratitude for roof shelter, no harm from me or mine to thee and thine. I come in peace."

The runes' light shone a little greater so that she took it as an answer. Steadily she walked through the doors, entering the great hall which spread before her. Down the center of that ran a huge ancient table. It was carved from wood, of a type she had never seen before. Dust lay thick over it, but when she brushed that away, the wood shone, polished, a red-gold whose grain seemed to glitter before her eyes. Chairs carved of the same wood were placed along it, but they ran along one side only, that which was farthest from the door.

Two huge fireplaces were set to the rear of the wall, behind the table. Eleeri stared. It would take a man working full time just to chop enough wood. Or had that been provided by some use of power? Water ran into a basin attached to the wall near one of the hearths. She crossed to it. A horn cup on a silver link chain still remained. Then she stooped to look. The water ran into the basin, but there was no outlet. From where did it come, to where did it go? The soft plashing made her thirst greater. She lifted the cup, filled it, and drank. Then she lifted it in salute to the shadowy hall. Was it her imagination, or did something stir at that acknowledgment?

Eleeri decided she wasn't going to question things here. She was sure she was meant no harm. That being so, it would be unmannerly to question whatever occurred. She would stay polite as a guest should and wait to be invited into the forbidden land of mist. In the meantime she was hungry, and growing tired.

She returned to her horse and hauled her gear inside the

hall. She rubbed him down, then left him free to graze with a gentle slap on his shoulder. Quickly she kindled a fire in the center of one of the fireplaces and roasted a rabbit on a spit she found there. She peered higher to discover there was also a rod which swung out above the flame. She'd heard of that. Gaily she hung her coffeepot from the upturned end and watched as the water boiled. She drank, leaned back against the stone wall, and sighed in satisfaction.

In the saddlebags she had looted from Gerae's followers, she had found a packet of dried leaves. They produced a sort of herbal tea with a taste of sweetened lemon. It wasn't coffee, but then she hadn't been crazy about coffee anyhow. This lemon tea was more to her taste. She had been running low on it, but within the lines of bushes outside she had seen perhaps four or five that looked to be the source of the tea leaves. In the morning she'd check.

Her mind moved on to Cynan. What was he doing? Was he still strong enough to manage with what she had left for him? She had liked him, and yet when the time came she had ridden, leaving him alone. She knew this had been his wish, but she regretted doing so.

Still, he was a warrior; it was for him to choose his time and his dying. That was the white-eye way to deny a warrior the right to make his own choices. To drag one off to a hospital, there to die slowly, growing more bitter as the body withered. Far Traveler had also chosen. He had not wished to die shut away from the sky, from Earth Mother, from all her scents and the sounds of the mountains.

She remembered his last moments. It was well, very well. He had died as he had lived, in the clean air, in freedom. She grasped the pendant in her left hand.

"Look down on me, kinsman. Do not forget one who

will ever love you. In this strange land let your wisdom guide me as it did in that other." For a moment she felt a hand caress her hair the way the old man used to do to bring comfort to a small child. She felt his presence then, and reassurance that she, too, was loved and remembered, even from the sky trails he now followed. She sank down into her bedroll, a smile curving her lips. She slept, and if her dreams were more than she would recall on waking, that, too, was right.

During the night it began to rain lightly. While she slept, the Keplians had entered the hall and now dozed comfortably under a sound roof.

This is a good land, kin-sister, the mare announced as Eleeri opened her eyes. *There is more grass than we can eat, the water is sweet, and no Gray One could pass the gate runes.*

"What about Keplians?" the girl teased, but the mare was serious.

I think few of the males could pass. Perhaps some of the mares, as I did. The foals: of them it seems to me that all would pass. They are innocent, having committed no evil.

Eleeri considered that. "You think that the runes measure innocence. That may be so, but what evil have you done?"

None, but we are of the shadow. The runes were not swift to let me pass until your mind touched mine. Then that which held me back was gone. Her sending softened. *I have wondered, kin-sister, if our meeting was not meant. Together we have overcome that which would have mastered us had we not stood as one. I—I feel toward you as I have never felt, even to one of my own kind. Kin-sister you are in truth.* She turned inquiring eyes toward the girl.

"I, too, feel this way." For a moment they remained still, gray eyes meeting the flowing red fire that were the mare's orbs. Then Eleeri chuckled softly. "All this talk makes me hungry. I plan to find a nice fat bird, to do something about that." But as she passed the mare, her hand slid out in a loving caress. Tharna was content. Her kin-sister understood.

Over the next few days they relaxed, sleeping when they tired, eating as hunger came. Eleeri found herself constrained to hunt outside the canyon but accepted this as common sense. In case of siege or illness, she would be grateful birds and other small game abounded within reach.

But as the time passed, they all grew restless. Hylan no longer needed to nurse, but ate the grass which abounded at his hooves.

They had been there several weeks when Eleeri and Tharna felt a drawing from the outer lands. They consulted silently. Then as one they acted, the girl calling her horse, tossing his gear up and swiftly bridling the willing beast.

Hylan remained, but together Keplian and human left the canyon and hastened down the trail toward the lower lands. They had wandered, moving slowly as they came, but now they struck straight for their goal, the river. After a day's swift travel, they were there. Eleeri climbed a ridge and stared out over the area.

What do you see?

"No reason to call us here."

We go on?

The girl climbed down and swung into the saddle as reply. In silence they marched on along the riverbank, heading ever deeper into the Gray Ones' lands once more. Both knew this to be dangerous, but the call continued.

They would be wary, and with no smaller, weaker foal to slow them, it was unlikely the Gray Ones would be able to catch them, if the two had any sort of a headstart.

Suddenly Tharna jerked up her head. At the same time, Eleeri halted the pony, seeking out the source of her unease.

"What is it?"

Death—death comes to those of my kind. She had no need to add that it was a death in pain and terror. That echoed in both of their minds. Eleeri nudged her mount into a slow trot as the sensation broke off abruptly. One was dead, but the sensations continued, although weakened.

They rounded a long line of trees together just as the feeling faded again, then again. Now there was nothing but emotions: terror, loss, panic. There was a youngness to those, a formlessness that signaled no adults remained.

Eleeri strung her bow in one flickering movement, laid an arrow on the string, and touched the pony with a gentle heel. He edged out from behind the bushes, Tharna at his side. Before them three foals stood shivering, as Gray Ones circled. To one side, Keplian mares lay quiet in death. The Gray Ones were playing, knowing they could kill at whim. The terror of the foals provided a vicious amusement until, in one flashing second, that changed.

7

*B*eside Eleeri there was a snort of fury and a roar of swift hooves. Tharna charged down on the foals, crying for them to follow. A Gray One thrust forward to intercept her, to be sent flying with a well-aimed kick. Another slashed at her heels, only to find she had swapped ends and he was seized in savage teeth. They met through his spine as he was hurled lifelessly aside. The foals screamed in terror, leaping for the big mare. They were too young to form thoughts into words as Tharna did. Nor could they send far. But at this range they were almost deafening mare and human with their emotions. Before they had reached Tharna, Eleeri had counted enemies. Nine, with two already down.

The girl had not waited to see more. Arrows flew; Gray Ones howled in pain and fright as they died or bled. Tharna had charged. To her the babies ran desperately and she stood over them, ready. Eleeri circled, continuing to shoot as the wolf-creatures attacked her. But they relied on tooth and claw, and the pack tactics. She swung the pony beyond them and shot again and again. Tharna was withdrawing slowly, foals clinging to her flanks.

The attackers slunk back, howling their baffled rage and frustration. Eleeri watched. They preferred to face safer odds, it appeared. She guarded the rear as her friend headed for the river again. With a sigh, the girl removed her leathers. She was getting tired of crossing this river. She grinned to herself. She'd better not say that; it was a safeguard, since the Gray Ones would not cross. She cantered after the Keplian mare and foals.

The babies were afraid of the water. They balked at the brink, but Tharna was not to be halted by juvenile intransigence. A swift nip sent a colt forward with a surprised squeal, more of fright than pain.

Eleeri pushed her pony into the water on his downriver side. He swam valiantly and her assistance was limited to a grip on his mane, which helped him find his feet again on the far side. The two younger, smaller fillies needed more. By now, too, the Gray Ones had recovered some of their confidence. But as they raced forward an arrow storm met them, so that they rolled screaming and howling. With the trembling babies behind them, girl and mare faced the remaining enemies.

"If I hold them, can you get the other two across?" Eleeri hissed.

If they do not panic, Tharna sent. *If they do, I have no easy way to aid them.*

Her friend snatched a look behind her at the two foals who cowered in their shadow. They couldn't be more than a few weeks old. Keplian foals seemed to be born small. True growth didn't come until they reached two or three months of age; then they seemed to grow as if they were being inflated. But these two—she hooked a foot out of her leather.

"Watch the Gray Ones."

Moving quickly, she released the stirrup leathers from her saddle and flipped one around each foal. Buckled into the last and next to last holes, they fitted. Good. Now if one did slip, the mare would have something to seize.

She swung back onto her mount. The enemy had begun to advance again, hoping she was occupied. Seeing her attention was on them once more, they backed away.

Keeping her eyes on them she signaled the mare. "Go! One at a time." She watched from the corner of an eye as mare and foal plunged into the water.

Among the enemy there seemed to be some dissent. Eleeri thought she could hear growls and occasional snarled words. She was correct; the gray ones were furious at the likely escape of prey. But they had died in sufficient numbers to make it clear these two were not to be trifled with.

Their current leader was making the best of it. "Watch them. If we can, we pull them down. If not, we still have three dead ones to feast us." His look boded no good to Keplian and human, though, and his memory was working busily. A Keplian with a human. It could only be the pair he had heard of a few weeks ago. A pack had hunted them, to find themselves the hunted instead. They had lost many of their pack as the prey escaped. Back in their own lands he would bespeak all packs that they should watch for these, kill if they could ever be caught off guard. It might be some trick of those from the valley. He would show them the Gray Ones were not so easily taken or tricked. His lips peeled back from fangs as he snarled his frustration.

His fellows were less interested in the escaping prey.

Behind them lay enough meat to feast on for days. Longer, now that half their number was dead. The wounded were thrust aside as the rest sought the best parts to begin their meal. The last filly gave a tiny whimpering squeal at the sight. Eleeri cursed the feeding enemy harshly and she reached over to stroke the shaking foal.

"Don't worry, little one, we'll get you to a safe place, and your mother can't feel anything anymore." The baby looked up and Eleeri was struck all over again with the red fire that swirled in Keplian eyes. Her fingers curled around her pendant, feeling it grow warm.

"Help me get her away safely," she whispered softly. "And I hope that meal poisons the lot of them."

Back in the old days, as she remembered, wolvers had poisoned cow carcasses with all sorts of compounds, but mostly strychnine. They'd been after stock-killing wolves, not Gray Ones, but by all the gods she'd like to see this lot killed by the very mares they'd murdered. Once, when she was a child, she'd seen a container of the deadly powder. Her hand tightened on the pendant as she recalled the descriptions Far Traveler had given her of its use and actions.

The third foal was safely across and the mare was sending impatiently. *Battle-sister—Eleeri! Stop thinking and get over here before you provoke them.*

The girl came to herself with a jolt. Wordlessly she swam her mount across the water, then led her group along the trail. One hand still gripped the pendant, its warmth unnoticed. Nor did she see that the tiny eyes glowed with a wicked fire. Long ago the girl had also seen the molecular structure of strychnine. Now that knowledge swirled almost to her conscious before subsiding again.

The Gray Ones feasted heartily before sprawling in the

shade. They snapped and snarled lazily, and the wounded were careful to watch their uninjured companions. At present there was enough meat for all. When the time came that there wasn't, they must be on guard.

Mare, human, and rescued foals were all well up the trail and out of earshot when the commotion began. A Gray One found his arms and legs had begun to shake. Then another began to twitch. The spasms increased in severity as one by one all fell into the pattern. Only the wounded that had not been permitted to eat were free of the trouble. They, in turn, trotted over; with their fellows occupied, now was a good time to feast. Their satisfaction was shattered in a short time as the first of them also began to twitch. The spasms became continuous until all gasped, unable to breathe. Finally they went limp.

Far up the trail, Eleeri still sat her mount with a hand on the pendant. Strychnine was a cruel death, so she had always heard. The worst of it was all the other deaths that led from poisoning a carcass. The stock killers died, but so did anything else that ate the poisoned meat, be it bird or beast. The wolvers had rarely bothered to clean up the lethal remains. That was wrong. No, on second thought, she would not wish such a death on even the Gray Ones, not if it meant the innocent dying with them.

Where the Gray Ones lay in death's rictus, a bird landed. It hopped to the meat and began to feed. It was joined by others. They ate eagerly and departed, to be replaced with others. All were safe. Sometimes wishes can be more powerful than the one who wishes will ever know.

In another hour the foals were beginning to falter. Eleeri consulted with Tharna and called a rest break. Then she drew the mare aside.

"What are we to do about feeding them, sister-kin? All

are young. The colt might manage on grass and water; he's no doubt been eating grass as well as nursing, from the size of him. But the fillies are far too young."

The mare was serene. *Hylan no longer needs my milk. I have fed him because it pleases us both, but it was not necessary to him. Now I will feed these instead.*

Her friend surveyed her. "That'll be a real drain on you. You've been nursing Hylan for months and now you switch to feeding two foals for months more."

True, but even if I can only give milk for another month or two, they may then be old enough to manage part of the time with grass. Eleeri nodded doubtfully, saying no more. She couldn't bear to see the foals starve, but still less did she wish to watch as her friend wasted away, her strength going to feed the babies. She glanced over to where the three slept, slumped on the grass in utter exhaustion. Poor little things would probably be grieving badly, too, as soon as their strength returned. She would push this trip as hard as they could handle. If they were tired out, they'd be less inclined to mourn.

It was so, although the foals may not have appreciated her motives. Hylan was delighted at their safe return, and with playmates. As the older, stronger, and smarter, he took leadership at once. Even the other colt deferred to him carefully. Indeed, his deference was so marked, Eleeri wondered.

Stallions kill easily, the mare enlightened her.

"Hylan isn't a stallion, and I don't think he's a killer by nature, either. In horse herds it isn't that unusual to have more than one stallion. Not if it's a large herd."

Tharna snuffled. *That's horses. With our kind, the stallions are very quick to kill any who appear to defy them, mares and foals alike.* She saw her sister-kin's eyes widen. *Yes, I tell you this. I have seen it happen. It was why I wandered far away from the lands of the Keplians.*

She saw that Eleeri was interested and continued. *I bred to one of my kind so that I was in foal to him. He was slain by another, who would have bred me, but I was heavy in foal. If the foal died, I would come into season at once and he could breed as he wished. He would have slain my foal at birth so that none of his rival's blood survived. I knew what he would do. I knew him, too, to be vicious and cruel to mares, so I fled from our lands. It seemed then that anywhere I would have stayed was claimed by another creature. I was pushed farther and farther to the south.*

She snorted. *Then that Gerae found me. I was ready to foal, so that he was able to place ropes about me. Then he dragged me back to his village, where I and my foal were to be tortured, then slain.* Her head came up as her eyes flamed red with remembered fury. *Hylan was born and they gave me an hour to love him. Murderers, twice cruel. Then they would have killed him before me, but that I fought them.* Her sending softened. *Then you came, battle-sister. I know humans are cruel, but I will always know, too, that they can be as you are. At first I hated you, also. I accepted your help, planning to kill you as soon as we were safely away.* She saw the quirk of her friend's mouth and blinked. *You knew!*

"It was—um—rather obvious."

Amusement gurgled between them.

Tharna curved her neck proudly. *I learned to know you, to trust. I am not ashamed to change, to alter my mind. You saved us both, but I feared some kind of trick: that you saved us only to use us yourself. Then you fought for us again, killed your own kind to save my foal. I saw that you would risk yourself. That is not the way of one who plans to use. I watched you with Hylan, saw that he loved you, that you loved him, also. I began to believe in your kindness. I, too, came to—*

Her sending broke off as Eleeri flung warm arms about her neck, hugging as hard as she could. The girl cupped her hands over the soft muzzle, giggling as powerful teeth nibbled gently.

"I know. I love you, too, kin-sister, you and Hylan. You're my family, and these three little ones, too, if they can accept that." Her voice ended on a questioning note.

The fillies will love us all. They are younger, more adaptable, and prepared to love any who are kind and gentle with them. The colt I am not so sure of. He is slower of mind, more ready to sly violence if he thinks we do not see. Her sending grew sad. *I fear it may be too late for him to learn love.*

"Do you think he recalls the way here?"

No, part of the way we came in the dusk. He was exhausted and did not think to look about him. She snuffled thoughtfully. *I do not believe he even knows for certain if we went north or south.*

"Then we'll see he doesn't learn, if possible. But we may have to make a decision sometime if he looks like he would be a danger to us all." Eleeri sighed softly. Things could never be simple. But that was life.

Weeks passed, then months. Outside it was winter, but within the canyon the air seemed to remain warmer. The fillies had grown, ceased to nurse, and gave their names trustingly. The colt, too, had given his, but the look in his eyes grew wilder as time went on. Eleeri marked her eighteenth birthday and taught the foals to enjoy celebrating their own. Hylan was smug; he already knew about birthdays. It was that smugness and the growing desire to dominate that thrust the younger colt into action.

Terlor flew at Hylan, teeth bared, hooves already striking out. Taken by surprise, Hylan nonetheless fought
back. He was larger and stronger, but reluctant to injure
his fellow. The younger colt had no such inhibitions. He
attacked with a driving fury that sent his enemy to his
knees. Tharna arrived just as Eleeri came running from
another direction.

"Stop it, *Terlor!* Stop it!"

Her voice went unheeded as the mare waded in. With
ruthless efficiency, her teeth clamped down on Terlor's
neck as she hurled him to one side. She stood between
him and her colt, eyes dangerous.

Eleeri marched up to the panting youngling. "What did
you think you were doing?" His ears went back and his
muzzle shot out, teeth grabbing for her. She evaded him
neatly as her hand slashed across his nose. She had handled biters before. But Terlor was no horse. Even dull-
witted though he seemed to her, he was Keplian. It had
been a feint, and a hoof upflung caught her hard behind a
thigh. She fell, rolling so quickly his next strike missed.

The mare came then in a drumroll of hooves, eyes suddenly crazed with anger. Massive hooves drove down, the
colt squealed in pain and fear, the sound cut off as hooves
crunched down again. Blowing through her nostrils, the
mare stepped back from the body. Her mind was sad.

*There was no choice, sister-kin. He intended to kill
you. He was too dangerous to allow freedom. He would
have been sure one of us was alone next time so help
would not come.*

Eleeri knelt by the body. Hands smoothed the black
hide as tears stole down her face. "I know." She stood.
"But now what do we do with this? We don't want it rotting here."

Without thinking, she clutched at the pendant. From it a

mist arose, silver, laced with soft golden glimmerings. It swept out and over Terlor. When it cleared, he was gone, as mare and human stood staring at each other.

"Automatic garbage disposal," Eleeri said, looking stunned.

What?

"Nothing. Look, Tharna, I hated Terlor dying, but you were right: he'd have killed me. If he'd stopped, we could never have trusted him. His mind was too clear just then. He wanted us all dead—you, me, and Hylan. That way he could have the canyon and the fillies."

She said no more, but departed with bow and arrows. Hunting would soothe her, and a fat bird or two from the lower foothills would soothe her stomach. As she walked, she thought. There was a surprising difference between the colt they had rescued and Hylan. Tharna's son was not only large and powerful for his age, he was also far more intelligent. Tharna was sure it was the constant companionship he shared with his mother and Eleeri. Colts were usually pushed away from their dams as soon as they were able to survive alone. This seemed to be partly for their own sake. A Keplian male never hesitated to kill a colt that wasn't his own. In fact, from what Tharna had said, he didn't hesitate long even if the baby *was* one of his blood.

As a result, the abandoned small colts learned savagery to survive. In turn they killed foals, used mares as they willed. The cruelty was self-perpetuating, and in many ways it seemed similar to the pack rule of the Gray Ones.

But what of a colt brought up with love, taught gentleness by a dam he loved, a human he trusted? Would he in the end revert to stallion behavior, or would he breed a new race of gentle intelligent Keplians? The partners to humans that Tharna thought they may have been created to be so long ago? At Eleeri's throat the miniature gave out a sudden light, a shaft of warmth that attracted her attention. She lifted it up.

"Is that it? We were called here to change things? Is Tharna right?" Secrets twinkled in the sapphire eyes, but she was suddenly sure her guess was correct. She grinned, strolling off along the faint deer trail. Well, it made for an interesting theory. But if they were to breed a new race with just Tharna, Hylan, and the two fillies, it would take rather a long time. Her own people had raided for children to strengthen the tribe. They'd accepted any child as Nemunuh if the children showed they wished to be and had the skills. Adults, too, had been accepted.

That sparked a thought. She'd talk to Tharna once she found meat and returned to the canyon. It sparked another as well. She found herself wondering as she trotted along: With all this breeding going on, where did she fit in? Was she to be barren, or did the plans of the someone who'd started all this include a mate for her, too?

She laughed, throwing back her head as she padded off on a fresher trail. Never mind a mate. If her other idea was right, she'd be too busy to think of anything else. She made her kills, a fat hill hen and a small half-grown buck. She could dry the meat within the huge old fireplace. There was a hook well up within the chimney, as she had discovered. In the meantime, she'd eat the hen while she discussed this new plan with her battle-sister.

The mare was interested. It would soon be spring, when trails opened again to the lower lands. It would do no harm if they merely scouted Keplian lands.

They set off together a month later. Hylan remained to care for the fillies. He was becoming a strong young yearling who thought as Keplian stallions had not bothered to do for generations. The fillies adored him. At present they looked up to him as a protective big brother. In another couple of years that would change. Meanwhile, Hylan enjoyed being left alone in the canyon with his charges. It made him feel important and removed some of the sting of not being permitted to accompany his dam and her kin-sister.

Down in the plains once more, Tharna cantered briskly along the river's edge. *I know all the places to hide once we reach our lands. If only you can persuade that horse to cooperate.*

She regarded the pony with scorn, and Eleeri grinned. The mare despised the sturdy little dun as a mere copy of a Keplian. She would never have wounded her friend's feelings by the obvious retort.

Two days later, they were drifting unobtrusively around the fringes of Keplian country. Twice Tharna wandered toward another mare and exchanged gossip. Self-centered as their race was, none remembered that she had fled under strange circumstances almost a year ago. As long as she remained out of sight of any of the stallions, they were safe. After several days of this, Eleeri was well bored.

"What have you learned so far?"

That nothing changes.

"Very helpful. When do we do something about it?"

The mare eyed her friend with amusement. She had seen the growing boredom and expected a demand for action would come shortly. She could provide that to some extent and proceeded to explain. Eleeri was slightly surprised.

"You mean she'll come with us just like that?"

Tharna's shoulder twitched. *Not so casually as you make it sound, kin-sister. But she *will* come. For her there is no choice unless she wishes to see her foal killed at birth. Her herd lives close to the old Dark Tower. The stallion lord was recently slain by a rival, who has taken the herd as his own.*

Eleeri nodded. "So according to stallion habit, he'll kill any nursing or newborn foals not his own."

Her friend sent sadness. *That he has already done. Only this young mare remains. She bred late and will not bear her foal for another month.*

"So she'll come with us to give her baby a chance."

More than that. She fears if the stallion attacks her newborn, she may not be able to prevent herself from attempting to protect it. A stallion is likely to kill her, too, for that.

For the remainder of the week, Tharna slipped out to speak with the distracted young mare. Choosing a time when the stallion was in a different part of his territory, the three trotted quietly for the river.

With the new addition safe in the canyon, the two comrades returned to Keplian lands. Over the course of a spring they added another young mare and two orphaned foals to their family. Eleeri surveyed the results with satisfaction. Three adult mares, three yearlings, and three foals. A nice balance of ages so far, yet still Hylan was the only male.

In fact, the girl had come to believe two ideas. One was that only a male foal raised with love from the very beginning would fit into canyon ways. The other was that with the way that stallions killed even tiny colts, Terlor had been something of a fluke.

Orphaned foals were simply left to stray or starve. Many fell to the teeth of the Gray Ones, others to the irritation of stallions. Life was difficult enough for a mare; few would accept a strange foal and risk shorting their own foal's nourishment. Yet Eleeri believed most of that was learned. In an atmosphere of peace and plenty, attitudes could change in a bare generation.

Summer followed, harsher than usual down on the plains, but in the canyon, water flowed and grass grew thick and green. Tharna and Eleeri spent a lot of their time now shadowing Keplian herds, watching and listening. Twice they managed to save orphaned foals and return with them. The girl had even made a short trip down through the lands to the southwest. There she had successfully bargained for several nanny-goats and a male. The milk might not be exactly what they were used to, but the starving foals would drink it.

By the time winter came, they were twice the number spring had counted. Still three adults, and three more than yearlings now. But the babies had increased to a dozen. At that point Eleeri had called a halt and taken the mare aside.

"Before we accept others, we need to look at what we have. How many of us can the canyon support? Even with no outside addition, we are going to start growing as soon as Hylan is old enough to be accepted as a stallion by some of the mares here. Once that starts happening, our numbers will go up like a startled hill hen."

Before that time we may have found other solutions. I have found a strange thing, kin-sister. Eleeri waited. *At first I had great difficulty passing the runes. Now I pass freely. Our friends, too, had to link somewhat with you before they were permitted to enter. Now the mares pass as freely as I do.* She paused, then her sending became diffident. *Could it be that the power here now measures us as of the Light?*

Her eyes were hopeful on the girl who stood there. Eleeri could not answer. She, too, had noticed this thing happening and wondered. But she would raise no hopes.

"I can't say. I've tried to ask the pendant, but no luck."

The discussion turned back to herd size, but there was a sad look in the mare's eyes. Later that night, Tharna drifted silently down to where the silver mist sparkled and coiled. What was behind it? What did it hold? She had no way of knowing, but it drew her. Somehow she desired to be part of it, accepted as one of the Light. She had never known when this desire had begun, only that it had been part of her as long as she could remember—as long as she had the hope that there was another way of life for her kind.

She blew softly through wide nostrils. That change she had seen here; if she lived long enough, she might see the other. Her mind yearned as the mist wreathed her gently. Had there been any there to see, they might have thought it a trick of the moonlight, as for a fraction of a second her eyes appeared to glow a soft gentle blue. Then the mist folded back into itself and there was only a fire-eyed Keplian mare standing quietly, moonlight silvering her hide.

8

*W*inter came slowly that year. The snows held off, the air remained warmer, and the land gave of berries, nuts, and fruit as never before. It all made Eleeri very suspicious. The wisdom of the Nemunuh said that a time like this was Earth Mother's warning: times ahead would be hard. Store food, eat well, and prepare. She did so, gathering everything she could in the large woven baskets Far Traveler had taught her to make. Dried meat she stored in one of the rooms above the great hall.

But if times were to be cold as well, perhaps she should think of more bedding. She had more hides than she needed; those could be traded for woven stuffs at the same village as where she traded for the goats.

Tharna was reluctant. *The way is far, the road dangerous.*

Eleeri laughed. "Both true, but when the land warns, the wise warrior listens. Come part of the way with me; Hylan, too, if he wishes."

There was an eager whicker from the young stallion, and the friends shared amusement. The girl stood, stretching slowly, enjoying the pull of fit muscles. It was a strange life, this one she lived, but it contented her. She had friends who were as family, a kin-sister and kin-son, a strong roof, and ample food. The water was clean, the air clear, and the hunting good.

A shadow swept across her face then. Who was she trying to persuade? She loved the life, the Keplians, but she missed human companionship. No, let her be truthful in this, since it was only to herself she spoke. Years were passing. She was almost twenty; her heart cried for a mate. She watched the Keplian mares with their foals, the pride of Hylan and his gentleness. Her body hungered, but not for food. She silenced it. What would be, would be. She must live with contentment if other joys were not granted. But there were humans she could visit.

She remembered her first trip to the lake keep, two days' ride down the stream and along the lakeshore. Originally, many long generations ago, it had been lovingly built. Then it was abandoned during the adept wars. Later, those who lived there now had given it new life.

She chose gifts to take. The first time she was sure she had been closely watched, but neither lord nor lady had appeared. Instead she had been offered shelter in the same stable as her pony. No one had challenged her. But she was eyed warily all the same.

Another trip would be fun. The village about the main tower was small: just a well-fortified keep, central tower, inner courtyard, and a circle of cottages about it. In all, not more than forty people. The lord, his kin, and the three families who served him directly, along with armsmen, lived in the central keep. Cottages served for those who raised the garden vegetables and tended the animals.

It was a small but happy community as far as she had seen.

She rode in close to sundown, the dun pony striding eagerly under his load of furs and hides. This time the stableman brought an invitation as soon as the pony was relieved of his burden.

"Lord Jerrany asks if you will dine with him and the Lady Mayrin. After the meal, they would be pleased to see what you have brought."

Eleeri's ears pricked up at this. Interesting. Last time she had been treated with a wary condescension. Oh, the people had been polite enough. But it was clear that although they asked her no questions, they wondered at a woman who rode alone. She had conducted herself carefully, showing only courtesy and some of the lesser furs she had brought on that first trip. No sense in exciting greed. But with this invitation it was as well she had chosen to pack a couple of gifts suitable for a lord and his lady.

She waited until the man had gone, then opened her pack. She would place those carefully chosen presents on the top before lacing the tough material closed again. For a moment she lingered in the stable, brushing the pony as he leaned into the slow strokes. She had learned enough from Cynan to know that in some ways this Escore was a ghost-ridden land. It was haunted by those who had died in the adept wars, those slain by the Dark and those who served it. But with the coming of others from overmountain in Estcarp, new life had sprung up.

Cynan had said that with the newcomers the Dark had been stirred to action once more. But also small places such as this which had been long dead, had risen to new life. Her eyes flickered about the stable. This would have been rebuilt. It looked as if the roof was new, but the stone walls were old. Her own hold was like that. Well, she would take a quick look about outside. Last time she had not wished to, in case they took it amiss.

She nodded to herself as she walked to the door to stand looking out into the growing dusk. The keep had been carefully situated by whoever had raised the ancient stone walls. It tucked into a tight curve at the far end of a lake. In addition, the builders had bounded it by digging a ditch deep into the rocky ground. This completed the encirclement, so that the entire village was surrounded by running water. A potent spell, as the girl had learned.

She walked to the edge of the stream. The water had cut deeper over the ages so that it now ran through a deep channel and must be crossed by a bridge. She studied the mechanism—clever! The bridge could be raised to prevent passage. She looked closer and grinned. The locking bar was of forged iron. So the lord and his lady knew that trick.

But then, in this land they'd be fools if they didn't.

She peered along the bridge, and her invitation to dinner started to make sense. At the far end, where she had crossed casually only a short time before, there was a new addition. It wasn't obvious from the approach side but could be seen quite clearly from where she stood.

At the far end, thin forged iron bars had been inset into the wood between the planking. They were recent; she was sure she'd have noticed them had they been there before. Ancient stone posts guarded the bridge's approaches, and from where she leaned, she could see a faint blue glow. It looked as if runes of protection had been placed there in slight hollows. They would be unseen by any approaching, even crossing the bridge. But it would take a Dark one of considerable power to cross. And such a one would set the runes to blazing.

So that was why she was now welcomed. The keep defenses had passed her as one who, if she did not walk in the Light, at least was not of the Dark. The sun was setting. She hurried back to the stable.

Shouldering the pack of furs, Eleeri tramped into the hall. A handsome man clothed in rich fabrics—obviously the Lord Jerrany—rose to greet her, offering a guest cup.

"To the farer on far roads, the welcome of this roof. May fortune favor your wandering."

Eleeri's hand went up as she allowed the pack to slip to the floor. "For the welcome of the gate, my gratitude. For the feast, thanks. To the lord and lady of this roof, all good fortune and a bright sun in days to come." As she spoke, slowly her forefinger traced signs of guard and good fortune. She allowed her mind to open to them, and the air began to glow. Jerrany would have leaped for her, but his lady seized him hard.

"No, look to them. Here is no ill-wishing."

The signs brightened into the warm blue-green of Light as the girl stepped back. She grinned cheekily up.

"Now that we all know where we are, would you prefer to eat or look at furs first?"

For a startled moment the two gazed at her. Then Mayrin's grin flashed into a startlingly close copy of Eleeri's smile.

"Come, eat and be very welcome. There is always time to look at luxuries later." She slipped around the table and walked to the girl. "Sit here." She turned. "Don't all stand there gaping; bring our guest food. Or do you plan to starve a woman of the power?"

Servants sprang into action guiltily. Mayrin turned back. She eyed Eleeri's pendant with interest. "You wear no jewel. Is this what you have instead?"

She had spoken without thinking, and now her hand

went up to cover her mouth, just as her Lord looked horrified.

"Oh, I'm sorry, I'm sorry. I know that was rude and I have no right to ask such a thing. I—it's so beautiful I just asked."

A soft chuckle. "Why not?" There was no need to speak of the pendant's power. "It was a gift from a friend." A thought came then. "Are either of you kin to one Cynan of the House of Bear's-Kin?"

It was Jerrany who answered. "Cynan? I am not sure I know that name, but my mother was of the house. All that was swept away in the Horning. Her kin departed the land safely, but when they would have returned, it was too late." Eleeri looked a question. "The turning came then. Soon after, my mother and her lord chose to take horse for Escore, called by geas."

"Would she have known Cynan?"

"I do not know. It is possible, with the house on both sides of the border, there was some coming and going before Karsten ran mad. You do know there were two houses of that name?" At Eleeri's headshake he nodded, continuing then. "It was thus. The house was founded by a landless man of good blood. It was on the border where land was easier come by, since Karsten was empty and the land was wild. Many generations later, another son of the house returned to Estcarp to build there. His keep was on the other side of the border, but close by as the hawk flies."

He paused to savor the roast set before him. Eleeri and Mayrin smiled at each other as he talked.

"The house in Estcarp prospered also, and for many years there was much travel and trade between the two. My mother was of the Estcarp house. Of later years, the trade had lessened, but she had said when danger came, her house stood by kin, as was right. I think that those of the Karsten house were given shelter, but later they moved on. I know little more. My mother herself was wed shortly before the Horning and dwelt not within the keep." He finished, reaching hungrily for the trenchers of bread.

"I thank you for that. Do you write to your mother?"

"Letters go with trade goods to other places. A letter may come to her hand in time."

"Perhaps then you could say that Cynan of her house in Karsten wished this to be known to his kin." She straightened, allowing her voice to take on an impersonal note. "I, Cynan of the House of Bear's-Kin, returned to my keep to die within those walls. The land is yet in turmoil, so I have survived. But age comes upon me, I will lie in the land that once was ours. Let my kin remember there are two houses, that one day they may return. This message I send by the mouth of one I name kin-friend, sword-sister. Aid to her at need is laid upon our house, even as she aided me when I stood alone. This I, Cynan of the House of the Bear's Kin, do swear."

She reached for her pack then, producing the two plump packages. Formally she laid them upon the table, undoing the twisted grass string which bound them. In turn she held each up so that the lord and lady might see.

"To the lord and lady of the keep, I offer guest-gifts. May they be received from one who would be friend to you and your kin."

Jerrany rose to bow. "They are received as guest-gifts," he said slowly. "Friends in this land are always good to have, but those who move too swiftly may stumble. Yet we, too, would hope to have gained a new friend."

Eleeri nodded, seeing that he did not move to take up the gifts. She laced the pack shut again and sat to continue the next course offered. As she ate quietly, she mused on the power she had displayed to them. It was growing, it seemed. When she had arrived in Karsten, she had been no more than a child with the horse-gift. But her time in Karsten seemed to have changed her. Meeting the lady in the place of the Old Ones. The gift of the warding stones. Cynan's teaching. All seemed to have brought growth to her gift.

Once she had crossed into Escore, found her Keplian friends and her hold, things had changed further. The hold had closed about her in warmth. It was both unfamiliar and oddly familiar. As if after long wandering she had returned home. She eyed Mayrin as the woman ate. She, too, seemed to have some of the gift.

Mayrin looked up, to return the glance and smile a little. Then she reached for the gift. She laid it out, biting back unseemly groans of delight. A vest of rasti fur, and another for Jerrany. Her eyes glowed at the soft feel of the fur as she stroked it.

Jerrany reached for his own guest-gift. He had seen the quality at first glance and had deliberately taken time so as not to show his own interest. Eleeri watched as he took it up.

But Jerrany was giving nothing away. He passed her more food, pressing wine on her as well. She drank sparingly of that; water was her usual drink.

The conversation moved on to hunting and Eleeri realized with some amusement that the lord was now trying delicately to discover her home territory. His questions circled cleverly. At one time querying if certain bushes would grow in her area, at another if hill hens were within her borders. She answered truthfully. It was unlikely he would find her. The canyon was high in the mountains where few trails ran. Nor was the entrance easy to find, even for one who followed the Light.

Once the meal was concluded, she reached for her pack, unlacing the drawstrings with swift fingers. Then she began to unfold furs, some the dazzling white of the mountain leapers, others the silver-tipped rich brown of river rasti in winter. She had had to work very carefully to get those last. Rasti hunted in packs and would attack anything that was food if they hungered. They were swift, cunning, and deadly, appetites on four legs, feared by even the most skillful hunters. They could be killed. But those who fell dead were at once eaten by their kin. To have cured undamaged furs proclaimed her far and wide as a hunter of unmatched skill.

Jerrany drew in his breath. There was now no doubt, this one was of the Light, but what a hunter, also. He must indeed write to his dam and kin. He would send word also to the Green Valley and she who dwelled there. His lady caught his eyes, speaking wordlessly with tiny movements, her eyes alight with hope. He nodded slightly, hand twitching in a signal that she should move slowly. For several hours they bargained over the finest furs either had ever seen. The girl had come from the mountains somewhere, that was certain. Leaper furs of this whiteness could only have come from beasts living in snow more than half a year.

He allowed the rasti furs to slide through his hands. But this was the puzzle. These were lowland animals; this type tended to live by rivers on flat land.

Eleeri retired to the offered room for the night while he still sat pondering. She *had* to be of the Light. She'd passed forged iron, runes of ward and guard; she'd then called Light in runes herself. But the pendant his lady had admired was that of a Keplian. Those accursed followers of evil had killed many over the years. Would it be wise to broach to the girl the matter of the missing one?

He shrugged, departing for his own bed. There he found Mayrin of no mind to let slip an opportunity.

"Where do you then think her to live?" he was queried when he confessed his bewilderment.

"I know not. She brings furs from mountain and plains. Aldred says she came from the east along the lakeside. Those rasti furs are of a kind that makes a home by rivers; maybe she followed the stream that flows into our lake. But I cannot be sure. None of us have traveled far to the east. Those are the lands of the Gray Ones and the Keplians."

"She is not evil," his lady was swift to point out.

"That is seen, but how she lives in such a place, I do not know."

His lady shrugged. To her it mattered not where the girl lived, as long as she was sure of her innocence. That she was, after the demonstration in the hall. She was sure of another thing, also. Eleeri had a sense of humor. She had marked the wicked twinkle as their visitor called power to her runes. It had been as if she were saying, *There, you misjudged me.* Mayrin had felt a sudden feeling of liking flow between them as eyes met. She wanted to know more of Eleeri as a friend.

She lay curled in her warm bed, mind drifting into sleep. But even as she relaxed, her heart wept, remembering.

She loved Jerrany. He'd been her idol from the time she was old enough to admire his youthful courage. He, in turn, had been kind to the younger girl who followed him. He had told her of his ambitions, to raise up a house again. His father had died in Estcarp's wars, and his mother fled to Escore with her new lord, a man Jerrany disliked. He would carve out new lands for himself, not be beholden to another.

That was as well, Mayrin had thought silently. Her hero's stepfather liked the boy no more than the boy liked him. Jerrany's mother had produced other children to her new lord. It would be they who inherited his holding, close to Mayrin's own in a dangerous land.

She herself had been promised to another, a man she feared. But her own father was adamant.

"What if you do not like him, silly chit? You know nothing of him but his looks from afar. You will wed him and unite our houses."

But Escore, too, warred, and the man died—to her very great and secret relief. Jerrany announced soon after that he planned to seek a new home. She had been heartbroken: she would never see him again. He was brother, friend, protector, and he was deserting her.

In secret she had learned swordplay from Jerrany. Now she bent her mind to gathering other abilities: knowledge of poison, the making of arrows, the setting of guard runes. Jerrany had come and gone, bidding her a gentle farewell. Her father had begun to cast about for another lord for her when Jerrany returned, jubilant.

"I've found our home. It's all a ruin now, but most of the walls are still there. We can build it up again, Mayrin."

"What have I to do with it?" she had asked bitterly.

She had met astonished eyes. "Why, it's our home," he had said simply. "Don't you want to be with me?"

Her heart had leaped up. Without caring for her dignity, she had flung herself at him, laughing and weeping at the same time. "Of course I do. You know I do. I thought you didn't want me."

He had taken her by the shoulders, setting her back from him so that their eyes met. "I suppose I always thought you knew. I love you, Mayrin. Why else would I have been seeking land and a home for us? Now I have a place and we can be wed."

It hadn't been that easy. Her father had first forbidden her to see *the boy,* as he had termed Jerrany. Finding that difficult to enforce, he had spoken to Jerrany himself, only to find a fighter who met him as an equal.

"I love Mayrin; Mayrin loves me. You may bring her to the altar with another. You cannot force her to speak vows, nor would such an attempt be approved in this place."

Her father had been furious, so much so that he had tried to goad her brother into an attack on Jerrany. But Romar had refused. Jerrany had been his friend since they came to the Valley of the Green Silences. He was almost the same age and together they had trained, fought, become as brothers in blood. Mayrin had thought at this point her father would suffer a seizure.

"Defied by one whelp!" he had roared. "Then by the other. By all the gods, you may go your own way, then. But expect nothing from me. Neither bride gifts, nor aid, nor anything I have. Go your way alone, both of you!"

They had done so, with Mayrin set in the care of Duhaun herself as her brother and beloved gathered what they must have. Others had chosen to join them, the lure of new lands being great. Some from Estcarp came still to Escore, and three families of those who joined them. Here and there single men added themselves to the group, bringing what they had in the way of goods and gear. More had followed later.

Romar—she remembered his gaiety. His laughter. He had been a rover, a wanderer across this strange and ancient land. It had called to his heart so that for months at a time he had vanished into its vastnesses. It was as if he sought without knowing, as if he hungered without being satisfied. He looked at none of the girls who would have been glad for his notice. Her father had raged to no avail. Those who led here valued the boy's skills, his reports of a land where evil was slowly being driven back.

Mayrin had loved her brother. It had delighted her heart when he chose to accompany them. But now he was lost, gone into that unknown from whence she feared he would never return.

Now from out of that same unknown a woman came. Nothing was impossible; perhaps Eleeri had seen or heard something. Maybe she could seek out some clue to Romar? Mayrin resolved to be careful, to move slowly, as her lord had said. But she would know all that her visitor knew. She *would!*

In sleep her mouth still held tight to that resolution. Romar was her brother beloved; no unknown land should reive him from her. She would befriend this traveler, leech from her any secrets she knew, use her if she must, anything to bring her brother home again.

The morning dawned bright and fair. Eleeri would have ridden homeward then, her trading complete, but that Mayrin pled with her to stay awhile. For the sorrow in the lady's eyes, Eleeri stayed. They talked and laughed together as lonely women will, finding in each other a friend unlooked for.

A day passed swiftly, and another. Glad to see his beloved so happy, Jerrany also pressed the visitor to remain. In all, Eleeri was at the keep for seven days before her need to return grew great. That last day Mayrin took her aside.

Her head hung in shame as she talked, but the younger girl smiled. "Don't look like that, Mayrin. I guessed there was a favor you needed. Whatever it is, I can promise to try if it not be against honor."

"It is not, I promise it is not." Mayrin ran lightly from the room to return with a small package. It was wrapped in a piece of fine cloth which she unwrapped gently.

"I've talked about Romar, my brother. He went from us into the lands to the east many months ago now. Nor has he returned. I fear for him." She stared sadly at the palm-sized painting she now displayed to Eleeri. "This was done before we left the Valley of the Green Silences. I have one of myself and my lord also. But this is dearer by far. It may be all that is left to me of Romar."

"The favor?"

"Wherever you go, wherever your home is, let you seek, let your eyes be ever busy searching, looking for one like this. I would give all I have to bring him safely home." Her eyes were desperate.

The woman she addressed nodded slowly. "I do indeed wander, as did your brother, sometimes to the east. I will watch for him, free him if he be trapped, bury him if I find his body, bring news to you if I have any. But only as I can. I, too, have those who rely on me. I cannot risk them for one unknown who may already be dead. But I sorrow for your grief. I will do what I can."

Mayrin flung her arms about the slender body. "That is all I ask. Come back. With news or without it, a welcome holds for you ever."

Eleeri turned away, but Mayrin's fingers seized her arm. Eleeri turned, brows raised questioningly. A small object was pressed into her hand.

"Here; you did not look truly. Look now, study the face. He may have changed a little if he has been treated ill by those of the Dark. Please, remember him, find him for me."

Eleeri looked down. At her previous glance the boy had seemed nothing special. Now she looked closer as her new friend begged. She guessed that Romar would have been sixteen when the limning was done. The same age as— She stared suddenly. No wonder she had no more than glanced. Why should she look closer? The image of this boy stood staring imploringly at her.

"You *know* he's alive somewhere, don't you?" Eleeri said. "You're twins."

"That is so," Mayrin said softly. "I feel him to be in great danger, but death has not touched him as yet. You are also right that we are twins. It is rare, very rare for those of the Old Race. Few there have been with any talent in our line, but Romar has an affinity with beasts. Horses in particular." Her fingers twined and twisted frantically, although her voice remained calm and quiet. "But we have the gift of twins. I would *know* if he were dead; therefore he is not. Find him for me, Eleeri."

For a long moment, Eleeri studied the portrait. Mayrin had changed, but not greatly since this was done. The boy here was young, untried. But there was strength in that face, pride without vice, power without the need to use it unjustly. The eyes were lonely, inward-looking. To an outsider he would have appeared as no great one to risk aught for. His face was thin, with fine bones and a determined chin. Eyes of a shade more green than gray, if the painter had not lied—but no. Mayrin's eyes, too, were that hue. The mouth was clean-cut, modeled with almost a delicacy, but there was no weakness in the set of those lips. It was the mouth of one who acted as well as dreamed.

It drew her in a way she had never felt before. She was no child to be attracted by any pretty face. She would have shrugged off the feeling, but even that would have

been to acknowledge it. Mayrin had been kind; her lord
had traded fairly. They asked only that she be alert for
traces of this one. It was not asked that she storm any
strongholds of the Dark. She glanced down again. Hmm,
a trick of the light . . . for a moment the painted eyes had
seemed to implore, to focus on her. Her face came up,
eyes measured Mayrin. Witchery? No, she did not think
so. Just a trick of the light.

This likeness must have been made ten years ago or
more. From what her friend had said during the past
week, Eleeri could piece some things together. Romar
must be about twenty-seven now, Jerrany some three
years older. She bit back a sound of contempt. Mayrin's
father must have been an idiot. Fancy expecting a boy of
sixteen to confront one who was older, more experienced,
and his best friend as well. Twenty-seven—about six
years older than Eleeri was now. She brushed that idea
aside. His age was unimportant. Let him be a child or a
grandfather, she had promised to watch for signs of him.
That she would do, but no more than that.

She rode midmorning, with Mayrin and Jerrany at the
bridge to wish her a good journeying. The women hugged
a final time and there was a genuine friendship in that.

The keep's lady wore her guest-gift proudly, the vest of
rasti fur glistening in the sun. Now and again her fingers
strayed to the pockets lining the inside. How clever, how
cunning. She would have these made for every gown now
that she had been given the trick of them. Jerrany, too,
would find them useful, in his jerkins. Romar should,
too—she felt a bitter pain. Romar might never know anything she would wish to tell him. She watched until horse
and rider vanished around the lake edge.

"Find him, please find him, bring him back to me," she
whispered into the air.

Eleeri rode around the lake. With all her trade pelts gone, she could ride again, and it pleased her. The walk to the keep had been long and tiring. In a day or two she would be back at the canyon with Tharna, Hylan, and the others. But as the pony trotted on, a young face intruded. Well, she would keep an eye open for the boy—man now. The gray-green eyes seemed to hang in her mind, hopeful, waiting. With a determined effort, she banished them. Winter was coming. She had things to do other than looking for some fool who'd probably only gotten himself lost.

She slept that night in wards, but in her dreams she saw him. After that he was gone. Eleeri nodded. Her mind was her own; it would banish what it was bid. If imploring eyes watched her, after that they were ignored. So she told herself, and who is to say she lied?

9

But she did keep her promise. She raided less often into Keplian lands, but when she did, her eyes were always alert for the boy who looked like Mayrin. The Gray Ones watched her, but after several disastrous meetings, they tended to look the other way—unless they were in full pack as they were one bright spring morning after winter was banished from even the mountains about Eleeri's canyon. They gave chase, but the tough fit pony carrying a light weight and the powerful Keplian mare stayed easily beyond their reach.

Eleeri reined in many miles later, laughing. "That gave them a nice run. Didn't they look disappointed?"

The mare gave her whinnying laugh, then sobered. *Kin-sister, have you not noticed, this spring they have returned to chasing us again. Before the winter, they had looked aside if we were in view. Now they hunt again.*

"That was full pack," the girl objected.

*They knew themselves unable to catch us, but they

still gave chase. Something builds; the Gray Ones do not hunt where the prey is worthless.*

Eleeri grinned. "I wouldn't say we were worthless, precisely."

Not if they could take us, no. But they have tried often in the past, failed, and ceased to try. So why do they try again now?

"I see what you mean." She sat her pony, looking thoughtful. It *was* strange. For most of the previous year the wolfmen had ignored them both. Tharna could be right. Something was building. But what—and why? Her mind made an intuitive leap. Romar! According to Mayrin, he'd ridden off in spring last year. They'd expected him back by late summer. Could the Gray Ones have taken him, found a use for him? But what sort of use, apart from food? Or torture? her mind added grimly. The pony had ceased to nibble at the grass. Now he lifted his head alertly. Eleeri gathered in the reins.

"I suspect trouble comes. Best we leave."

The mare nodded, then stiffened as the gust of changing wind came to her nose. Her eyes met Eleeri's in deepening surprise. The pack still followed. Eleeri led them to the river. Let the evil ones stick their noses into all that running water. It might cool their brains. The river ran higher than expected, so that the girl was becoming worried. It would be dangerous to cross, it must have rained higher in the mountains last night.

Moving with decision, she swung the hunt upriver, heading now for the stream that fed the lake. That, too, was high, and the crossing was difficult. They paused to rest on the other side as the pack snapped and snarled in frustration.

"Better keep going, kin-sister. I have a nasty feeling

that if we stay in plain sight, it may impel that lot to do something stupid."

The mare shrugged. *If they try to cross, they die.*

"And if it dawns on them this stream has an end?"

Tharna looked startled. It would be well out of the territory, but there was actually nothing to prevent the pack from circling the lake to continue the hunt.

It is far—many days, even for them.

"True, but if they are driven, they might not care about that. There is food to be hunted and when they round the lake there are also humans."

The mare nodded silently. Humans unaware of approaching danger. As they talked, they had moved away from the stream, hooves clicked dully on the rocky trail. They traveled several hours in silence, each recalling the events of the day. There was little doubt that something stirred in the land once more. Tharna was apprehensive; her kin-sister would insist on poking her nose into it, whatever it was. She would that Eleeri was better armed. Not with her bow only, but with the gift and powers. They walked slowly, so she had time to decide. A flick of her mind alerted the girl that there was something the mare wished her to consider.

Eleeri listened. The golden mist at the canyon end had almost ceased to interest her. It was forbidden to enter; nothing answered calls from without. Her pendant warned her away from it and even her own common sense advised caution there. There had been so many other adventures and paths to follow, the mist had been relegated to the back of her mind. Now she protested.

"We are still refused entry."

How long is it since you tried?

That was a point. Eleeri thought back. Months, many months. It must have been—she counted on her fingers—

why, it had been early last summer. Well, she could try again. It would do no harm as long as she was polite. At least she hoped it wouldn't.

She did try, to receive the clear impression of a barred door. Whatever was within the mist wasn't welcoming her in today. She walked away slowly. Would it ever allow her in? Was there something she was supposed to be doing to pay for the privilege? She chuckled. She didn't want to get in that much anyhow; it was just curiosity.

Farther down the canyon, Tharna waited. She noted the return and the deliberately casual air. It seemed the gate was still barred to them and her kin-sister wasn't of a mind to try again in a hurry. Tharna said nothing but returned to grazing.

Eleeri noticed both the attention, then the studied disinterest. It pricked her so that she turned on her heel and returned to the mist. There she stood formulating what she would say. The Gray Ones' unusual behavior, the sense that something was wrong in the lower lands. The feeling of an approaching storm, not of wind and sky but of power and danger. She fixed the feelings in her mind, then did what she felt was the equivalent of knocking on the mist's door.

In a burst she sent her message. Attention sharpened on her. She felt a sudden exhilaration. *That* had interested it.

Query?

She sent again her surprise at the way the wolfmen had followed them so tenaciously. This time she included all events, mental pictures of the terrain. The way they had been hounded right to the very edge of running water. The way she and Tharna had felt they should move away even that after crossing—as if the desperation of the pack to reach them was communicated. The sudden fear that the

Gray Ones might decide to circle the lake, move into territory they did not know. Endanger the humans there who were friends.

She had the impression then of having her mind winnowed. The rifler was interested in the Keplian mare. They were friends? Yes, they were, and was there anything wrong with that? was Eleeri's sharp response.

In return she received a burst of amusement. On the contrary. The mist or whatever dwelt within was pleased. Eleeri blinked, sending her own query in turn: *Why?* Now there was a sense of duality touching her, not one thing communicating, but two. Male and female. She received the impression they were human in some way, more than human in others. Adepts, then? she queried. In reply the touch vanished. The image of the barred door returned and she found herself backing slowly away again as the mist writhed and coiled.

She retired hastily to share the experience with Tharna. They stared at each other when she had finished. Wordlessly the mare began to graze again. She liked to consider things, to chew over thoughts as she did grass. Eleeri was not so eager to think about all this. In several ways she wasn't even sure she had liked the way her mind had been invaded. She had suffered no injury, but they could at least have asked, she thought resentfully. She didn't even belong in this world.

That brought her up short in her mind. Didn't she? This world had allowed her to be herself; it had given her a home, a roof and friends. Here she rode as a warrior as she could never have done in the world she had escaped.

It had been an escape. She had run here. Entered willingly along the road of the gone-before ones. For a single moment she felt a terrible longing for Far Traveler and their home. But her great-grandfather was gone, their small home no longer hers. Even if she could go back, nothing would ever be the same. Tharna and Hylan could not travel with her; in her world they would be treated ill. She fingered her knife. She could not ride as a warrior there. That thought alone could sway her powerfully.

Life was hard in this land she had chosen. She must fight to survive, to eat. For food and trade she must hunt, and all she owned was from the work of her own hands. She drew in a deep breath of the spring-scented air. Then she marched into her keep. It *was* hers, hers by right of finding, by use. The decision had been made. For all this time in many ways she had been living as if her sojourn here were only temporary. Now she knew in a burst of wild gladness it was her home, her keep, her land. No one was going to take anything away from her without having a fight on their hands. And that, she added with mental ferocity, included any Gray Ones or their masters.

She swept inside to begin turning out winter-musty furs. Bedding she hauled to the stream and washed in the stone basins designed for that purpose. She looked properly at the basins for the first time. Clever: whomever had dwelt here hadn't intended to live without amenities. She trotted back inside to add her own clothing to the pile.

She left the grass spread with her work, as she returned to her keep. For too long she had used only the great hall. On very cold or wet nights many of the Keplians would join her there. She had never bothered to search the upper rooms.

She snorted. That had been the faint remembrances of Far Traveler's tales. Of how it was not well to accept a roof where the owners had died. She didn't know that the owners *had* died here. It could have been far away. They could even be those who lived behind the mist, and hence not dead at all. She tramped up the narrow stone stairs.

You could tell this place had been built by those expecting a war. The stairs had no rail and twisted in a way that allowed a defender free sword-arm.

Upstairs, she counted as she moved down the narrow passage. It must run the length of the keep, above the center of the downstairs hall.

No wooden furniture remained, if any there had been, but stone tables furnished several of the rooms. Hearths were placed to warm bedrooms. Two large alcoves shelved in stone may once have been linen closets. She wandered through the rooms, tapping idly at the walls. Cynan had showed her the small hiding place for jewelry in his own hold. Had they had one here? she wondered. She drifted down to the end of the passage and found, to her surprise, that it continued in a flight of stairs leading downward again. She orientated herself. Strange. She'd seen no second set upward from the lower floor.

She trod down, eyes and ears alert, hand on knife hilt. Down, down. By now she had to be below ground. She glanced up and suddenly understood. Once there was probably extra planking level with the stone floor, hiding the continuation of the staircase, probably with a hidden trapdoor there. The light had faded so that she stumbled, retreating in search of something she could use to light her way. Feet padded swiftly back up the stairs—there, that would do. She'd used branches to sweep upstairs the previous summer. Now dry, they would burn to light her way. She glanced at the armload. Would it be enough?

Surely she could manage. She hurried back down to where she could no longer see, then lit a branch. As it burned, the amount of light was small, but it did allow her to see the stairs. She padded on down until a door appeared before her. Stone, but so well crafted it could be opened by a firm push. She peered around the edge in wonderment. A vast expanse of paved floor met her gaze.

There seemed to be nothing but that floor stretching into darkness on the far side. Making a mental note that she must make better torches for this, she advanced. Stone-paved floor, stone block walls, and no other entrance. That didn't make sense. Why would they have this down here with no escape? Perhaps it had been only storerooms?

She padded around the perimeter, holding up her branch. It was beginning to die; she lit the second and continued to walk. She guessed this area was almost as large as the keep above. Something caught her eye, a rusted remnant of metal on the floor. She stooped to find she was holding a dagger. From the studs that surrounded it, the steel had once been within a leather sheath. She faced the stone wall, thinking. Was this a weapon dropped in flight, or had it a deeper significance?

Cynan had taught her several words in common usage as commands. This keep had been built as a fortress, but those who had lived here might not have used more than simple locks.

She faced the wall, lifting her voice in clear command. "Ashlin!" Eleeri said. There was a soft creaking, a grinding, as the wall opened.

Behind it, protected from time's hunger, hung weapons. Here and there were gaps as if a portion of the collection had been snatched up in haste. The woman studied the array carefully. Bows, quivers filled with arrows, swords, daggers, honing stones, everything one could want to defend this place. She smiled. Would her word continue to work? She walked to the edge of the open section, then took two more paces sideways.

"Ashlin!" There was no response. She paced sideways

again. Still no response. But on her third try the wall again quivered into life.

This time it was mail. Mail in a wonderful metal that held the sheen of oil on water. She lifted out a piece and admired the work. The mail—no, she remembered now, when it was rings like this Mayrin had said it was called chain. The chain was wrought by a master, surely. It hung heavy but limp as velvet in her hands. There was a smaller shirt there which she found her hands drawn to.

It fitted perfectly, as if some long-ago smith had made it for her measure. Once on, it didn't feel so heavy, either. She lit the last branch—now she had light enough to leave, and that was it. Facing the open sections, she spoke the word of closing and watched as they snapped shut again. She'd be back. There was more here to be discovered. She hurried up the stairs as her branch burned low. Was it possible, her curiosity suggested, that the commands would work in some of the bedrooms as well? Were there other secrets she might have overlooked?

She soon found there were. Mayrin had taught her other commands, and these opened what must have once been clothes closets in several of the rooms. She gasped over the wealth of silks and velvets exposed to her. From the sizes and other indications, she guessed there had been a lord and lady of the keep. There looked also to have been babies.

For the remainder of that day, she trotted from wall to wall all over the keep trying her commands. Even the kitchen yielded up cupboards of pots, pans, crockery, and other minor items. Eleeri retired to bed, her head whirling with delight. From being a beggar in someone else's keep, she now felt true ownership for the first time. It was as if the keep itself had let her in.

Early the next morning she was back down the stairs

again with torches. She circled the walls, trying each of the words she knew in turn. One opened a small door to stables she had not known were there. By the afternoon, she was exhausted with her work. She retired to the great hall with a charcoal stick and a large piece of white bark. There she attempted to make a plan of the keep. As she drew, she marveled. Why had it taken her so long to explore? It was as if she had felt herself an invader. That by remaining in the hall alone she would not anger those who had once owned this place.

In some ways she understood her own actions. It had been the canyon with its runes and strange mist. She had felt that to trespass too greatly would be to see them all driven forth. But now that they had lived here for a time, she felt a gradual welcome begin to close about her. As if she was known now, recognized and accepted. The keep was hers: she would accept its gifts, its shelter, the comfort offered by the strong walls and runes at the gates.

For the next weeks she was busy going over her new-found keepdom. She began sleeping upstairs in the bed-room that must have belonged to lord and lady. The kitchen shone with burnished pots and pans hung on the walls. From cupboards now open to her searching eyes, she retrieved tapestries, hanging them with much labor and cursing. It puzzled her that the cupboards appeared to have protected their contents so well. It occurred to her to experiment with fresh meat placed inside the closet in a bedroom. The attempt explained much to her; the meat remained fresh for weeks. After some trial and error, she found that the more often the cupboard was open, the more swiftly the meat would decay. A spell? It had to be. Some magic to preserve from time whatever was placed within. Good. The cupboards she did not need would do well to keep her food against the summer heat.

Meanwhile, the Keplians had not been idle. Hylan had taken to quiet visits into the lands his dam had once known. From there he had returned with news gleaned from his kind. The last visit, Tharna had traveled beside him. Now she came in search of Eleeri.

Kin-sister, there is news, nor do I like what I have heard.

The woman stood up to stroke the soft nose. She waited. Tharna would speak in her own good time.

In the center of our lands there rises an old shadow. Evil lairs once more in the Dark Tower. My people fear it, obey it, yet still do they fall to its hunger. It is possible it is the reason the Gray Ones hunt us far harder than ever before. More and more Keplian fall to them also.

Eleeri had known of that. The Keplians had always been small in numbers, the fault of the treatment meted out to orphaned foals by the stallions who killed so casually and the mares who refused to aid the helpless. Now she listened to Tharna and Hylan as they told of foals and birth-weakened mares taken almost under the noses of herd stallions. Even of young bachelor males pulled down by many Gray Ones working together.

They are run mad. They kill and kill until all our lands will be empty. Hylan's breath hissed in. *They even attack the rasti. But they lose doubly in that. The rasti are not such as should be trifled with. Many died—on both sides.*

The woman smiled broadly. "It is well said that when evil ones fall out, good may profit. Let us hope they slaughter each other until none remain."

Unlikely, the stallion commented. *They say in our lands that that which dwells in the tower spoke to them harshly, saying that if they war again, he will punish both sides.*

Eleeri glanced up. "That won't get it far. Rasti care nothing for threats. If the Gray Ones attack them, they will fight."

Tharna nodded. *But the wolf ones do care. They fear that which is in the Dark Tower. They will not again attack without word. I fear that it may be your friends who are to be prey next. There was some talk of a gathering of the pack, that they might hunt out far toward the edges of their territory.*

Eleeri gazed out from under the trees where they were standing. Her mind was suddenly made up: she would ride to speak of this to those of the lake keep.

That is well, kin-sister. But ride wary.

That the woman was more than prepared to do. The sturdy dun was saddled and Keplians mind-sent affection as she rode past them. The runes flared at her passage. Impelled by an impulse, she leaned over as she passed, fingers tracing the main runes of guard. A word came into her mind then as if gifted to her. By now she had learned not to speak such aloud, but in her mind she stored it against need.

As she rode from her hold, she thought about the runes. From what she now knew of the land, the gift of power was common. Even those who had little were taught to use what they had. All homes, keeps, strongholds, were warded, the Valley of the Green Silences most strongly of all. It was an ability native to the people here.

Her mind turned to the Gray Ones. Unpleasant creatures that they were. They and the Keplians had been enemies from time out of mind. It seemed that the attempts to control them, perhaps to draw power from them, was driving them mad. The tower might demand they cease to fight; the dweller there would not wish his meager resources wasted casually in a war he did not approve, and one moreover which killed his own side only. But he wasn't having much luck there, Eleeri thought. That suited her. Friends profited when enemies fell out, Far Traveler had been fond of saying. If the Gray Ones continued to irritate the rasti, too, it would be useful.

She shivered. A rasti pack-ground was no place to be. They looked rather like weasels to her—weasels grown to three feet in length, with wonderful fur. And like weasels sometimes would in the depths of a hard winter, rasti hunted in packs.

They had no true intelligence, but they had an animal cunning all their own. Nor, if their territory was invaded, did they seem to care how many of their own kind died, so long as the intruders were expelled. The dead were food, their own dead or the invaders. She shivered, thrusting the thought from her mind.

She rode steadily downstream and along the lake edge. That night as she slept, she dreamed as she had not done in many months. A dark-haired man looked at her with a wistful hope. He had aged beyond the boy of the small painted picture. But she knew him . . . Romar, twin to Mayrin. His face twisted in his efforts to reach her, to speak, perhaps to warn.

Then strength visibly drained from him and his face went slack. She leaned forward; her eyes studied him. He was thin, pale of skin, as one who had been indoors too long. But resolution still showed in the firm set of jaw, the folded lips. In her sleep, slender fingers slid to her throat, there to twine about the Keplian pendant. She strained to see more clearly. Warmth rose from that which she clasped.

Her dream sight cleared a little. Now beyond the man she could see a window, blue sky spread above, gray stone surrounding it. He sat held to a great carved chair by leather straps. Yet she sensed he was held by more than the bonds she saw. About him spread a circle. Runes flared red, smoked in black around the outer line. Eleeri shivered. There was no mistaking what she saw: Romar was captive to an evil that sought to use him. His eyes opened again, and in them there was a desperate appeal. The runes flared high, veiling him in a smoke that reeked even in her dreaming, of power and danger.

She pulled back. The scene began to fade, but as it did so, it shifted. Now she looked down as a bird might upon a tower below. Confirmation. That was indeed the Dark Tower, deep in Keplian lands. She rode on at daybreak, the dream repeating over and over in her mind. She feared the effect on Mayrin, did she speak of this. The woman would insist on an attack, but Eleeri felt that this would bring only death. They must be clever. Attack, yes, but as thieves in the night, not as warriors. The fighters of her people had once esteemed such battle cunning.

Her face flickered into a brief dangerous smile. She would keep her own counsel, but she would speak of the warnings her friends had brought from Keplian lands. That would be sufficient to place the keep on guard. As for Jerrany—there, too, she would not speak, she decided. He loved Mayrin dearly, too much to hide anything from her. Once she suspected, Mayrin would have the story out of him as a sea-dog shelled sea-snails.

Eleeri rode into the keep days later. From across the bridge, her friends came running, Mayrin laughing happily.

"Oh, it is so good to see you again. What has happened since last you came? Has the hunting been good? Are you tired?"

Jerrany seized the reins. "I'll take this fellow to be cared for. Go you with Mayrin before she bursts with her questions." He touched her lightly on one shoulder. "She speaks for us both, though. It is good to see you once more. I'll bring your pack to the hall." He strode away, leading the weary pony.

Mayrin had her friend by a sleeve. For the first time she realized that there was a hard material under her fingers. "Why, what is this?" She turned up the outer fabric. "Chain, you wear chain, and such craft! Where did it come from? Have you found another place to trade? What —"

Eleeri held up a hand laughing softly. "Let me answer one set of questions before you ask me more. As for the chain, it was found, not traded. I will tell you the story another time. The hunting has indeed been good, and yes, I am both tired and hungry. I have no news of Romar, but something that may bear upon you and the keep. Feed me and I will talk with you and Jerrany of it. This is in part why I have come."

Late into that night they talked. Jerrany did not take her words lightly.

"I will have all put in order. We do stand ready, but there are many small things which might yet be done to prepare for siege or attack." His face grew serious as he thought. "What have you brought to trade?"

"No luxuries this time," Eleeri assured him. "All good deerskins, sinews, and a gift for you, another for Mayrin." She reached for her pack. "Ask me not where these came from. They are for you, a gift of Light." She allowed the first bundle to unroll, revealing a matching chain shirt which would fit her friend. Mayrin gasped, touching it with wondering fingers. Another bundle unrolled to spread half a dozen swords across Jerrany's feet. They were unadorned but of superb workmanship. The keep lord picked one up, closed his hand about the hilt, and tried a pass or two. Then he spoke as one who offers a pledge.

"We will ask not whence these came. That they are of the Light is enough." He eyed his wife sternly when she would have spoken, and Mayrin's lips closed again. "They shall be used against evil, to protect that which is good."

He was more sober than was his custom the remainder of Eleeri's visit. When she departed, he watched as her pony rounded the lake edge, gradually disappearing from their sight. Then he strolled inside and called for a trusted armsman. To him he handed a letter.

"Take this to the lady who rules the Valley of the Green Silences, and none other." Hoofbeats died on soft turf as he stood at the keep door. Silently he went to his armory and from there to check provisions.

Little enough of the gift was there in his line. But now he felt the chill as of a coming storm. He had heard Eleeri's warnings with belief. He had mentioned it neither to his wife nor their visitor, but a hunter for the keep, ranging farther than usual, had seen Gray Ones. There was more the woman was not telling, he was sure. Perhaps she was not certain of the import herself. There would be no ill reason for her silence.

He stared out over the land that lay before him as he passed an arrow slot. It was fair: here he had planned to live, to see children grow. Would his bones lie here before his time instead? And what of Mayrin? She would not leave did he try to send her.

He looked out over the land to where blue-tinged mountains lifted far in the distance. Here they had come to build a house and a name. Here they would stay, for life or death. If the valley could send help, well enough; if not, then they would fight alone. Sunlight glinted far down the lakeside. No, not quite alone. Eleeri, too, rode to war.

He sighed. Always Romar had been his right arm. If only his friend were here now to stand beside him. His step was heavy as he left the window. Behind him there were none left to care about him, he thought. His mother had long since turned to her new lord and her growing brood. No, here were his only friends and loves. But he missed his sword-brother Romar with every fiber of his being.

He found he was standing in the middle of his bedroom studying the window once more. Through it he could see a long sweep of land toward the Valley of Green Silences. He sighed. This had been a lonely and dangerous place to choose to live. But hitherto it had been free from the Gray Ones. It was a sign the Dark was growing in strength, and a danger to all who rode for the Light.

Many years ago, a different Dark lord dwelling there had tried to seize the mind and heart of a witchmaid—the daughter of Simon Tregarth. She had been freed, and evil turned back on the man who would have used her. But the tower was a place which seemed to call to those small ones of the Dark who would be greater. A pity it was impossible to tear it down completely so that none might rise there in Dark power again. He had suggested that once; it was Duhaun herself who told him they could not. Some reason rooted in the things of power. He had not understood half the explanation, only enough to know she was right. It could not be done without endangering the land itself.

Far down the lakeside, sunlight flickered briefly from bridle mountings as Eleeri rounded the stream bend. She, too, was remembering—a harsh-planed face weary beyond words, and gray-green eyes that pleaded for aid.

Over the past few days her mind had been made up. There comes a time when a warrior must ride. Along with Romar's face, those of Mayrin, Jerrany, Tharna, and Hylan arose along with her other Keplian friends. Too many innocents. If she must don war paint, take oath to ride pukutsi, to ride slaying until all who faced her died, or she herself fell, then let it be so. She found she was humming softly as she rode. Far Traveler's death song. She smiled. She would be ready.

10

Over the weeks, things settled to quiet again, but no one in keep or canyon was deceived. The feeling of danger grew as the Gray Ones were seen more often, always deeper into the lands that bordered their own. Eleeri took to sitting alone where they appeared. Bow in hand, she waited, patient pony grazing ready. From ambush her arrows slew in ones and twos until the wolfmen were nervous about the whole fringe of country toward the mountains.

Hylan did his share to make other Keplian males as wary. Twice he fought and defeated stallions given over to the Dark. He had seen their treatment of mares and foals. Now he knew why his gentle mother had fled to find refuge. All honor to her kin-sister who had protected them. As a foal he had looked up to the human; as a colt he had listened to her. Now as a stallion he spoke equally but accepted that she was the forethinker, the one who made plans, watched for consequences. Now he quite simply loved her, as did his dam.

To see a Dark-given Keplian stallion was to see power and majesty embodied in evil. To see Hylan beside one was to see the difference. He was larger still, his lines cleaner, and the power shone from him like an aura. In the canyon all bowed to his will, save his dam and her battle-sister. Even other Keplian males who met him on their land tended to back away. Unlike them, he had not struggled for food as a colt. He had not been fed by a dam thin from constant breeding, who would chase him from her as soon as possible to save his life. He had become magnificent but also intelligent. In him the potential of his kind was realized.

He glanced up from juicy grass as Eleeri passed. *Where do you go this time?*

"The river. The rasti are disputing with the Gray Ones again." She grinned evilly. "It's a saving on energy. If I shoot anyone at all, it's a kill, since the opposition finish them for me."

The huge beast was amused but worried. *When enemies fight, it is well for us, but walk warily. The rasti are stirred by all this intrusion on their territory. Even I would not wish to meet them where I could not flee.*

Eleeri could agree with that. A rasti pack was death on many feet. She had seen too many others fall to them when injured to take chances. She swung up and nodded. "I'll be careful. You keep an eye on things here and I should be back by sunhigh."

She was gone, cantering past the runes, which flared into life as she passed. Hylan watched, listening as the hoofbeats faded. Then he walked slowly toward the entrance. At his approach, too, the runes began to glimmer, a soft blue-green glow that strengthened, warmed. He eyed them wistfully. He was of the Light; all here in the canyon were so acknowledged by the marks of ward and guard. Yet still he wished for more. To any eye who knew him not, he was of the Dark, a Keplian, follower of the evil. If only there was something to distinguish him in his outer form. He sighed silently, returning to his grass.

His dam wandered over several hours later. *Where did Eleeri go?*

To the river to tease rasti. The question's import dawned. *She said she would be back by sunhigh. It is past that. You worry.* The last was a statement.

His dam nodded. Both knew her kin-sister's custom. If she said she would do something, it was done. If not, there was good reason. Both were suddenly afraid what that reason might be. They looked at each other and in accord trotted from the canyon and down the rocky trail toward the river. There was no sign of Eleeri there, but her pony's scent lay on the grass. They followed, taking it in turn to guard as the other laid nose to ground. Tharna found the first place and reared to a halt.

Here there was trouble.

They scented the pony's rush of fright. His hooves had scored the ground as he leaped away. But why? Soft noses leaned downward, scoured across nearby ground in an outward circling. Gray Ones! A whole pack, as many as two dozen, perhaps, and all males. This was no casual wandering; this had been a trail. They had been going somewhere with a purpose—and the trail led toward the lake.

That is, it had. Now it led into the higher foothills as Gray Ones turned to hunt woman and pony. Eleeri had run, but no swifter than necessary, saving her mount's strength.

The Keplians trotted along in pursuit. They would find

her. The scent was fresh; the wolfmen must have her cornered somewhere.

Eleeri had left that morning with no intent beyond a few enemy deaths. She fought cautiously, using the land itself and pitting enemies against one another. She had been greatly successful over the past two months. She had hunted deeper into the lands toward the Dark Tower than her Keplian friends knew. She had seen nothing of Romar, but clues told her he was held there or nearby. She had discovered the tower was guarded; that alone told her that something was there to be protected. Time and time again over recent weeks she had approached, searching out what she could find of the defenses.

But this morning the sun had been warm, the sky blue. There was no thought of towers or prisoners. She would twist rasti tails, kill Gray Ones if she could.

She allowed the pony to pick his own way downhill toward the river. For a short time she watched the rasti, but none were careless today. Far across the stream she could see movement. She pushed the pony into a steady walk as she paced the distant shifting. Curious, she crossed to move closer. From the long grass almost at her feet, Gray Ones rose up. Mad with fear, her mount leaped and whirled, fled with all the speed in a sturdy body kept fit and well fed. The Gray Ones had moved to cut her off from the running water. In his panic her mount was carrying her farther away, bearing almost directly south so that her distance from the stream widened.

She fought him savagely, driving into his mind as she never did. But this was desperate; she must send him back to the running water. A swift glance had told her the deadly danger. A full pack of males loped behind them. She turned the sweating animal in a long slow curve and reached the river. Not good: on the other side, the rasti waited; behind, the Gray Ones closed in. The pony could outrun them, but his endurance was far less than theirs. They had only to keep between her and the water wherever she could safely cross. Split the pack and they had her. But mad with the hunt, they were not doing that—not yet. Her mind worked feverishly as she scanned possibilities.

Her hand went up to close around her pendant. Behind her the hunt faltered, and in that short time she had fled the closing ring. She thrust the unwilling pony into the water. The river was still high from spring thaw, and he protested. She understood that, but it was risk this or be eaten. She hurled pictures at him until he swam, terror at his heels. A greater terror rose before him as the rasti now gave chase, leaving the Gray Ones pack howling in frustrated rage on the bank behind them. The pony was tiring. Eleeri was a rider who knew how to lighten her own body as she rode. But he had come far and fast, with panic sapping his strength, leaching the stamina from his muscles.

He began to falter. The rasti were closing in on them now. Still he staggered on, his fear of them so strong he would run until he died on his hooves. Eleeri was turning and shooting, keeping her weight balanced. At each arrow another of her pursuers died. Those who were only wounded were swiftly taken by their companions. Each death slowed them so that the exhausted pony remained ahead, but for how long?

Eleeri counted her arrows and shivered. Without her weight, he could escape. With it, they would both die. If she'd been sure the followers would leave her if her mount went down—feast while she was free to run—she might have acted. She was deeply fond of the small horse who carried her so willingly, but she would sacrifice him to survive. A quick knife thrust would ensure he did not suffer.

But she was under no illusions. The rasti took only minutes to eat those she slew. But always there were a few who continued without sharing the feasts. They seemed to be taking turns to eat. Would they all halt to share a far greater bounty? Somehow she was sure they would not and she could not bear to kill without that certainty. The pony reeled on, his hooves only yards away from teeth that now gaped in bloodstained anticipation.

Eleeri had decided. When the pony could no longer stay ahead of the rasti, she would act. Kill him cleanly, then run for a place where she could make a stand. The body might draw off sufficient of them for her to give a good accounting in her final battle. *Hai!* She would be able to stand before the gods as a warrior. Her lips curled back in a battle rictus. Let them come, the first to reach her should be the first to die. She hurled fear away, allowed rage to flood in. Adrenaline surged as she turned to shoot her last arrows.

From the hillside nearby came a sudden burst of sound. The Keplians had not followed far into the lands of their enemies. A wind shift had revealed enough for them to know that the hunt's direction had changed. It neared them swiftly and to their nostrils came the deaths of the rasti, the stink of blood, sweat, and terror. They could smell the growing weariness of Eleeri's mount. Below them the hunt came into view far down the mountainside. If they left the trail and followed another they knew, they might yet be in time.

The pursuit gained on Eleeri. As they moved, Tharna and Hylan dropped obliquely down the heights, gradually reaching the lower lands. So intent on the race were those involved, none looked up to see that others might be taken into account. Hylan and his dam reached a lower trail. It was smoother and they leaped into a gallop, huge bodies straining as they sped along. With their far greater speed, they reached a bend that turned in the direction of the hunt, and were still ahead of it. They had time to see and understand Eleeri's decision. In a few more minutes the pony would go down and she would turn to die.

In the woman's battle rage she was mind-sending. Her intent struck like a sword as the pursuit raced toward the Keplians. There was an instant of wordless communication between them, a decision made. It was against all they knew, but they cared nothing for that. A friend, a kin-sister would die unless they aided her. She would do this and more for them.

Hooves blazed a path down the last slope toward her. Minds screamed warning, pictures too fast for ordinary mind-speech. In one jump Tharna ranged beside the pony, Hylan on the other side, keeping the faltering animal straight as he ran.

He shouldered hard into the smaller beast. His mind flung an order. For a moment Eleeri herself faltered—was he sure? He was! Tharna had slowed, and her hooves now shot out viciously. Teeth snapped as the leading rasti went down. Their followers swirled in eddies as they ate and ran on again. But the Keplian raced faster than any rasti could run. The unburdened pony kept up, terror driving him beyond normal endurance.

Astride the Keplian stallion, Eleeri thrilled as they outraced death. She crouched low over his withers, her weight balanced, feeling the great driving muscles under her. Her mind unconsciously reached out, seeking that oneness she had always found with a mount.

It came, in a flood of imagery and power. It was as if, reaching for water, she had drunk unwatered wine. The

Keplian, too, was stunned by the union. For him it was Light, a blaze of it that lit corners of his mind, showed to him things for which he had no words. He felt it run through him, cleansing, healing. He remembered the terror of his birth, his bewildered pain and the hatred for those who hurt him, kept him from his dam. Now all that was healed. He understood their ignorant fears. Accepted that to them he had been of the Dark, and that the Dark was killed where it was found.

Beside him the weakening pony ran. He felt only pity for it. Before, he had scorned it as a pale copy of the glory that was Keplian. He was sorry for it now; it could never have this, the power and blaze of the Light blending two into one. He had feared to take Eleeri upon his back, feared that he would feel degraded, humiliated by a rider. He flung up his head, and the wild savage scream of a fighting stallion broke forth as a trumpet blast in triumph. He was not bound by a rider; he was freed. This was not emptiness, being used. It was a fullness, and in the Light he knew at last this was his creation.

They swerved uphill, following a faint trail in the direction of the canyon. Linking by mind-touch, Tharna felt a pale echo of the ecstasy of Light the rider had brought her son. She wondered sadly if this pleasure was felt by those who carried the Dark ones. If so, then she could better understand their acceptance. Denied by the Light, they had chosen to still be greater than they were alone. She followed her son, hooves dully sounding on the rocky path. Next time it would be she who carried her kin-sister, who shared the union of Light. But she would be generous. She felt a gentle amusement at that. Yes, she would allow her son to carry a rider—sometimes.

They reached the entrance to the canyon, the rasti long since left behind. Ahead the runes flamed brighter than she had ever seen before. Higher and higher until they were as torches that lit even the day. The blue-green changed slowly to the golden shade shot with silver that was the mist of the lower reaches. In it Eleeri could feel a gentle welcome, a tugging. She shrugged it off. Her pony had carried her, given all he had. What kind of rider would she be to leave him neglected, lathered, still saddled and bridled? She dropped from Hylan, turning to lay her head against his shoulder for a moment. Her hand reached out to pull the mare in so that they stood together.

"I know what you did."

Tharna stirred. *He did no more than I would have done. Next time *I* will carry you. I am your battle-sister; it is right.*

Eleeri felt the faint note of questioning. She hastened to send reassurance, then love. "Next time, kin-sister. You shall both bear me as you choose. Who would be borne by a horse when they could have the greater?"

This close she could feel both thinking. The idea drifted through the three as they leaned together, touching. Maybe they had been right. Perhaps it had been for this that the Great Ones had created Keplian. Eleeri pulled herself away briskly then. "The pony—I have to see to him," she explained to the soft complaint. Agreement came reluctantly. Her friends followed as she tended the small leg-weary animal. As she worked, they kept up an amused mind-send of comment. Finally the woman found the jests at the uncaring beast's expense a little too much. She turned to face them, the look in her eyes serious.

"Listen to me. I know he is not Keplian. I know he has no mind—speech, no great brains, and not the speed or beauty of either of you. But he does his best always. He would have died, running to save me out there today. I value his gentleness, his hard work, and his honesty. It does not mean I value my friends any the less." She fixed them with a stare and waited.

There was a long period of silence. The pony moved away to graze. Hylan's head came up.

You are right. You value him for what he is, as you have always valued us. We are more, but—

His dam picked up the words. *But one does not ignore the moss just because the grass is juicy. Both are edible and of value to one who hungers.*

The woman nodded. "Just so. Now, would you keep what we have done from the rest of our friends here?"

The Keplians consulted, noses touched. Tharna turned great eyes on her friend. *Let them see; let them know. What have we to be ashamed about? If I carry my kinsister, it is no more than my wish and hers.* Her head lifted, neck arching proudly. *I ask the permission of no one; nor does my son, who is lord here to them. Let any see. We care not!*

Eleeri knew the step they took then as she vaulted lightly to the mare's sleek back. In full view of all those who lifted amazed heads, she clung as Tharna whipped into her floating gallop down the canyon's length. As they approached the mist, it seemed to shiver, blazing in golden shimmerings that beckoned. The mare shied away, circling to race back down the grass. Eleeri bent to her neck, crooning the ancient words that tied rider and mount. Tharna did not understand the speech of the Nemunuh, but the love behind the words, the caring and affection, those she understood fully.

Two minds reached out, touched, clung closer than ever before. This—this was destined. Together they gloried. Eleeri could feel Tharna's great heart pumping, joy in the speed of her powerful legs; she *was* the mare, the mare was her. Tharna, too, explored, it was as if her mind expanded. She had never understood the concept of far time. Now she did. She saw possible futures laid out before her. All the misty worlds that could be if—she leaned into them, peering, striving to discover. She realized the relative frailty of her companion. Eleeri must store food for winter, make herself coverings against the chill. She could not travel as swiftly as a Keplian. That was why she so valued the pony. Ah! That she now understood.

She saw their differences, and their likeness. Felt friendship course warm through both. Slowly as she halted, a picture formed which explained much to her. A human was frail in comparison to Keplians, Gray Ones, even the beasts. Therefore they must always think of tomorrow. They must make weapons, change the land they lived in to fit them so they could survive. Since they could not live naked and shelterless, they must find or make shelter, stitch clothing, store food for the places, the times when there was none close at hand.

Tharna felt strange, as if her mind were expanding, filling with new thoughts and ideas. Whole chains of logic built up and broke to re-form anew in different patterns. She stood, head hanging, a long slow shivering rippling along her body as the bonding continued.

Hylan nosed her gently. *Is all well with you?*

She roused herself, pulled back a little. *It is well, my son. So many new things, so much to think over.*

Eleeri's laughter tickled both Keplian minds. "I, too, have learned a few things I never considered. Your mind is treasure, kin-sister."

The truth of that touched them all for a moment. But the emotion was becoming too strong. The woman disengaged herself, sliding from the broad back. She trotted away across the grass toward the ancient keep. She was starving, and thirsty. She would eat, drink, and sleep on the day's events. Behind her the Keplian knew what she would do. Without discussion, they moved away to drink and graze.

That night Eleeri slept the sleep of the dead. The day had been more than exhausting. The full sharing with Tharna had drained her until she could barely remain awake long enough to cool her throat, fill her empty belly. She fell then into a sleep so deep that she lay motionless, utterly limp within her bedding.

Into that sleep the man came walking. Tall and lean, eyes the gray-green hue, with black hair. The strong planes of his face denied the gentler molding of his mouth, matched the determined jut of chin. He was worn thin and the pallor of his skin betrayed a captivity, but pride still showed in the set of his head, in the litheness with which he yet moved.

About Eleeri's throat the Keplian pendant flared to life. In her sleep her fingers clutched at it. His mouth opened to speak and she strained to hear. Nothing. He was speaking, but she could hear no sound. It was as if a thick pane of glass stood between them, walling off all he wished to say. But she came from a people to whom the hands could speak as eloquently. Without her willing it, her fingers lifted and signed. For an instant, blue-green fire hung in the air, and his fingers rose to trace the rune. The fire deepened.

Sound came then, so faint she must strain to hear, each word seeming to drain him. Quickly she signed that he should use his hands instead, remembering the sign language Cynan had taught her. He nodded, beginning quickly so that she understood they might not have long before what they did was noticed. She knew his name, but hesitated to give her own. Names had power in this place of dreaming, perhaps even more so than in waking life.

He saw her thought and nodded. Eleeri grinned then. A name common enough to catch her attention, but no name of hers, that she would give.

She touched her breast. "Tsukup." It was the Nemunuh word for an experienced warrior. One who had learned wisdom where the arrow flew. It was a word that might draw her, but never too strongly, since it was only of her people, not of her. Then she stared at him until his eyes rose to meet hers. Silently she shaped his name with her lips. He started back, a question showing clear. She began to sign, her hands flowing in graceful dance. Ah, he was nodding again. He grasped that she had learned of him from his sister. Gradually, with much signing, they were able to exchange some information.

But all the time the sign hanging before them faded. Suddenly it was gone, and even as it faded, so did Romar. His last look was one of despair. He might have been asking himself what good they had done, save to hold out a hope that would die before the Dark.

Eleeri came blinking awake in her bedding. She sat up cross-legged to ponder. Now she knew more of Romar. His limning had showed a boy, but it had been no boy she fronted this night. A man, a warrior had faced her. The boy had shown a sensitivity, an imagination in the lines of his face. This one might yet have those, but if so, they were deep buried.

She counted over the points he had been able to tell. He was indeed captive in the Dark Tower, but who or what his captor, he could not say. He was used as a—the only word she could think of was *power-line*. Using Romar's strength, the captor fed his will to the Gray Ones and those Keplian males who served it. Recently the drain had become far greater; Romar was failing as his strength was pulled from him to serve evil purposes. If he was not soon freed, there would be no more than a brainless husk remaining. The desperation he felt had come across to her strongly, as had the despair.

She considered carefully. All her original reasoning still applied. More so now that she knew more. From hints she had received, she could guess that Mayrin, too, would be of use to the thing. Brother and sister could be linked to be far more than either was alone. But Eleeri could not be so used. She was not of Romar's kin or blood, not even of this land. She had some of what they called the power here. But somehow she felt it was different, that the tower could not turn it against her. She marched to the beat of a different war drum. Her songs were not the songs of this place, but of another. Of a people tied to a different land, to other powers.

Best she move carefully in this. Allow the enemy no crack in which to slip a lever. She would learn what she could. Tharna had been able to tell her somewhat of the powers. She would continue to visit the keep also. Mayrin had some of the minor gift. She could tell more and Eleeri would learn. Then, when Eleeri was ready, she would try to call Romar. Two heads were better than one. With greater knowledge and some preparation, there might be a way they could free him.

11

But she was not ready when Romar intruded on her dreams once more. His face was thinner, and his eyes weary. She watched as his fingers wove back and forth, paid attention to his words. Why did he waste strength so? Then she saw past the warrior who warned her of dangerous paths, to the fearful man within. He had been isolated, bereft of friends and family. He came to her out of simple loneliness, came to the only one he could reach to share with. In turn, her hands flashed in the sign language they were mutually building.

"The Gray Ones fear you," Romar signed.

"That we have ensured. But what of your master? Does he recognize our enmity?"

Romar nodded slowly. That which used him did indeed know something opposed it. As yet it was not greatly disturbed. It was confident in its own power and strength. The deaths of the Gray Ones were minor. There were always more.

Eleeri grinned. "One day there may not be. We'll see if we can't thin their numbers to where that thing does start to worry."

"Well enough, so long as you do not cause too much notice to be taken. Better an enemy secure in its own mind."

To that she nodded. Warrior sense. She would keep a balance, kill as many of the enemy as possible without alarming the leader too greatly. The talk turned to other things. Romar was eager to hear of his keep and kin.

"You have not told them?"

"It seemed unwise."

He bit his lip saying nothing.

"Be assured that if danger rises, I will ride to warn them. They have become my friends. It is just that—" she broke off, shrugging.

"That you fear Mayrin's reaction. You believe she will demand you storm the tower for me and at once, unprepared?"

"Yes," Eleeri admitted.

Romar's head bowed a little as he considered that. "You are probably right. Keep your counsel, then, but do not forsake me, I beg of you." The last words were forced out through stiff lips and the woman was touched, although she allowed nothing to show.

"I have no intention of that. I pause to gather knowledge and test the gifts I have. Already we can talk longer and more easily. This may be of aid when we come to free you. Gather your own strength and wait. The time of your freedom may not be far from you."

Before them the sign faded into nothingness, and Romar with it. Eleeri sat in her bedding, thinking hard.

She hoped he could last out. It would be folly to attack before they knew more about the tower. To be truthful, even then she was not sure she wished to risk all she had. Romar drew her strangely, but he was not kin for whom she must shed blood. She shook her head. Captivity wore hard on him, that was plain. She could still speak to him whenever he came. That much she could and would do. She lay back again and allowed herself to relax. Sleep claimed her once more, a restful dreamless drowse so that she woke refreshed and eager to hunt.

That night she slept peacefully, but the next night and the next, Romar was there. Gradually she came to know him until at length he was able to speak of his deeper fears. Of his pain and humiliation.

"It is as I had always imagined rape to be. An invasion not of body alone, but a tearing at the spirit. Each time it uses my power, I retreat deep within myself, yet each time the place I have free grows smaller. One day it will wrench from me all that I am and there will be nothing left but a shell that walks and talks in my image."

Eleeri heard the bitter fear that edged the words. Without thinking, she responded. Let him know that he was not alone in his fears; she, too, had been abused and cowered beneath that terror. She spoke slowly of her aunt and uncle. Of their hatred for her blood and race.

Romar was caught by her tale. "Then you are different in the world you left?"

"So they counted me. But I am human, as were my people. They fought for their land, to keep the way of life they valued. No more than that." Her hand movements slowed. "Too much hate; always there is hate. Why cannot people live in peace? Why must they always covet what other have?"

A tired smile broke over the face of the man. "Because they *are* people. I sometimes think the urge to own and take what you do not is inbuilt in us all. A growth upon the animal need to hold territory." He glanced at their sign. "Tomorrow night let us debate more of this. If naught else, it takes my mind from my own fears." He was gone then, leaving Eleeri to her own dreaming. Two nights later, she was able to reach him once more. She had spent the time considering. Now she signed busily.

"How were you taken?"

"I do not know, I was struck on the head and remember little. I was hunting. I recall a campsite, lying down to sleep; then I was where I am now. I think perhaps I was taken as I slept. I did not know another had begun to use the tower. Therefore I slept no great distance away." He shrugged. "It was folly. But I had hunted well and my horse was very weary. I camped to allow him time to recover. For that, both of us paid."

Her hands went out to him as her fingers flicked through the signs. "Do not blame yourself. But what of the tower? Can you tell me more? What of he who uses it?"

Romar eyed her. "It is a place of very great power from the Dark. It seems to call to those of its kind who are lesser and would be more. They lose and are destroyed, but always there seems to be another. But I am called, dream well." He was gone and she slept more deeply.

Nights came and went after that. Sometimes they brought Romar and together they pondered philosophical questions, shared lives, and even small jokes as friendship grew. She knew her company was enabling him to hold on with more strength. Perhaps some of her own vitality was leaching across the barrier to replenish his own store. Whatever it was, he had come to appear less worn as the nights of comradeship passed. By now they were as old friends, each comfortable with the other.

Yet still Eleeri wavered. She knew this friendship had a

claim upon her now. But so, too, did the older friendship with Tharna and Hylan. Was she to risk them, perhaps even those others who shared their home? The Dark Tower was feared by even the evil that served it. How much more, then, should those of the Light stand back from combat?

Yet in her heart she knew what held her back. It was fear, quite simply—not of dying, but of losing all she had found here. The more she put the knowledge from her, the more it returned to nag at the fringes of her mind. At length she made a decision. She would wait. Once, long ago, she had heard some joke about that sort of decision. That put off, either it would grow to where something *must* be done, or the problem would solve itself. With that decided, she was more relaxed with Romar when he came again. She did not know he, too, had seen the battle and understood it.

He would not demand of her more than she could give. He had long since realized that she was one who walked her own path. To urge her against her own wishes would only be to harden her mind against the thing he asked. Nor had he any rights in this. She was not even of his race, let alone his kin.

He studied her as they talked. She was beautiful—oh, not by some standards, but he was not of a kind which lusted after a plump and witless prettiness. He admired the swift litheness of her movements, the slender body, pride in every line. His maleness was not challenged to anger by her weapons skill. She was one to guard a man's back, to stand as an equal in an uneasy land. With her a man could be himself, not watching his tongue for fear of alarming a soft frail female.

At first he had been drawn to her by a terrible need for some kind of companionship. Now it was more. There might be for him no tomorrow, no future, but if there were, then he wished to spend it with her. Still he allowed nothing to show, neither desire nor understanding. He would make it no harder for her than she was already making it for herself. He watched as she battled with her own fears. Watched her waver between wishing to storm the tower to his aid, and fearing she would lose all she had won in this new land.

Then the power began to draw more strongly again upon him so that for many nights he must stand alone. Eleeri guessed the reason he did not walk her dreams. Outside the canyon the Gray Ones bayed the hunt more often. The rasti seemed to grow in ferocity so that for some time she left them in peace. A warrior did not fight against foolish odds. But her heart burned to ignore the teachings of a lifetime. She soothed herself often, reminding herself of Far Traveler's tales. So many had been warnings against the impetuousness of youth. But still she longed to see the face of one who had grown to be friend. To share her mind's thoughts, to share her— No. A warrior did not fight against foolish odds. As for her heart, let it be kept for one with a better chance of life.

In her distress of mind, she roamed wider than ever before. Once she met a scout, at least so she believed him, though he said nothing of his reasons for being in the Keplian lands. She spoke with him politely before moving on. Something moved in his eyes and she was wary, keeping the pony beyond reach of any hand weapon. Tharna joined her a short time later.

He follows.

Eleeri swore irritably. "I don't like this. What's the man after?"

He hunts. Minds shared the scent of a predator on the trail. Eleeri turned over possibilities as they trotted on.

Her eyes scanned the terrain they had been traversing as the man had appeared. Then she understood. Wordlessly she conveyed it to her friend. The mare faltered in her smooth gait as she, too, eyed the land and its contours.

He saw us together. He will believe us both, then, of the Dark.

"So I think. The question is, do we attempt to lose him or will he attack?"

A mental shrug was her only answer. The woman nodded. The mare was right. They could only wait and see. One thing she decided: she would not allow them to be trailed too far in the direction of the canyon. If others found them there, they, too, might leap to conclusions. That she would not risk.

She became aware that Tharna was distressed by the human's assumption that the mare was of the Dark. Eleeri reached out to stroke the rough mane, to scratch gently at the base of the small erect ears.

"It isn't your fault, kin-sister. We are in Keplian lands and not so far from the tower. He would have assumed I was of the Dark even if he had not seen us together. He knows me not; my clothing is not of the kind his people wear." She glanced down at the hackamore she used to guide the sturdy dun. "Even my bridle is not of their kind. I remade this into one I preferred, and close as we were, he could see the differences. Let him hunt; we will lose him quickly."

But in that she proved wrong. Whatever else the man might be, he was a tracker. He was falling back as the dusk deepened, but still he clung grimly to their trail.

"Best we do not return?"

Unspoken agreement.

Eleeri swung the pony away from their homeward trail to move instead parallel to the stream. Better not to approach their ford, either. The tracker might see enough to follow that across the stream and into the hills. She wavered, wanting to drift back in to cover and slay him as he passed. The man was a danger to all she held dear. If he followed them to the canyon, he would doubtless return with others to kill them all. Yet she was unwilling to kill him out of hand. They fought on the same side in this battle. Medicine could turn against one who killed his own.

He still follows, Tharna observed.

Eleeri shared her indecision. Perhaps if they continued they could make a wide circle around the Keplian lands, lose this one in the rougher foothills far to the southeast. That was if he would follow them on a trail for so many days. But if he would, then they might lose him without the need to slay. On that last they were in accord. They dropped to a steady walk, leaving clearer signs as they moved on. Let him trail them now—it was their wish.

That he did for two more days. But on the third night he seemed to have lost the trail. Woman and mare halted on a small hill to study their back trail.

"No sign of him. The last I saw was last night's fire."

Do you think we've lost him, kin-sister?

Eleeri looked doubtful. "There's no reason we should have. He's followed us through more difficult tracking than this. Why should he lose us now?"

Perhaps he has wearied of following?

"Maybe, but I have an unpleasant feeling there's more to it. I think I'd like to backtrack."

You think he's run into trouble. Surely we would have heard or seen something. Eleeri considered as she recalled the night. The wind had shifted soon after dark so that it blew from them to their follower. It had increased until by moonhigh it had been blowing hard enough to take any sounds away from them with ease. By dawn it had fallen to a light breeze, but if there had been an attack on the man around the middle night . . .

Is it for us to seek him out? He walks these lands by his own will. He chose to hunt us both.

"I know that, but I'm curious."

Her friend heaved a loud sigh, then turned to retrace their tracks. With a grin, Eleeri heeled the pony up with her again. Tharna was just as curious; she'd never say so, but she was as interested in reasons as her kin-sister. They moved cautiously, watching any cover they neared for signs any hid within.

Ahead lay the larger patch of taller trees in which their hunter had stopped the previous night. Both halted abruptly as the breeze switched directions. To their noses came the stink of blood, death, and Gray Ones.

"So now we know. Your nose is keener. Are any still there?"

None living. They moved forward slowly, both alert to danger.

Within the grove the scent became stronger. Eleeri held her nose. "What *is* that smell? It *can't* be bodies; if the man is dead, it was only last night it happened."

The mare fiddle-footed nervously. *It stinks now of power. Be wary.* They slid closer, eyes flicking from side to side. To their surprise, the grove was hollow, a thick triple circle of trees about an inner clearing.

I knew not that this was here, kin-sister. It is on the edge of our lands, but I rarely traveled this way.

The woman shrugged. "It feels like power, but nothing dangerous?" Silently Tharna sent doubt. Many things in this ancient land felt safe—to prove as deadly as any obvious danger. Eleeri moved closer to the bodies. She counted thoughtfully. Whoever their hunter, he had been a fighter. He lay sprawled in the clearing; around him four

Gray Ones lay. Somehow she had no wish to go toward them. There was still no feeling of danger, but something about the way the bodies lay was ringing alarm bells.

She stared at them as Tharna fidgeted. About them the turf in the clearing was short, almost groomed. The trees, then? She studied them. Interesting that it was a triple circle. Perhaps this place had once been some kind of temple.

I smell power, but no danger as yet. Let us remain still and think. Eleeri's eyes went back to the five bodies and it was then that she realized what had troubled her about them.

Although the grass was a bare inch high, the figures lying here seemed to be half hidden within it. She moved to one side; from a new perspective the view was the same. Tharna, too, stared as the idea was passed. Eleeri stepped forward delicately to pick up the hunter's sword. A soft grinding made her jerk upright. On the west side of the clearing something they had taken to be a boulder was slowly unfolding. It turned dim black eyes on them.

"Mine!" A rusty voice proclaimed. "Not take mine."

The woman bowed. Politeness cost nothing, and here it could save lives. As she straightened once more, her eye was caught by the nearest body. Surely it had slipped deeper into the grass? Understanding came. A temple of sorts, yes, a place that the dead might find honorable burial in a self-maintaining system.

She bowed again, more deeply. "Guardian of the Dead, we came only to retrieve the personal possessions of this one. We seek nothing else. Will you give them to us, then allow us to depart?"

Never mind those bits and pieces. Let's just leave, Tharna sent. Eleeri shook her head slightly at her friend.

The thing that faced them might take it amiss if it believed they had come for the wrong reasons.

The grating voice came slowly. "Give gift."

Hoping she had understood that, Eleeri reached for the bundle tied to her saddlebow. It was second nature to her to hunt as they rode, even with one who pursued behind them. Three of the plains leapers hung there on a plaited grass thong. These she carefully laid out on the grass before the guardian.

"These three for the possessions of this one and free passage," she offered.

The leapers were already sinking into the grass, so small they could be utilized at once. The dim black eyes closed and the thing began to curl into boulder-likeness again.

"I guess that means we've made a bargain."

The mare snorted softly. She turned toward open land, the pony following obediently. Eleeri bent to gather the hunter's sword and saddlebags. She wondered what had happened to his horse; the poor thing was probably meat in Gray Ones' bellies by now. Still, it was odd none of the wolf-ones had plundered the dead already. An unpleasant thought crossed her mind. Maybe the guardian had other defenses. It had been very clear that she should not take anything without a fair exchange. She smothered a chuckle. It was possible the Gray Ones had tried that and got the worst of the bargain.

She headed for the gap through the circle of trees and turned to take one last look. By now the bodies were almost gone. Her pace suddenly quickened and she all but thrust Tharna from the grove. She continued to urge haste until they were well away from the dense growth.

The mare protested, *Why are we hurrying now? We're away and free.*

"I know, but a few points occurred to me."

Such as—

"Such as the bodies in that clearing were vanishing almost as we watched. But only the bodies of the Gray Ones. I'm sure the hunter's body wasn't disappearing nearly as fast and it seemed to be straightening, almost as if it were being properly laid out."

Tharna looked baffled. *I do not understand. Why do these things bother you?*

"Because they lead to a couple of conclusions. One: If the Gray Ones' bodies vanish that fast, it is possible they were not the ones who killed the hunter. This is supported by a fact. They appeared to have no injuries. If they had fought him and been slain, surely they'd have wounds. Two: The thing in here demanded a gift before it allowed us to leave. I was able to pay, what if I hadn't been? Just how capable would it have been of punishing us?"

The Keplian was nodding by now. *You believe the Gray Ones tried to loot the bodies and leave,* she sent quietly. *You think the Guardian of the Dead killed them.*

"I have no proof, but that's what I think. I also think that grove would be a good place to steer clear of in the future—unless we have a few dead bodies we don't happen to want." She swung into the saddle. "Let's get out of here. I'm tired, dirty, and hungry. If we move fast, we can be home by dark, with luck."

They held to a brisk canter toward the mountains. During much of the hunt they had traveled in a wide curve, which they now cut across. By nightfall, they were leg-weary but safe within the canyon. Eleeri lit a candle and opened the saddlebags she had retrieved from the grove. As she ate and drank, Tharna and Hylan crowded in to see what she uncovered within the supple leather.

Eleeri paused to take another bite of wheatcake. Then she tumbled the contents across the floor. There was little of interest, just the usual small odds and ends carried by any traveler. Nowhere could she find a name or information. But this was not like home, where every pocket carried papers, every bag identification. She turned the sword over in her hands. It was a good plain weapon, well cared for but never of great value.

She looked up at her friends. "What should I do with this?"

Hylan was practical. *There is nothing to say who this one was. He could even have been of the Dark. Pass all before the gate runes closely. If they give no warning, save the possessions. If fighting comes, one may need them. But I would speak of the human to no one, lest others come seeking more of you. He is dead and guardian-buried. Let him lie.*

It was a long speech for the stallion, but before he ended, both listeners were nodding agreement. The runes passed the rescued gear as innocent of evil. It was stowed away. Sooner or later it would be of use.

Eleeri retired to her bedding, her mind still mulling over the recent events. One thing she had not mentioned to her friends still troubled her. She was sure the hunter had been of Mayrin and Jerrany's race. His face, too, had been thin with strong cheekbones, his body lean in the rough clothing. The wide-open eyes had been the gray of slate, and the hair black. For one horrified moment as she first saw him, her heart had slowed, then raced in fear. He had looked so like Romar. As she looked again, she had seen it was merely the likeness of kind, not kin. But that spasm of fear had chilled her. Even now as she recalled it, she shivered.

Her mind turned over this knowledge. Romar wasn't

kin to her. She owed him no kinswoman's duty. But he had become a friend—and more?

She had known when she looked upon the dead hunter's face that she loved Romar. Through the long nights of talking, of sharing hopes, beliefs, and dreams, she had grown to feel for him. But was that sufficient for her to risk all she was in an effort to free him? Slowly she decided it was.

She rolled over onto her back and stared up at the stone ceiling. This new land had given her so much, perhaps now it would give her love. Her thoughts wandered to Far Traveler, who had shown her the path. She had taken it knowing that she could never return. Yet so far she had held back from a full commitment.

Gradually she made her decisions. She would need power to free Romar, help from others. The help was easy. Mayrin and Jerrany would aid as soon as she spoke of Romar's captivity and danger. It was time and past time she shared all she knew of that with them. But the power . . .

Still, the powers here had answered her in minor ways. She shook herself free of the blankets, walking steadily down toward the entrance to the canyon. There she placed her hand flat against the runes.

"I am not of your kind," she said slowly, thinking as she spoke. "But I go to do battle against the evils you guard us from. I am not of your blood, but I stand with those who are against the Dark. I am not of your world, but I choose to be now, to remain for good or ill as it befalls me."

She waited, watching as the runes showed a little more clearly. Their light grew, gathering as a soft mist sheening against the dark rock walls. Her fingers traced the signs of ward and guard.

"Show me what I should do."

The answer came in a blaze of light so great she shut her eyes against the flame. Power seemed to pool about her, to gather like a shawl across her shoulders, to drip jewellike from her hands. Then the light shifted. Before her a great arrow stretched down the canyon. It met the golden mist and a path opened. Eleeri bowed her head. A question asked—and answered. She would follow the path the power showed. She began to walk toward the mist.

12

From either side of her Tharna and Hylan came then, to walk with her. From their minds she received no fear, only a growing sense of excitement and anticipation. No fear, only the belief that beyond hope they were about to receive a greatly longed-for gift. They reached the edge of the mist and paced slowly down the path the power had carved from it. Deeper and deeper they plunged. Behind them there was no sight of the canyon, only the mist closing in. It felt strange, Eleeri thought. As if she walked in a place that was not quite of this world.

Shadows formed, to vanish as the three came near. Then one came which grew more solid as they closed in. Eleeri strained her eyes but kept to the steady unhurried walk. There was nothing to fear, nor would she show any, for the power might take that as an insult. Beside her the Keplians moved, hooves almost spurning the ground. In them the joyous sense of hope lifted higher. Before them the mist darkened, developing edges, columns, a peaked roof carved with hanging vines and laden with fruit. The mist drew back then as they paused to stare in awe.

A sense of warmth gathered about them, a greeting to friends arrived. The Keplians waited as Eleeri moved; surely the welcome was not for them also, children of shade and shadow? A shaft of the golden mist curled out, drifting to encircle them like a lover's arms. They were welcome, thrice welcome, let them enter where others of their kind had once stood in friendship with those who dwelled here. Eleeri felt the surge of joy from her friends, and her own mind echoed it. She slowed her pace so that her friends might walk beside her once more.

By now the entire structure was clear, and they halted to study it. Unused to buildings, the Keplians had nothing to compare it with save the Dark Tower and the ancient keep in their canyon. Eleeri had seen far more in reality and in pictures. The building reminded her of the many photographs she had seen of the ruined temples of ancient Greece. It was not one of them, but had the same air— great age and a lost power hung over it. It was built from massive blocks of some warm honey-colored stone. Within the stone, silvery streaks laced the rock—the colors of the mist that had finally parted to let them in, Eleeri noted.

Was this place even here? Could the mist have become solid to show them something which in truth was not there? Her eyes came back to the entrance. She drifted forward to touch the steps. Under her fingers the stone appeared real. She lifted her head. She'd been wondering what lay behind the mist ever since she came to the canyon. Now she would find out and no fear would stay her steps. She trod forward boldly, past a great bronze door cast with detailed images, although she would have loved to stop there, to peer at the tiny perfect scenes she saw out of the corners of her eyes.

Tharna and Hylan flanked her as she entered the great hall. It seemed to stretch forever to her startled gaze. Mist curled and lingered here so that she could not see the walls or far end of the hall. Light shimmered from that mist, brightening as they walked forward. It pooled about two oblong shapes that were raised above the floor on a small dais.

Slowly the three approached. Was this right? Were they called to this place? The welcome grew again: reassurance, friendship. This was very right, let them come forward, let them see and know.

Around Eleeri's throat the pendant became heavier. Her hands went up to lift it away. As it ceased to touch her flesh, mist gathered there also; the weight fled but before her stood the pendant's Keplian once more. The perfect stallion, eyes gleaming sapphire in the mist's light. He reached out to touch noses with each of her companion Keplians and the woman caught the wonder that filled them. Her own hands went out, not to the stallion but to her friends. Minds met with power. Around them light shone brighter and from the dais came a great cry that echoed in their minds.

Be welcome. Come to us and be welcomed, blood of our blood, children of kin.

Eleeri allowed her feet to drift forward, up the seven shallow wide steps of the dais, until she could see what lay there within the cradle of the golden stone. The stallion of the pendant, too, had moved. He mounted the steps on the other side of her and reared high. Not a threat, Eleeri noted, more as if he paid homage to those who lay there. She laid one hand on the stone bed, felt the power which ran here. Whoever these had been, they had been Great Ones.

Ah, for that we thank you, blood of our blood, but none were so great as to be invincible, be they of Light or of Dark.

Involuntarily she stepped back. They Great Ones were *not* dead. Unless—unless in this land the dead could still speak? Gentle amusement met that thought. Encouraged, she moved back to look down at the two who lay there as if asleep.

She stared, blinked, and stared again. If you took from them the clothing, the fine jewels, the aura of power that yet lifted about them, the woman looked like—she had seen her own face in a mirror often enough. They might have been mother and daughter. The man, too, looked familiar. She studied the lines on the thin face, the weariness at mouth corners. Ka-dih, but he was Romar! Romar as he might appear worn thin with living and twenty years older. She cried out then.

"Who *are* you? What do you want of us?"

Pictures came in reply, as if they happened before her eyes. No sounds came, but what she saw gripped her, drew her in so that she stood motionless.

The two before her lived, loved, and laughed in a world that had once been. Lived here in this building of golden stone, loved each other, wed in heart, mind, and body. Laughed with—ah, yes, laughed with their children, a boy and a girl, twins, barely old enough to toddle upright. She saw the enemy their bright happiness made, saw him plot and scheme to bring them down, these kin to the Light he feared and hated. She watched as their lands fell prey to the evil he sent. She saw how at first they would have reasoned with him. They wanted no enemy, no battle, no blood shed on green grass. But it takes one only to begin a war, and war came to them from this enemy adept, steeped in Dark power.

At long last they understood that in this enemy there was no mercy. They turned from laughter to tears, weeping as their friends fell, as those who looked to them for guidance were slain. They created others. Meddled in the stuff of life to find friends who might stand with them. Called on powers and ancient names for aid.

That aid was given. Keplians came to walk with them as friends and companions at need. To fight beside them, to stand against the Dark at the side of Light.

"Then how . . ."

She was shown. Saw the enemy as he crafted an answer. The Keplian had come from power which was neutral, but it could be twisted, changed. This he did, yet what had been created for the Light could not be turned to Dark save by its own will. The race were of the shadow by his evil, but of the Dark by theirs alone. Those who chose differently could turn again to that which had created them.

A surge of emotion shook her. Her friends saw even as she did. Beside her the great black mare knelt on the steps. Her mind was clear: no words, but a cry—need, longing—let them return to the Light!

Patience, child of kin, patience.

The pictures swept Eleeri away once more. She saw how the forces of Light failed. Good did not always win, or why would evil strive? She watched as the lord and lady's forces fell back until the canyon alone was held in safety. That last stronghold would not yield: the enemy knew all his power would not force its gates. But he could starve them out, keep them pent within forever. This he planned, but no plan is safe; it may be known, guessed at.

And this was so. In their hall the two sat, their children playing about their feet.

The enemy had not known. One by one, two by two, they had sent those who were loyal away to safety. The Keplians had gone, the humans, the Flannan who shared their home. Even the horses and dogs, the two cats in whose friendship the lady had delighted. The hall was empty now save for the four who sat there. Eleeri was somehow privy to their conversation, but not in words. She simply understood as they decided. The time had come to send the children, then to leave their beloved home themselves. To join friends who were also of the Light.

She saw the rainbow play of power, saw a gateway open and the small boy toddle through. Then something struck. The gate shimmered, twisted, turned aside in dimensions unknown as the tiny girl entered. There was a cry of terror from the lady. Power roared—everything two parents had to save their child. Eleeri caught a glimpse of coast, of waves that hurled themselves in unending battle with the rock. With an almost audible snap her mind recognized the scene. She had been shown photographs more than once. From those who sent her the pictures there was a rising sense of warmth. Yes, yes!

Eleeri allowed it to sink slowly into her mind. Cornwall! That had been the Cornish coast. She understood what they showed her now, and why the path of the gone-before ones had opened to her. But—why had she been called here? Was there a purpose, something she should do?

Patience. Watch.

She saw the gate fade, saw the lady slump, weeping into cupped hands, her lord comforting her. The child had lived. She would continue to live even though the world be strange to her. Their son, too, was safe with friends. But the power had gone. They no longer had enough to build another gate for their own escape, or the escape of the great stallion who was brother-kin to the lord and had remained to carry them to safety at need. They conferred. If they could not leave, neither could that enemy which prowled outside enter. Not so long as they lived. This last place they could deny him, though they might not escape.

They chose, all three of them, to keep inviolate the home they had loved. Eleeri watched as they worked power to bind the Keplian into the small image. Something so small would be overlooked. Only when it touched the flesh of one of the blood and kin would it answer. She saw the stallion shrink, saw the lady stoop to mold a lock of mane in her fingers, add the silver loop. Silver, a metal of the Light. Any who found it would know this was no image from the Dark. They used the last of the greater power to send the pendant—somewhere. Then they stood hand in hand.

She felt their sorrow, their pain that all they had loved was gone. They would never see their children grow, never run laughing beneath the hot sun to plunge into cool water. Never blaze across the lower lands on the backs of kin-friends who bore them willingly. Slowly they turned. Power flamed about them; stone answered as they crafted the dais. A long shallow cradle topped it, a bed that might hold the last of those who dwelt here. They lay down. From them power poured upward, curved to meet in a shimmering shield, then faded into nothing. It was there, but unseen.

The enemy came boldly as it faded. He could not enter in power, but he would use the remnants of theirs. Build power again once past the runes. He would use this place as his stronghold now. He saw the dais, marched up the shallow steps, and bent to smirk at those within the cradle. He had won! He laughed, then louder until his mirth rocked the silent hall, echoed oddly from the hangings that still lined the walls. He had won! This land was his to do with as he would. The Light had failed, fallen. The Dark was triumphant. He lifted his hands to a howl of exultation. Then he stooped again. One last thing. He would destroy those two who lay here powerless. He drew on power, smiled, and cast it from him.

It lay over them, but they did not wither from the blast. Its master had turned away, avid to see what he would get from this conquest. His eyes inventoried the tapestries, the furniture. There would be more yet in other rooms. He would have it all. Behind him power moved. He had cast off his own to enter; this was the power left within the walls. He had seized it, tried to make it destroy, but it was not for his using. It gathered, then, as he turned, it struck. He cried out, reeling from the awful blow. Stumbling, staggering, he sought safety, fleeing the anger he had raised.

Beneath him his body crumbled. The two who lay there heard the echoes of his cry, the rage at his defeat. Now only a thin film of dust lay over the floor, veiling the gold of the stones. A small wind arose, lifting it, bearing it forth past the entrance of the canyon, there to disperse it among the hills. A Great One had lost his gamble; the Light was strengthened thereby. But that malice had not died. In another form it would return, ever seeking to destroy.

In the canyon, all was silence. All that could be done had been. Now let them sleep away the years together until release came. Here the Dark could not enter. One day the Light would return—the Light, the kin, and a child of the blood. Until that day they were together; it was enough.

And the story was not quite finished. Eleeri watched as slow time took the tapestries, the delicate fabrics first. Then the wood, powdering, falling into dust, the swords that had hung on the walls slowly changing to rust, sifting to the floor. Only the stone remained. Stone of outer keep and stone of inner place. Faces flashed before her. The two here could not show her her own heritage, although that she could guess. They could show her of Romar—a little. Their son had prospered, wed and bred sons in turn, marrying the daughter of the house that had sheltered him. Other faces, other men, all with that look of the man who lay before her. Daughters, too, of that line, with the look of the lady.

But in the end, all bloodlines fail. She was the last in direct descent of the daughter who had gone strange voyaging. Eleeri felt horror strike at her. They had not forced her life into this pattern?

It was none of our doing, far-daughter. Your life was always yours to live. We did but open the gate when we felt the call of your spirit.

"How? I thought your power was all gone."

The answer flowed through her; tears sprang to her eyes. They had used that which had remained to them. Down the centuries it had kept their bodies intact, their spirits within them, waiting. Sensing her need, they had given all to this, their far-daughter. Even as they spoke, the bodies crumbled slowly, inexorably. Spirits strained to leave. But they had gathered the rags of power, held to await her arrival. Now she was here; she knew.

Find our far-son, free him, take this land. It goes to those of our blood to be held for the Light. Bring back the kin-friends to that Light also.

From the woman a question. Warm laughter reached out to surround her.

Mare, stallion, come forward. They did so, trembling. *Far-daughter, look now at your kin-sister, your kin-brothers.* Behind them the stallion reared high, hooves silver-shod. The Keplians lifted their heads to watch—and sapphire eyes blazed. Eleeri stared in wonder.

Amusement. *Darkness cannot live where love and Light are.* The voices pealed up in a great cry of triumph. *Behold, the kin-friends have returned to the Light. Our daughter's blood is come again. Great Ones, let us go now to be at peace.*

Tears flooded down Eleeri's face. "Don't go, not yet. I haven't even had time to know you."

To all things there is a time. We have waited so long to be free. Would you bind us still?

She bowed her head. "No," she said softly. "No, go in peace and I'll find Romar. I'll free him, too; half of this place is his. But"—she looked down at the golden stone—"how can I? I don't have the sort of power you had."

Love reached out. *You are our far-daughter; you will find the way. As for friends, two you have here who will fight beside you. Another who will bear you for a little. Beyond this place I think others wait. Accept them, lead them.* A hand lifted to touch her own. *May rich feasting come from this, far-daughter. Food for mind and spirit and heart. Our love to you always.*

The hand slipped away. Both faces smiled at her for an instant. Then the fires blazed up to surround them. They died—to reveal an empty cradle. Eleeri bowed her head and wept silently. Now she was alone.

Two warm noses thrust indignantly at her so that she staggered. Sudden happiness flooded her. No, she was wrong; not alone, never alone. She flung her arms about the mare, then the stallion.

"I know . . . I knew them for such a little time, but I think I'll always miss them." She sniffed and wiped her eyes. "Well, life goes on. We have to find Romar, free him, tell him he owns half of all this, and make Mayrin and Jerrany happy."

She laughed. "A mere nothing. I can do it all tomorrow."

A hoof struck stone; sparks flickered from that blow so that she stared. Behind the dais the pendant stallion remained, his eyes glowing softly at her. What had they said? Ah, yes. *Another who will bear you for a little while.* She approached him slowly and his nose came down to touch her enquiring fingers. But when she would have touched his mind, there was only blankness there. She drew back. Surely he could not be evil, not here in this place. Not one who had been kin-friend to the lord and lady?

Denial. She nodded. Then it must be that he simply wished to stand apart.

Agreement. Along with that came a feeling. That he must do this, that they might not share minds in friendship as he, too, would have wished.

She smoothed the tumbled mane. She would trust him. She would not intrude on his thoughts save when he offered them. The mare thrust in beside her, her son at her heels. The pendant stallion moved back. Idly Eleeri wondered if he had a name.

No longer—call me what you will.

Eleeri grinned. "Then I name you Pehnane—'Wasp' in my tongue. Let us go forth to sting our enemies."

Even so, far-kin.

Hooves followed her as she paced back through the

mist. Once again it parted slowly before her, closed in behind. She had gone in knowing so little, been given such a treasure to fill her mind and heart. Would she be able to return, she wondered, or would the place sink now into ruins and dust behind her? She shrugged. What did it matter? The canyon, the keep, they were hers. Let the lord and lady hold the place in the mist. She would not intrude. From her friends she felt approval of that decision. Even Pehnane touched her lightly with agreement. Good. Then that was the way it should be.

She stepped from the last curls of mist and strode over the turf. The Keplian mares and foals parted for her as astonishment exploded in their minds. She whirled to find them staring at Tharna, Hylan, and the magnificent Keplian who followed. Hiding a smile, she left her friends to explain. The day had been exhausting; she would relish a dip in the stream, then food and drink. In the morning she would ride again. They should scout the boundaries of the Gray Ones' lands, see how far the evil had moved.

But the night brought Romar to her. His eyes more desperate, face more worn, his body lean to the point of gauntness. Hands traced the sign, his voice came to her faintly.

"If you cannot aid me soon, it will be too late."

"I know where you are," she said softly. "What I don't know is how to free you safely. I could not bear to see those I love dead in this attempt."

"I will tell you of a door. My master—" his face twisted in pain and anger, "plans to move against the Light soon. You could act then."

"How much attention would it call to us?" Eleeri asked practically. A back door was all very well, but not if it had alarm bells.

"I may be able to turn his attention aside while you

enter. He is stronger than I, but his power is not so much greater. That is why he uses me. Once inside, if you attack him and I also strive to be free, it may be that we will succeed." He said no more, but she understood the thought. If he died in the struggle, he would still be free; it was merely a different path. But what of her? She had no wish to die facing something of the Dark. Yet—yet this was Mayrin's brother, Jerrany's friend. Her far-kin—and she had promised the lord and lady she would try.

She gathered all her determination. "Show me all you can."

He did not speak for a long minute, but the look in his eyes was enough. Then he spoke quietly and swiftly. The door was one unregarded. Once it had been a secret, but to Romar, linked with the Dark mind which used him, knowledge had come. To use can be to let slip secrets as well, and so it had proved. With the right word it would open. Now that word was hers.

Along with it came warnings: she and whoever entered with her would be tested. She must remember that much would be illusion, but perhaps not all. Outside there would be no posted guards, although the Gray Ones roamed the area. Inside the tower there were those who served the Dark. Not all their weapons would be obvious. All the time the sign which hung in the air between them faded. Finally he had given her all he knew.

"It will take power to open," he warned. "I cannot say how much. Go to Mayrin and Jerrany, beg their aid." He sighed. "I would not draw them in as I have you, but without help, the Dark grows. I fear for them even if they cannot help."

Eleeri lifted her hand to trace the sign. "I swear. I will tell them of you, and ask them to ride with me to lend what they have. I have little doubt they will come. Always they have sought you, fearing lest you had been slain."

She said nothing of the long hours in which she had wrestled with this problem. Mayrin might be slender of body, but that slenderness concealed an iron will. Jerrany was quite simply Romar's sword-brother as well as his brother-in-law; he would have stormed the Dark Tower on his own were there no other way to free Romar. If she spoke of the man she dreamed, this would happen. Twice she had determined to join forces with them. Each time she had returned to her canyon and seen the foals, she had weakened. How could she risk all she and her friends were building here?

Besides that, over the months there had been long discussions with Tharna, Hylan, and the other Keplians. They had slowly learned the joy of being truly free of fear and cruelty. Now it would please them to teach others, to bring more of their kind into the canyon until they had learned kindness. The adult stallions would be time wasted. But mares and foals could be taught. Was she to dismiss all this to ride to war? She might lose everything they had gained, and win what? A single man. One she had no need of.

In those flickering seconds before she answered Romar, her mind hardened in final decision. To buy a good life at Romar's expense would be wrong. He was her far-kin. She owed him aid. Her eyes swept over a face grown slowly more dear to her.

If she left Romar to die, she would not be able to live with the decision. In the end, it was as simple as that. If he was rescued, Mayrin and Jerrany would understand her silence and forgive it. If she died, no one would know why she had said nothing for so long. Jerrany at least would understand, if he survived.

The sign faded, wisping into nothingness, and Romar was gone. She stared into the gray, remembering the desperation in his tone. The one who used him must be close to draining everything. Soon Romar would die in body and mind. Before then, she must have summoned help, taken the path to him for freedom or a clean death.

In her sleep her hand clenched savagely. If she could not win him free, she could do that. He should die at her own hands that the evil one might bind him no more. At her hands, death would set his spirit free.

There would be no time for scouting Gray Ones in the morning. With the light she must ride. But first—her mind busily turned over various plans and supplies.

A deeper sleep claimed her then. But always as she drowsed, Romar's face watched her. Pleading for freedom, hopeful, believing in her. How could she have thought to stand back? This was a warrior. It was for her to ride with him in battle. Here was one who could accept her as she was. Her mouth curved in a smile that made her sleeping face briefly that of a child again. *Far-kin, hold on, I am coming!*

13

She woke with that determination still burning. She breakfasted, then went in search of the Keplians.

"Battle-sister, I must have speech with those at the lake. Will you come?" The mare stood thoughtfully, enquiring. "I dreamed again last night. Also I swore to my far-kin within the mist that I would aid Romar. It seems the time to fulfill that vow is come."

Dreamed?

Eleeri smiled affectionately. Tharna always did like to hear it all in order. She began to explain. Hylan stood by in silence as he listened closely.

He found a point and broke in. Eleeri halted to hear him. In the Keplian lands Hylan had traveled widely over the past two years. He knew them as even the mare and woman did not. He was younger in battle and perhaps less wise, but he knew things they might need to learn. They listened, eyes intent on him. This would help them still further in an attempt to free Romar.

"But I need to ride for the lake, to tell Jerrany and Mayrin all this."

What then, battle-sister? You cannot bring down the Dark Tower by direct assault. It will need cunning. Cunning and power. Tharna queried.

Eleeri began to talk again, quietly. Her friends nodded approval as she did so. It was hazardous, precarious, a chance and no more. But no less, either. The influence of the tower was spreading, the strength of its new occupant growing. Once Romar was gone, the evil one would seek others to use. Some might even come willingly.

"Enough talk. I ride now, this morning. Do either of you come, or do I go alone?"

Unnoticed by the three, mares and foals had gathered around them. They, too, had listened. Eleeri suddenly stepped back, jumping a little as she saw them for the first time. Her eyebrows rose and she glanced from one to the other. A lean scarred mare stepped forward. Theela seldom spoke. The scars had come from a vain attempt to protect her foal from a stallion. She had been found wandering dazed, bleeding, and bereft, to be gently guided back to the canyon by Hylan. She was a loner, most often keeping to herself, but her foal by her rescuer was now half grown and one of the finest in Eleeri's lands.

Her head lifted. *We will go.*

The words were few, but with them came a quick flow of images so that the woman understood. While she, Tharna, and Hylan had conferred, the remaining mares, too, had been in conference. They had scores of their own to settle. Forced matings, murdered foals, savaged friends among other mares. Here in the canyon they had found another way of life. Hylan adored his foals, condescending to play games with them and treating their mothers as equals. They might understand less of the issues. But one thing they did understand: it was the way of life in the canyon, against the way of life out on the plains. To keep the new way, they, too, were prepared to do battle.

Eleeri reached out, allowing her fingers to brush the soft nose. "What of your foals?"

Grown some; others stay.

The woman leaned against Tharna as her eyes swept those who crowded about them. That was true enough. Over half the babies were of an age where down in the lower lands they would have been driven from the mares for their own safety. Here in the richer pasture even the smaller foals were larger and stronger for their age than their lowland kin. The mares had ample milk. Should any of those who came with her fall, their foals could still be fed.

From one side a colt shouldered his way to her. They had brought him back from a foray the previous year. His dam slain by rasti, the foal torn about the legs, still they had found him doing his small best to fight. The rasti had been toying with him before the kill. Eleeri's arrival had put an end to that. Now Shenn faced her, intelligence gleaming in the red-fire eyes.

He reared slightly, his hooves thumping emphatically to the ground. *I go with you. I have no foal, no dam, no mate.* He snorted. *I will carry a human, if that will aid.*

There was no intake of breath from those listening before Theela nodded. She made her meaning plain, her intent clear.

I, too, will carry a human. I will carry one so that they do not fall. I will carry one to fight. If they are injured, I will stand beside them. Bear them home again. She reared, her hooves slamming into the earth. *Kill those who murdered my foal, kill those who hurt my friends, kill the ones who would take this place away from us.*

With each sentence her hooves slammed back to earth. The colt was the first to follow her, but others took up the cry. Hooves thundered against soil, thumped dully against rock. Eyes shone red as sweat sleeked black hides. Foals bucked and whinnied in excitement as the mind-cries went up.

Into this Eleeri's voice slashed. "You say you will bear humans—will you bear them to the rasti burrows to fight? To draw off the attention of the Dark one, to drain his power? Will you stand off those of your kind who would fight against us, even kill them if you must? Be wholly damned by them, hated and even hunted?"

Theela reared high. Her belly gleamed in the sunlight as it showed the wicked scars marring the smooth hide. *I will do all these things. What does their hatred matter? As for being hunted*—her head tossed, ears flattened wickedly—*I have been hunted before. Let them hunt if they will. They may even find me.* Her teeth were bared, her eyes madness.

If any enemies find her, they may not live to regret it, Eleeri thought, seeing the ferocity. *This one will fight pukutsi when she fights. She may go down, but she will take many with her.* She took a breath.

"Go, think of this. I ride now to talk with the human keep. We must make plans. An attack must be made that is coordinated so we waste none of our strength."

She saw the colt nod slow agreement to that thought. The scarred mare nodded, trotting off to graze. Eleeri noticed that she was no longer alone though. With her Shenn had gone, his flanks brushing hers as he grazed beside the mare. She met Tharna's eye and a gentle amusement flickered between them for an instant. Then the two were all business.

"Will you both come with me?"

Tharna moved closer. *I will carry you.* Her tone was a little jealous so that Eleeri was touched. Hylan crowded up.

I can carry you back? His mind-send was hopeful and Eleeri laughed.

"Even so, kin-brother. We are three, but I'll have to bring the pony." There was an irritable snort but no objection. Swiftly she saddled the willing animal, balancing packs of hides and weapons she would take for the lake keep. She vaulted to Tharna's back and they trotted toward the canyon exit. Seemingly from thin air Pehnane materialized, eyes sapphire flames.

Where do you go?

In a few quick words Eleeri explained, guessing he wished to hear it from her, although surely he must already know. Approval came to her.

The plan may work. What of those who say they, too, will fight?

"What of them?" Her voice was hot. "They have a right to protect what they believe in."

His sending was mild. *I did not say aught against that. Do they fight for the Light?* There was an odd intensity in the sending of that question.

From behind came a snuffle as Theela joined them. *I hear.*

Pehnane swung his head to her. *And you answer?*

Her head dropped as she considered, then lifted again. *To kill foals is evil. To mate with mares who do not wish is evil—wrong. To live as we did in our lands was . . .* she fumbled for the right word.

Tharna supplied it. *Dark.*

Yes. If that is Dark and how we live here is Light, then I fight for the Light. I die for the Light. Her sentences stopped, but her mind still sent—a bitter litany of pain and sorrows in pictures that tore at them all. *I stand with the Light.* The mare repeated slowly, as Pehnane looked at her. Her mind sent a sort of grim satisfaction. *I know what I say. So do those others there.* Her nose indicated the grazing Keplians. *They do not hate so greatly, but they *will* fight.*

I believe. Come—follow.

Trailed by the mare, he paced slowly toward the exit. At his approach, the runes blazed into life. His nose went up to trace one, then another, and finally a third.

Do this also.

For an instant she gazed up at the flaring signs. Then her nose, too, traced over the ancient signs. They blazed higher, blue mist swirling and condensing, smoking from them to cast a veil over Theela's head. It cleared and Eleeri bit back a gasp. The mare stood proudly, her eyes yet fire, but now the clear pure blue that marked the other Keplians standing with her. The colt moved in slowly from where he had waited behind his friend. His head lifted to study her, then the signs.

I stand with Theela. He said no more, but before they could prevent it, he was tracing the first sign. Eleeri drew in her breath in wonder. The blue mist swirled out to take him in its embrace. The power knew its own and all hearts. In that fraction of a second as he touched, it judged and sentenced. A colt with sapphire eyes faced them, shivering a little still at his own boldness.

Hylan's mind-voice was dry. *If we are done here, can we now leave? Or must we wait while everyone lines up to rub noses with a wall?*

The colt pawed the ground. *I would journey with you.*

Eleeri dropped from Tharna's back and stepped toward him. Her fingers went up to stroke the mane from his eyes. Wordlessly she sent a picture. Mayrin—laughing, playing with her children. Looking down at Romar's limning, pain in her eyes. Pictures, memories of gentle laughter, of the essence of her friend.

Shenn's ears perked. *I would carry her. She is like you.*

Theela strolled over and waited. Now Eleeri sent Jerrany, of his strength, his caring for his mate, his small ones, his anger at cruelty. His kindnesses.

A nose thrust into her hands. *I will carry this one if he wishes. If he will trust me.* Theela sent.

"Then come. At the keep you can meet him and make your decisions. Pehnane?" She turned to find the stallion had vanished once more. "I wish he wouldn't do that. It's like having a ghost about the place." There was a soft mental giggle from her kin-sister as Eleeri remounted.

That one does as he will. We do not need him. She moved into a gliding walk and, followed by the obedient pony and three of her kind, paced away along the trail.

As they traveled, the woman was making up her mind. To simply arrive with four Keplians might cause some— well, surprise at the very least. It might even provoke someone into an attack before they thought. Better to ride in on the pony, explain it all to her friends, then call in the Keplians. Jerrany could be as lighthearted and as giddy as any boy. But under that he was a warrior of a warrior people. He would see the advantages to all of this.

She had only to tell them both of Romar and her dreaming. That would be to drop stones on one side of the scales. If they knew there was a chance to free Romar, to defeat the Dark Tower in the doing—to make safe their lands for a while longer—then they would go to battle with goodwill, taking allies where they offered.

She glanced sideways to where Shenn pranced, unable

in his youthful high spirits to prevent himself from a few caperings. The stunning blue of his eyes struck her anew. A sign of the Light. Seeing them, she was certain Jerrany would be able to keep any from acting foolishly once she had spoken to him. The keep had its own runes of ward and guard. The Keplian should be able to pass those also. Another demonstration that they were now of the Light. She nodded to herself. So long as she moved carefully, all should be well.

They wended their way along the trails, always keeping a lookout. Here in the higher hills they were far from the Gray Ones' ranging, but there were other things which dwelt here. Some were of minor darkness, others quite simply dangerous. The rasti colony was many miles away, but solitary males often wandered up into this area. One rasti was no danger to five warriors, but even so, a bitten fetlock would be no light problem should the teeth go deep. However, they saw no one and nothing over the several days of journeying.

They worked their way down toward the lake on the third day and the keep tower came into view as they topped a small rise. Part of the journey had been spent in discussion, so all knew what they should do. Eleeri dropped from Tharna's back, calling the pony to her. By now she was skilled in the uses of her gift. As her power had grown with experience, she was finding she could do far more than she had ever imagined. It was now that Cynan's patient months of teaching and his stores of shared information were coming into their own. She swung into the dun's saddle, leaning over to pat first Tharna, then Hylan. Then, gathering the reins, she rode down the hill to where a sentry was announcing her appearance in stentorian tones. Mayrin and Jerrany came running.

"Eleeri, welcome, but—" Mayrin paused, "you look so grim. Is something wrong?"

"Not wrong, no. But let us be private quickly." She saw the way both faces looked then. Eager, yet half afraid to know. She swept them into the solar, where Mayrin slammed the door.

"We are private here—speak quickly. Oh, Eleeri, have you found him? Have you found Romar?"

"Yes!" Eleeri said baldly.

Then she found herself grinning as Mayrin seized her hands, dancing her about the room. They subsided, panting, as Jerrany smiled down.

"Tell us everything you can," he requested gently. "Then we can make plans."

Eleeri talked. Her friends listened until she was done with the tale, including those of her blood who had waited so long in the canyon. Then it was Jerrany who commented.

"We can expect no help from the valley or its lady. I have been sending information all along to Duhaun. She knows all that we know of you, Eleeri. And I have written of the spread of evil into these parts where it was not before." He smiled. "Indeed letters have been flying like hail between our keep and the valley's lady. We made plans should this time come. Now we move to put them into action and little time shall be wasted."

"What plans?" Eleeri asked practically.

"For a start, the valley can't help because they are already fighting elsewhere. The evil has grown strong near the Forest of the Mosswomen and it is taking most of their strength to protect the outlying stronghold and keeps in that direction. However the children are to be sent to the valley, to Duhaun. To help she has sent us five men-at-arms. She has also sent a gift."

He held it out as Eleeri took it gingerly. It was a tiny lovely thing. A carved piece of crystal in which living colors seemed to swirl and blend.

"What are we to do with it?" Eleeri questioned.

Jerrany's face became almost boyish again as he grinned cheerfully. "*What* it is I do not know. But if we prevail, we are to break it. I told the lady we may have to storm the Dark Tower. This is her reply."

"In other words, we have to win to use it?"

"Just so."

Mayrin reached out to take it. Quietly she busied herself threading it on a chain, which she placed silently about her own neck. Eleeri hid a grin. It was clear Mayrin intended to ride with them.

Eleeri could imagine the arguments which had taken place before her arrival. Jerrany had been convinced Romar was captive somewhere. Once he found that place, he would attack. Eleeri had seen, too, that Mayrin would never allow herself to be left behind. Why should she? The woman was trained to bow and sword, and as good a rider as any. True, Mayrin was ten years older than Eleeri, but Tehnup—experienced warriors far older—had ridden to war in the days of the Nemunuh's glory. From what she had heard of Estcarp, women did not usually ride to war. With the coming over-mountain to Escore, many had chosen to don breeches and take up sword.

She stood, pulled her friend into a strong warm embrace. "I greet a warrior who rides."

Mayrin's face flushed half in pride, half in embarrassment. "Jerrany doesn't approve."

He was quick to repudiate that. "I approve, dear heart. Given the choice, I would have you on my left, Romar on my right. It is the children I fear for. Who will care for them if we fall?"

His wife snorted inelegantly. "Who will care for them if you lose and evil comes howling about the keep walls? No, they will not be here but safely in the valley with Duhaun. *I* will be with you."

Eleeri patted his arm. "You're doing the right thing." Mayrin left the room to prepare the nurse and those men who would accompany the children. She turned to Jerrany. "How did she convince you she should come with us?"

His look was wry. "By convincing me that short of binding and gagging her, I could not keep her at home. She quite simply said that she went with me; if I refused, she would follow anyway."

He said nothing of the hot words added to that. Mayrin had been rude in all earnest to her usually adored husband when he had suggested she remain behind. She had reminded him—in words that seared his ears—how she had chosen to oppose her father in wedding Jerrany. She had then come into a dangerous part of the land with no other neighbors, no one to stand with them should evil find them here. Shoulder to shoulder she had fought beside him to clear small darknesses and dangerous beasts. She had never complained.

In this wilderness she had made a home, borne his children, cared for their people. And for all that time her brother had been with them. Romar was her brother in blood. Her twin. Half of her heart. She had believed Jerrany cared for him, as sword and shield-kin. Through all the years of battles and hard drudgery, Romar had aided them. The keep was not his. He had no share in it, but he had hunted for food, fought beside them as if it were. Eyes flaming, she had demanded if she was now supposed to forget everything.

Jerrany had protested. They were only making contingency plans. Romar might be dead. He might be somewhere they could not find to attempt a rescue. There were no assurances that Eleeri would ever return with word of Romar. And if she did, there were no guarantees he could he saved. If she were killed fighting beside him, the children must grow up without either parent.

Mayrin had ignored much of that. Was she to be no more than a brood mare? she had demanded. A subservient wife and keep mistress? Her father had cast her off for her refusal to wed where he chose. But he would take in his grandchildren and treasure them. Her head had jerked then, her eyes meeting his in defiance. She would *not* be lessened! He had accepted her as shieldmate as well as wife. Even Romar had been willing that she should fight beside them in those days. Now she would fight again—for her home, her brother, and the future of her children. Let him try to prevent her if he dared.

He had not. Rather, he had gathered her into his arms, filled with pride in her and fear for her.

"I would rather have no one else at my side," he had told her. Yet within him his heart chilled. So many things could happen in such a battle. He must seek ways to ensure her safety even though she fought.

He smiled up at her as she returned now, taking her hands to draw her down beside him.

Eleeri was able to draw them maps both accurate and detailed. Once those were completed, Jerrany called an armsman.

"Take these to Ternan, tell him to make copies. I want two and they must be exact. Our lives may all depend upon it." He glanced at Eleeri. "The man's too old to fight, but his father was a scribe and a copier. As a boy, Ternan learned well of him. Now he serves us thus and as a tutor to the children." He stood, moving restlessly about the room. "One set can go with the children. The other we will leave here in the muniments room as a record. I will also have Ternan write all that we plan."

He saw the glance they gave each other. "No, I am not a fool. It is true if we die, dark may come. But think of this also. We may fall but in falling take our enemy with us. The land may be cleansed for our children and those who come after. I would have them know by whose hand and whose deeds this was accomplished."

Eleeri nodded. To her it was natural. The Ncmunuh had always sought to drag down the enemy who had slain them. To use one's final strength to slay in turn the slayer was right and proper. She also made a mental note to visit the great room below her own keep once more. She would look for a weapon she could hide. Something unsuspected and easily hidden. If the time came she must use it, there would be something available. She hid a shiver. Better to die by her own hand if she was left helpless than to fall to that which held the Dark Tower.

Of course, she added to herself, if the enemy was so stupid as to suppose her helpless, it might approach. Her lips drew back against strong white teeth. In which case, it would not be she who died at her hands. She returned to listening as Jerrany went over the maps. Twice he called in men to give orders. Once Mayrin pattered away to return with more of the scarce paper. Finally they retired. The groundwork of their plan was laid; it remained only to add flesh to the bones.

With firstsun they were risen again, her friends watching from the bridge runestones as Eleeri saddled her pony in the courtyard behind them. She mounted, trotting across the bridge to join them.

"I will be just a little while." She eyed those who gathered in the courtyard now. "Do not allow your people to act in haste. I swear to you these ones I bring are of the Light and will fight with us."

Jerrany looked up, his eyes searching her face. "Always you have been of the Light, passing our runes of ward and guard. I do not think you are easily deceived, either. We will draw back to the keep when you come. Let your friends pass the bridge and they will be welcomed with all good seeming."

She nodded, nudging the pony into a walk. Behind her Mayrin's hand slid out to take Jerrany's fingers in a hard grip. If these were true allies, Romar might yet be brought home. She strained her eyes as pony and rider diminished in the distance.

They waited. Then slowly something grew again before their eyes, resolving into one rider with a mount and four loose beasts who ran smoothly about them. Murmurs rolled up from those who watched; the sounds were doubtful but not yet hostile.

Taking Mayrin's hand in a strong grip, Jerrany drew her backward. Now they stood waiting within the shadow of the arch that led to the courtyard. The group neared the bridge and from the dust began to resolve into its component parts. There were gasps of awe as they realized Eleeri was astride a Keplian mare. The mare pranced, arching her powerful neck and curveting proudly.

On the woman's left a Keplian stallion paced, larger and finer than any could have believed. The pony trotted busily to her right. At her tail came a scarred mare and a younger stallion, only a colt yet already grown to rider size. At the runes they halted. Eleeri dropped casually from her mount to reach up toward the stone nearest her hand. The runes flared blue-green as she traced one of the signs. She stepped aside to allow the mare to approach in turn. A soft nose lifted to trace a sign, the light flamed higher. The stallion stretched out—with his touch the light became mist rising about the Keplian's hooves. The other two closed in to touch and the mist rose like a tidal wave to engulf them.

Then it cleared. Before the wondering gaze of the keep's inhabitants, all stood unharmed. Eleeri leaped to Tharna's back, her sword lashed free of the sheath. In the sunlight it flamed gold and silver; blue fire dripped from the edge to splash over Keplian shoulders.

"With friends, allies, kin to the Light, I come. Shall we enter in welcome?"

Hand in hand keep lord and lady moved forward. "Enter in welcome!" Jerrany's deep voice came.

Mayrin's lighter tones counterpointed his acceptance.

Hooves passed over the bridge. The Keplians stood staring about them as they reached the courtyard. From the center of his people Jerrany walked forward. His hands lifted; Mayrin stepped to his side. She, too, raised a guesting cup as in unison they spoke the words of acceptance and welcome.

Then for the first time in a thousand years they were truly answered by one of the race who fronted them. Tharna's head lifted.

For the welcome of your gates, gratitude. To the lord and lady of this house, a fair day, good fortune, and a bright sun on the morrow.

There was a long silent pause—then the cheering began.

14

*E*leeri stood back to watch. The Keplians had understood the sound, she smiled to see their surprised pleasure. Then she drew Mayrin aside.

"You have a small amount of the gift. Is it enough for you to probe into the deeps of a mind?"

Her friend shook her head. "No, not with any but kin." She laughed then. "Although Jerrany and I do share thoughts sometimes usually at just the moment we shouldn't."

"Oh?"

Mayrin giggled. "It was at a dinner for the Lord Terne of the Valley of the Green Silences. He's a nice old man but very stuffy and pompous. It was kind of him to ride all the way out here and he only came to go over our fortifications for us. But he would keep on about the importance of having escape passages. We should have at least two, one known only to us. We were both sitting there trying to look interested and he just kept on and on. The next thing, I had this picture—" She broke off to snicker again while Eleeri waited patiently. "It came from Jerrany. It was of Lord Terne as a burrower, digging tunnels madly all underneath the keep until the whole thing fell in on him. Then this burrower with his face sat up in all the dust looking so surprised. I couldn't help it." She was laughing again, and visualizing it all. So was Eleeri.

"What did you do?"

"Muttered something about being needed urgently and ran. I got outside in the passage and just collapsed. Nurse came by and stood staring. That set me off all over again. It must have been almost half an hour before I could go back. Nurse said she hoped she was raising the children better. But when I told her, she was laughing, too."

By now so was Eleeri. She'd seen burrowers. Small stout animals who did indeed have an air of surprised pompousness about them. She giggled along with Mayrin until Jerrany turned to look.

"What are you two hatching?"

His wife grinned. "Nothing—yet. I was merely telling Eleeri about Lord Terne."

Jerrany grinned. "I remember that. I thought you were going to burst before you got out of the hall." Then he sobered. "Since these ones say they are our allies, let us make plans with them. The evil spreads and grows as it drains power where it finds it. If we are to act in time, it must be soon." He spoke not of Romar, but all knew what he meant. His heart ached for his friend Romar, who had always brought laughter and Light. Romar, who could not bear to be caged, and was now caged beyond his nightmares. Jerrany shivered.

"Let us make our plans quickly."

His wife nodded. Eleeri moved forward. "The plans have already been made. These Keplians are the friends I spoke of last night. They it is who will attack to draw off the attention of the enemy. No normal mount would approach the tower, therefore my kin-friends have consented to bear the three of us thither. But us alone. Let your men, those you can spare, ride on ordinary horses to fight beside the Keplians who distract the enemy."

"A reasonable plan, but will these two bear us willingly? I would hear it from them."

The scarred mare moved up to reach out with her nose, touching his hand. *I will carry you to fight evil. To strike the Dark I will bear you willingly.*

Shenn nuzzled at Mayrin's hair. *I, too. I will carry *you*.* He moved back in a half rear. *But we bear no human gear. You must ride us as we stand.*

"That seems fair." Eleeri said nothing of her thoughts: that he was yet too young to carry the weight of saddle and gear as well as that of even a light rider.

Eleeri faced her friends. "One thing I would say. Beware of seeking to force your minds into full rapport with these. Their minds are not as ours. I think it is that difference that has moved gifted humans to slay them before now." She gestured for silence when Jerrany would have spoken. "Yes, I share hearts with my friends. But from the beginning I never saw them as evil. The first time our minds touched, I was stunned, shocked, but then I opened my eyes and saw only those I loved before me. I no longer fear deep mind-touch. But your people have responded to it with such hatred that to my belief it is better you do not attempt it. Do you agree?"

"If you are certain of this," Jerrany said slowly, "then you are right and it is safer we do not try. But we can speak ordinarily?"

"Yes. Speak aloud, and Theela and Shenn will answer by mind as they have already done with you both."

He nodded. "Then let us check preparations." He called and one of the men-at-arms came running. There was a swift consultation before Jerrany turned back to the waiting women. Most of the orders had been completed. If they busied themselves before nightfall, they might be ready to ride by dawn. Eleeri grinned cheerfully. Not too fast. She would have to return to inform those of her canyon that the humans agreed to company them. Then she could ride with Tharna and Hylan to meet her friends at the stream ford.

For the next few hours the Keplians stood studying the bustling humans with deep interest. They had moved carefully to the side of the courtyard, half hidden in the shadows as the light began to fail. From a half door a girl emerged then, a child of perhaps seven or eight. Behind her came a boy bearing a sheaf of hay. A water bucket swung heavily from the girl's small hands. She bowed politely.

"Food and drink to the travelers, in the name of the Light."

Tharna stepped up, and drank gratefully. *Thank you.*

Shenn had reached for the hay and was happily chewing his mouthful. The small boy giggled and stroked the soft nose within reach.

"He's beautiful. Ask them what his name is."

I am Shenn, human.

"I am Kiren and she's Shevaun."

The young stallion meditated a moment as he chewed. *You are the lady's foals?* With that both received a brief picture of Mayrin.

They giggled. "Yes," the girl agreed. "But humans say children, not foals." She, too, stroked him gently. "You're so soft. Do all Keplians have such soft fur?"

Shenn preened slightly. Beside him Theela snickered, a

mental sending received only by her kin. Shenn tipped a warning hoof at her. He was finding these humans more than he had dreamed. The four Keplians listened as the children prattled on. It amused them to find they were at once treated as friends and equals in the conversation. There was no fear smell, no distrust of those who were different. The mare peered down at the intently childish faces.

How do you know we are good?

The girl appeared surprised. "No one could pass the gate runes who was not."

One who had great power might? A great Dark one?

The child shook her head knowledgeably. "He might, if he was very, very strong, but the runes would still warn us. I heard Mother telling nurse about you. She said the runes answered to your touch, that they showed you to be of the Light."

Theela absorbed that. The human girl was ready to trust easily, yet who was to say she was altogether wrong? Let them see how far she would move along that path.

Would you care to ride?

There were instant squeals of acceptance. Both children scrambled onto the mounting block in the courtyard center. The mare paced alongside and small light bodies squirmed into place on her sleek hide. She carried them carefully around the cobbles as her kin watched in amusement. From the door came a heavy step as it opened to reveal an outraged nurse.

The storm broke over the children's heads. They should have been in bed; she had been hunting for them for too long. Already her bad leg was aching, and she had much to do yet before she could rest. Even the surprised Keplians came in for a scolding. They should have known better than to keep the children up so late, no matter how they brought up their own kind.

Still muttering, she swept the heirs away, but not before Shevaun had flung her arms about Theela's lowered neck.

"Thank you for the ride." She pattered off hastily after her brother as the mare stood motionless. So they were human foals. It was strange, and interesting, that the children had no fear of Keplians. They might have been taught to fear the abstract; but face-to-face with reality, they had trusted. Tharna had felt the first horrified recoil of her kin-sister as their minds had touched for the first time. That had changed with a second meeting and acceptance. She had watched and listened earlier as Eleeri warned the keep's lord and lady. It might be that those two could never do more than read the surface safely.

But—her eyes gazed at the door through which the children had vanished—it could be that with a younger generation who had not learned the fears to hold them back . . . She reached for the remainder of her hay. There was no hurry; she would think on this for a while.

It was far into the night before all Jerrany's preparations were done. Finally he returned to the solar where Mayrin and Eleeri waited. They, too, had been busy so that a pile of carefully chosen weaponry and items were stacked in one corner. A quick conversation brought all to a knowledge of what had been done by the others. Jerrany studied the marked candle. It was late. If they would ride early they must— His comments were interrupted by Eleeri. It would be she who left, but alone. Her friends should allow her time to reach the canyon, alert the decoy party, and ride back to the stream where she would meet them all.

"Bring the extra things you think to need on a couple of packhorses. They can be held to the rear of the battle with your own beasts as spare mounts should your men require them. Once the battle is joined, we ride hard for the tower. The Light go with us."

At the nods of agreement she strode for the door. She would sleep, then rise to eat well. Warriors never knew when they would eat next. She left with the Keplians amid a rising clamor of excitement within the keep. Hylan had insisted on his turn to bear her. He cantered lightly over the rough ground, reveling in the dual sensation as their minds linked.

Some echo of that pleasure reached the mare and young stallion who paced them. Theela mourned it. For her there might never be a rider who could be truly kin. Her head came up. Yet, there might be, once the tower was beaten.

They reached the canyon, passing the runes that flared as mares and foals crowded around. Eleeri dropped to the ground and began to explain the plan. One by one they understood, absorbed, considered, and agreed. They had long since decided who would fight, who would remain to care for the smaller foals. Now the mares who chose thrust forward. Eleeri counted. Almost twenty would hunt beside the humans. That was well. The Keplians had an ability to handle evil at closer quarters, where humans would faint from the stench of the Dark. She went quietly to her keep. There she took up a bundle of torches twisted from dried grass around a core of a slow-, strong-burning wood.

Her steps led now to the great underground room below the keep. At her command doors opened, shelves revealed their burdens. Once again she chose weapons, mail to take for Jerrany. Then she stood allowing her mind to fall blank. It was like the sleek surface of a lake; no ripple marred the surface of her mind as she stood motionless.

In the deeps of her mind something stirred, like the movement below the waters of a huge fish that does not break the surface. She allowed it to sink again and waited. It returned with a silvery leap and before she could lose it, she shouted aloud the word that came.

"Ceearan!"

Light blazed from points in the ancient stones. Behind her there came a slow soft grinding as one final door opened. She spun, her eyes seeking eagerly. Despair suddenly filled her. What was this? Nothing but— She peered more closely. It looked like old damp clay. Damp? Her mind queried; it must have been here since the original owners left. How could clay remain damp so long, even hidden within such a hiding place? She remembered the bespelled cupboards upstairs; this might be as they. But why would the owners hide clay in such secret? Her hands went out as her shaking fingers were drawn into the surface.

Blank-faced, hands moving in a blur, she did what was laid upon her. Then she bundled the results into a cloth. This must come with her, a geas laid, but she did not fight the command. She half understood the reason, and within the geas she had felt the touch of she who had once been keep's lady. She would trust her far-kin. Carrying the cloth and its contents, she tramped up the stairs again to eat and sleep.

By sunhigh she was far down the mountain trail. With her the Keplian mares paced, the obedient pony following with laden saddle. Eleeri was astride Tharna as the mare pranced smugly. Hylan trotted well ahead, scouting the track as they traveled.

They reached the lower hills without incident and Eleeri halted them to rest. They would wait the night out here; at dawn they could descend the final slopes to meet with her friends at the ford. Several times as they moved she had shot leapers disturbed by the passage of hooves. Now she paused to walk apart. Each time she had bled the beasts, and now she skinned and gutted them quickly. The entrails were buried, the bundle of skins hung high in a tree fork and covered with strong-scented leaves. If she returned safely, she would take them with her. Survival in this land required that nothing be wasted.

Swiftly she placed two of the small bodies on sharpened sticks over the fire that now crackled within a circle of stones. The remainder she jointed and placed in a pot half filled with water. To that she added such greens and herbs as she had. In the morning she would not wish to waste time cooking. But there would be no need; the stew would have simmered all night in preparation for her breakfast. She waited until the leapers were nicely roasted, then she ate, tearing the well-cooked meat from the bones with strong teeth.

In the center of the dozing group she laid out her bedroll and slipped within. Her dreams were vague but ominous. Far Traveler with grave eyes approached, his fingers gesturing warning signs. She saw Cynan and her mind focused, reaching out. He had been her friend for so short a time—but a friend all the same. What had befallen him with her going? Was he still alive? She was certain he was not. Did he, too, come to warn her? The figure faded into hills and she recognized the land about his Karsten hold. She seemed to follow as he made with faltering steps for the small graveyard that held his line.

She saw him reach out to where the flowering bush blazed in glory. The blossoms lit the sunlight to a greater beauty and his lips shaped her name. A small wind blew through the bush and bright blossoms fell to lie sprinkled upon the gray stone. There was a sense of peace, of a long journey accomplished at last. She did not weep then; it would not have felt right to mourn him. He had chosen his own time and trail. In the end he had remembered her. She would remember him. She slipped into a deeper sleep without dreams and woke refreshed. As she ate, she conversed with the four Keplians who were closest to her now.

The breeze blew warm; the sun already betrayed heat to come. She vaulted to Hylan's warm back and the group trotted down the trail to where the rapids foamed and bubbled. Above them the water purled at the ford. Behind a clump of trees they waited until sounds spoke of their allies' arrival. Eleeri waved, to be joined by her friends then.

"Let's not waste time. My men all know what we planned. They have agreed to fight beside the Keplians."

Eleeri nodded, sending the message to those who waited. Hooves thumped as they swung to the ford. Human riders moved out to join them, those last in line now leading the three ponies hold and canyon had discarded. Eleeri turned back, opening the heavy bundle she had removed from her beast.

"Jerrany, I found this in my keep. It is twin to the one I gave Mayrin. I ask that you wear it. The one who once owned it battled the tower in his time. It would have pleased him to know he has some part in this." Under her hands the chain shirt fell free, gleaming in the sunlight. There was a subtle shimmer to the metal links, a shifting of colors like oil on water.

Jerrany reached out and donned it wordlessly. He had owned no more than the usual metal rings sewn to leather. But this . . . this was a great gift. How many of these did Eleeri have? he wondered silently. He knew of three now. Were there more yet? But he would not ask. It was enough that they all wore one, and Mayrin was safer so. That was all that was his proper concern. He glanced down, to see that their friend was not quite done.

From the same bundle she now drew daggers. The blades gleamed in the sun, a soft silver glow so that he sucked in his breath sharply.

"Silver?"

She smiled. "Silver and some way of tempering that makes them steel-keen. Wear them. They are doubly dangerous to the Dark."

He removed his own dagger to replace it with one of the proffered weapons. Mayrin followed suit. His leather ring-sewn shirt he hung on a branch, the daggers hooked into its belt. Then he turned to the waiting Keplian. He bowed and stepped forward. Theela stood as he jumped for her strong back, then as his legs curled about her, she curveted a little, testing his seat. He laughed, stroking the proud black neck.

"I know, I am here only so long as you will it. I'll remember." He watched as his wife mounted, the young stallion bending his haunches to sit so she could mount, heavy in her mail.

Eleeri swung onto Hylan, sending him pacing slowly into the rushing stream. In the breast of her mail the thing she had been driven to make lumped uncomfortably. She eased it with a surreptitious hand. They left the stream and ford behind as they struck out in a direct line for the tower. Soon the decoy party would reach the rasti to begin their attack. The attention of the tower would be drawn away. They must make the best time they could without being noticeable until then. Into a growing heat they moved, hearts high.

Far to the northwest ten men-at-arms traveled with eighteen Keplian mares. One of their number was a mere

boy who led the three spare mounts. The others were sea-
soned fighters, but their eyes were nervous as well as
alert. Even the blue-eyed Keplian leader failed to completely convince them that their companions were of the
Light.

Pehnane was silent. Humans believed as they wished.
So long as these fought, he cared not *what* they thought.
He had joined the party just before the humans rode up. It
was for him to lead this group to the rasti. Then he would
leave to be with the far-daughter. He trotted slowly on toward the territory of the rasti pack. Soon he would be with
those he loved.

Now burrows were appearing where the females laired
to give birth. The boy's pony was sidling and stepping
higher, nostrils flared. One hind leg slipped into the
mouth of a burrow and the pony squealed as it staggered.
Unprepared, the boy slid over the heaving shoulder to
land flat on his back. Two mares whirled as with a chitter-
ing two female rasti hurtled forth to attack. Their teeth
were at the boy's throat as he scrabbled to regain his footing in the rough soil. Before the rasti could sink teeth into
the soft flesh, the Keplian mares arrived. Flat-eared heads
snaked out to seize, to crush as the rasti were flung backward. Hooves stamped the life from them, satisfaction
reaching all who watched.

At the head of the column, a warrior relaxed. These
might be odd allies, but allies they were nonetheless. The
boy lurched to his feet. Clumsily he bowed low to the
mares before remounting his sweating pony. Honor where
honor was due—he owed them a debt. The group moved
on in better heart, the tenuous beginnings of battle-trust
established. Soon they were close to the main burrows
where the soil was turned.

In the tower, that which dwelled was enraged. Had he

not given orders that strength was not to be futilely wasted? He would punish these fools in such a way they would never forget. He drew on his captive to drive home his wrath on the defiant ones. His attention focused powerfully northward, where in a running battle the Light gave good account of itself.

Both humans and Keplians had followed a suggestion of the war-wise oldest man-at-arms. Now they ducked often into the running water where the rasti could not follow. From there they could emerge to strike again and again. Many showed wounds, but none as yet had fallen. The enraged tower concentrated in an effort to discover the enemy. All its attention flowed outward to the north.

Then to the base of the tower came seven to be joined by a great stallion. His eyes glowed an incandescent blue as he reared to a halt. Into their minds came a cry like a trumpet blast.

Now, now is the time! His form shrunk and twisted. Eleeri dropped to the ground to seize her pendant. With that clutched in her hand, she approached the tower's base. Lifting the pendant, she ran a tiny hoof lightly around a block of stone, murmuring a word. A faint gleam followed the path of her pendant. The stone creaked, groaned, and slowly slid aside. Before them was a wide smooth path leading into darkness. She turned to the Keplians.

"Hold the gate for us until we return or you know our deaths."

She reached up to hug each of them lovingly, then with squared shoulders she led the way through the arch. Mayrin and Jerrany followed. Their footsteps faded into silence as the Keplians took up guard. They would wait.

15

On the riverbanks the fight raged. Trust was by now established. Too many incidents had occurred for the humans to doubt their allies further. Time and again a Keplian mare dragged a rasti from a dismounted man's throat, to be repaid with a spear thrust to the rasti hanging onto her sleek hide, its teeth relaxing only in death. The archers took toll from their position on the rise. Then, the last of the arrows fired, they joined the battle, spears stabbing viciously downward. They had been less than thirty against more than two hundred. But intelligent use of the ground had aided them strongly. As had another fact that their leaders had taken into account.

Many times their swift retreats into the running water had saved them from a massed assault. The rasti were not intelligent. They were hunger, filled with blood rage, without tactics. They fought to overwhelm by sheer ferocity and numbers. They were now hampered by the blind anger and arrogance of the tower, which was demanding they cease their fight.

The mind there had not realized that the rasti fronted its own enemies. Rather it believed that the Gray Ones feuded once more. It drove power against the rasti, slowing them as they attacked. Mad with blood and battle rage, they ignored the orders hurled at them. But the power slowed them even as it took all the tower's attention from its own place.

Down a tunnel deep within massive ancient walls, three humans hurried. Torches flamed in their hands; they would save any power they had until it must be used. Within Eleeri's mind hung a bloodless face, strained beyond humanity. Eyes implored her to hurry, and hasten she did, trotting as swiftly as she could along the slime-covered stones. In line behind her ran Mayrin and Jerrany, daggers drawn. Finally they halted at the sight of what lay ahead.

"Are we traveling in circles?" Jerrany was bewildered. From the outside the tower was large, but not so big as all this. They'd been following the tunnel for almost half an hour in an apparently straight line. Now before them was a huge cave. Above them the roof arched out of sight. The worn path led down into its depths while at the edge runes showed faintly on the inset flagstones.

"Romar showed me the path. He was certain it led to our goal," Eleeri said quietly. "He thought it would be safe for us, since the tower is afraid of this place. Perhaps we have allies here?"

Something tugged at her throat and she slipped the pendant from its cord. Placing Pehnane on the ground, she stepped back, waving her friends to silence. Mist flickered out from the water-glistening walls to surround the pendant. It cleared and in front of them the great stallion struck the stones with a hoof.

Follow

They fell into line again and trod warily down into the cavern. As they traveled, all noticed that the runes on which they trod brightened with each footfall. The light seemed to spill over into tiny glittering motes which whirled up, clinging to the higher walls. Eleeri was sure these were forming other runes in turn. She felt as though she were shrinking as she walked. As if the cavern grew in size until they were insects who crawled along an endless pathway to some strange future, which insects would not understand. But ahead paced their guide, and they followed trustingly.

Without warning the motes of light coalesced before them, outlining a gray stone pillar. Nervously Eleeri halted. Were they required to do something here? She looked to the stallion, who stood motionless before the pillar. He gave no sign, so she waited patiently, eyes fixed on the specks as they crawled over the surface. She blinked. From their movement a figure was appearing—or was it a trick? At her shoulder, Mayrin drew in breath.

Eleeri turned. "What is it?"

"Long ago when I was a child, we visited Duhaun and she told me a tale of a Great One who had lived far to the other side of this land. He wasn't a bad man, just careless. He hated the warring and in the end he withdrew after some attempt of his went wrong and hurt those he'd loved."

Eleeri's mind leaped ahead. "Would he have known those of my far-kin, I wonder? Could they be passage for us?"

"I don't know. But Duhaun showed me an old limning. It had his own runes along the lower edge." She peered at the pillar. "I thought that they looked just like this." She pointed.

"What was his name?"

Silent, Mayrin crouched to write it in the dust that drifted now in a thin film on the stones. Eleeri understood. She had long since learned the power of a spoken word in this land. She drew it into her, spoke it in her mind several times over until she was sure of it. Then she straightened and approached the pillar. The light had settled so that she could see there were runes indeed. The last of them was the name. This she traced gently with her finger, then she sucked in a breath.

She spoke it. Light came then in a rush like lightning. Power roared and it seemed as if some presence opened drowsy eyes to study them. She stood firm, allowing it to see, to know who they were and what they did in this place. It was gone, but in turn she saw Mayrin stagger, then Jerrany as it searched out truth. It withdrew as quickly as it had come.

At their feet runes brightened one by one, showing a path. There was a sense that while they were not unwelcome, their absence was to be preferred. But to Eleeri there was yet one thing to do.

She stepped forward, speaking conversationally as if to a friend. "You did not ask, but I am far-daughter to those you might have known." Into her mind she brought the faces of those who had once held the canyon. She felt the sudden surge of power, of interest. Carefully she allowed her mind to picture all that had happened on the day the mists had permitted her entrance. She shared her grief that she had not known more of them, had kin for less time than her heart had asked.

Now the power was alive, seeking to know her whole story. It winnowed swiftly, seeing her arrival into this world, her meeting with Tharna and Hylan. Then it returned to watch and listen again as her kin acknowledged her as far-daughter and heir to their place. It sifted through her dreams of Romar and she could feel a dim anger that evil dwelled above its resting place.

As Romar had said, sharing is a two-way road. In turn she knew that there was little here of the person who had long since gone. Most of the power had drained away. The man this had once been had moved on seeking another home, but still some remnant had remained in the place he had loved. The man could not return, but his power had been very great. He could yet be a giver of gifts.

Her head shook slowly. "We ask nothing save passage and no ill-wishing."

Amusement at her pride. Then a memory. Her far-mother had been kin to him. Let the daughter of his line take up her right. Light motes rose to fall gently across her, weaving themselves into a covering that wholly embraced her before fading. Into her mind came words. She listened, agreed. If this one was truly of her blood, then kin-right was laid upon her. She raised her dagger and watched as the light motes sank into it. Her head turned.

"Jerrany, Mayrin, unsheath your weapons."

In turn they, too, saw the glittering points of light drift out to cover first them, then the upraised daggers.

Eleeri faced the pillar, now bowing but as befitted a warrior. "Sleep well, far-kin of my far-mother. What I can do, I will." She lowered her dagger until it pointed at the stone. "Earth, Mother. You heard my promise." The dagger lifted to point upward. "Sun, Father. You heard my words. Let me die within a season if I lie." Her hand came up in a brief warrior salute before she turned, leading the way forward.

Behind her there was a gentle sliding sound as the pillar crumbled to dust. The runes still held light, but the three humans and Keplian must hurry, already it began to fade.

They trotted swiftly. Where the stones allowed it, they ran, dropping back to a trot when the path roughened again. Neither of her friends asked what that last speech had been about. It was none of their business, and power was an ill thing to offend. The stallion had made no sound and now he merely paced before them. Eleeri grinned to herself. They were a motley group, in truth, but maybe their very diversity would help to confuse their enemy.

Now of a sudden their road sloped upward. They passed through an arch and halted abruptly. All turned to look. At their very heels a rough rock wall faced their gaze.

"Well." Jerrany ran fingertips across the harsh surface. "I gather we won't be coming back this way. There's even a different feeling in the air."

Mayrin nodded. "This is no longer the place of our friend's far-kin. This is the enemy's home and our battle-ground. Let us go forward, for now there is no retreat even did we desire it." Her face hardened. "And that I do not. Romar is ahead. He shall be freed or I shall die in the doing of it." Her eyes met those of her husband.

He nodded grimly. "Your brother, my friend and sword-brother, neither of us turns back now. But what of you?" His gaze touched Eleeri.

She sought for words to make them understand. Then— "I am geas-ordered and bound by my own oath. Better I die in battle than betray either."

Before they could ask further, she strode forward. Shod in soft calf-high moccasins, her feet were soundless on the smooth floor. Her friends followed, and none of them thought it strange that the stallion ahead made no sound as his hooves met the hard marble. He seemed rather to glide, nose seeking toward the walls. Then he signaled.

"A door?" Jerrany moved up to look. "Yes." He thrust gently with no result. Studying it, he hooked fingers into a carved rose and pulled back. The door swung open, allowing them a glimpse of a roiling mist that began at once to creep toward them. With a shiver he allowed the door to swing closed again.

"*Not* that one, I think. Spread out. Look for others."

They obeyed, something in the feel of the long corridor making them keep silence. Twice more they opened doors which showed them nothing they sought. One opened into a vast waste of scrub, sand, and hard-packed pebbles. The air was dry and heat smote them savagely. The other opened into snow, whirling in great flakes above a black and bitter sky.

Eleeri had been walking, running her fingertips along the wall. Under them a break caught her attention. She moved in, eye intent. A prancing Keplian was carved deep into the door's surface. She beckoned Pehnane. He looked at it. Something in his eyes was sad as his nose touched the nose of the carven beast. The door swung open.

They gazed in. Mayrin would have cried out then and run forward but for Jerrany's grip.

"Be still, beloved. Bait a trap with what the prey desires most. Better we look this over well before we walk into a spider's den."

He tugged her backward, a jerk of his chin sending Eleeri to the doorway to look within. She studied the figure that lolled in the chair. To her eyes it was Romar, but—she peered closer. This Romar looked a little too well fed, too well cared for. His clothes were of good quality, his hands soft. She nodded at that. Soft, yes, but not the softness of one who had done no work with them these last months. They were the softness of one for whom they had never been bruised on labor. The wrists were not the strong-tendoned sinewy strength of a horseman, but lay weak and limp in the figure's lap. Softly she pointed this out to Mayrin as the woman strained against her mate's grip.

"It is not Romar."

"Then who?"

Jerrany guessed, "A fetch, a made thing to lure us in."

His wife shook her head. "Perhaps not. I have heard of images made without features. Look you at the way it is dressed. That could be the clothing of either sex."

Eleeri raised her gaze and began to concentrate as she ordered, "Turn your eyes away, quickly. Do not look until I say."

She called Cynan to memory. He was gone, his spirit in the lands he sought. She could do it no harm, but his memory might now aid them. Slowly she drew from her mind the memories. Cynan as he sat cross-legged teaching her the languages of this new world. Cynan as he groomed one of the ponies, big hands gentle on the rough hide. Cynan as she had seen him last in life. His arm upraised in farewell, his body clad in her gifts. Into that last she allowed her grief to flow. Then she stepped to front the open door. Before her on the seat Cynan lifted his head to beckon her in.

She turned away. This thing was a mockery of her old friend. She longed to destroy it, but her duty as a warrior was to her friends. She would have explained, but they had guessed.

"It wears now the face of the one you called?"

"It does."

"Then the question is, do we attempt to destroy it or pass by?" Jerrany queried softly.

"Pass by. I think it is only bait; it has no power of its own. If we are not called by it, it will wait for others to come," Mayrin answered. "The true question is, does it have some way of telling its maker that a trap has failed? If so, it is best we hurry." Wordlessly Pehnane moved on. They followed in haste and silence.

The corridor wound on without windows, but Jerrany was sure it rose a little with each circle. A feeling of apprehension began to possess him. About him as he walked, the walls glowed. At first the light was unnoticed; then it brightened. Eleeri gave a small cry as Pehnane faded. She ran forward to pick up the pendant.

"Why? Why would he leave us now?"

Jerrany turned, searching for a reason. "The walls," he said quietly, "look at the walls."

Fire crawled up the ancient stones. It smoked, leaving filthy black trails behind the dull crimson glow. He advanced a hand cautiously. "That's power, not real fire; there's no heat." He glanced ahead, then back at the pendant in her hand. "Maybe he can't pass this as he was. You can carry him past as a pendant, though."

"Maybe." Eleeri was worried. "But I don't like the look of it."

Mayrin stirred. "Nor I, but we have only two choices. Go back or go on. I will not leave here without Romar."

Eleeri shrugged. "We go on, then, and the Light be with us." She marched forward, followed by Jerrany, Mayrin in the rear, daggers at the ready. They padded slowly along as the fire grew about them. The blackness spread rapidly until the whole of the way through which they now walked was black laced with the fire trails that formed runes on which they did not wish to look. From the floor a mist began to rise. It, too, was black, shot with the lacing of dull crimson that was now all that gave light. Eleeri drew her dagger and dropped the pendant into the empty sheath. She was drawn. Now that she thought about it, she had had the feeling for several minutes. Ahead lay the caller, Romar or another.

She reached out with her mind as she had learned to do with the Keplians. The calling seemed to strengthen, but she could not be sure. She allowed his face to rise in her memory. Then, walking slowly, she brought up the image of her dagger. This she touched to the face. The power flowed in with a rush.

She caught a warning. There was danger ahead, but here in the tower time was not as it was outside. If they moved forward steadily, did not falter, there was yet a chance they would be in time. Romar's strength was draining; that which dwelled here drew hard on him in its efforts to halt the battle far to the north. It would take much to turn its attention back now. Many of the tower's defenses were automatic. If they could pass them, they might come to its core unnoticed.

The sending faded, but not before Eleeri had read the weary disgust at his being so used. She clenched her hands. Better dead than enslaved to the greater Dark. If all else failed, she would pray to Ka-dih she could give a clean death as her only gift.

She turned to speak to her friends. Behind her the mist curled and shifted. There was no sign of them. She cursed savagely.

She'd allowed herself to be distracted. Could she have taken a turning they had not? Or had something crawled out of the walls and dragged them in? In a place like this, you couldn't be sure. She would have walked back, but something told her then it would be a mistake. Maybe that was the idea, get her tearing back along the way they'd come so she would forget why they were here. She set her teeth. She'd made a promise. She'd go on, alone if need be, and pray her friends found her again. She gripped her dagger and marched on, face toward the faint thread that called her.

The mist deepened, darkened, as out of it figures came. For a moment her steps faltered, then sturdy common sense came to her aid. These were dead or in another world. They could not be here. They were scarecrows raised to turn her back. She would not be so turned. Ahead of her Cynan bent a bitter smile upon her face.

"I loved you as a daughter. I trusted you and you left me to die alone." The accusation stung. She had thought long and hard before she had left the Karsten hold. Had she gone to be free of him? Her head came up. No! Her reasons had held then as they held now. Cynan himself had agreed, sent her on her way with goodwill.

She faced the figure now. "I grieve that I left you. I grieve that you died alone. But I bear no burden for my choosing. It was yours also."

"Because I saw I could not turn you aside."

She shook her head. "Because you loved me. Love shuts no doors, holds not the loved one captive. I have not called you here. Go now with my love and good-wishing." She walked resolutely forward as tears ran down her cheeks. The figure faded back into the mist and was gone. Another formed ahead. She flinched as the mean eyes fixed on her: her uncle. Mist formed a second figure to stand by him: her aunt. Cynan she had loved, therefore she had spoken gently to his image. These she had hated.

She walked forward, giving no way to them. They must let her pass or halt her as they could. She met them breast to breast as chill crept through her. Their hands gripped her wrists. Long-remembered insults hissed into unwilling ears. They despised her.

But she was no longer a child. This was a trick, an evil that sought to turn her from the proper path. She would not be driven back by these tatters of an outworn pain. She willed their fingers to loosen. Her dagger lifted to lie as a bar between them.

"I owe you nothing," she said quietly. "As you gave nothing, so I owe nothing. I did not call you; I do not hold you here now. Be free of me as I am free of you."

She knew then that it was true. They had feared her strength, hated her for the spirit that did not break. She had been the stronger all along. An unwilling pity rose as she met their gaze. They thinned and were gone as her emotion made itself known. Against fear or hatred they could stand; against pity they had no shield.

Then came the figure she had expected. Far Traveler with the eagle feathers in his braids. Before her he twisted into horror. Rotting flesh on brown bone. Breath stank from exposed teeth as his voice slid into her ears. Behind him came another: the pinched face of the social services woman. It was her voice that overrode.

"Now I've found you, you'll have to come with me, girl. The law says you can't live alone so young."

Eleeri hit back with an angry retort. The power below had given warning. Emotions could be both a weapon and a danger. She reached for calmness.

"I've lived here for years now. I am not a child any-more. The law has no claim on me and you have no power here." She felt the old fear as the figure seized her arm. "The law is against you," she repeated. "You have no law to back you in this. You stand alone."

The figure hunched its shoulders nervously. It looked at

her in disbelief. Eleeri gathered herself and flung her words at it.

"You walk in the paths of legality. Would you act against it now?"

The figure shrank back. With a look of puzzled anger, it shook its head. She was a social worker; the law was her work.

"Then leave, or you shall face the law itself that you break." It seemed to shiver, falling in until there was no more than another coil of mist.

Eleeri faced her last challenge as her hands went out to take those of her kinsman. Tears flooded down her face as she embraced him. She ignored the stench, the appearance; this was her protector, her teacher, her blood. She listened as he began to speak.

"Eleeri, Eleeri I named you, and strange are the paths you have chosen to walk. But there is no need for further struggle. Come with me and rest. Be my daughter's daughter once more."

"I follow a word given."

"Given to one who had no right to bind you. Come with me." The voice was full of tenderness.

"I gave the word. Shall I break my warrior oath? Is that of your teaching?"

With his arm laid about her shoulders, she looked up into the beloved face restored. Longing was in his tone then. "I miss you, child of my heart. Would you leave me to walk the spirit world forever without you? Leave these who are no true kin to you and come."

Almost might the spell have worked, so greatly had she loved him. But for that final sentence. Gently she freed herself, drew away from those loving arms.

"Kin of mine they are, and it is for me to aid. I gave warrior oath to one who trusted me. My friends are here.

Am I to leave them to fight alone? Nor will I leave one of my blood to die."

"You stand alone. Your friends have fled." His face moved in anger. "You were always a stubborn fool." Now he showed fear for her. "Do not walk this road. Come with me and be safe."

She eased her shoulders as if resuming a great load. She wept, but walked steadily forward. "I cannot. You yourself taught me that an oath may not be broken, that blood stands by blood, that even if friends betray you, yet shall you hold by the word given."

"I may not come to you again if you do this."

She dashed away the tears. "You have not done so now. You are the memory I have, but not the man I loved." She stood facing him and from her mind she banished his figure, letting him go as he had once released her. Mist billowed and was gone. Before her the passage stretched out wide and long with marble walls that showed no signs of the power. Under her moccasins the floor was stone paving.

She heard steps behind her and she spun to see her friends approaching. Both were pale, but their eyes were determined. As they came up each reached out to take a hand. For long seconds they stood there savoring friendship. They had been tested and not failed.

"I saw those I loved and feared," Jerrany said quietly. "I was offered choices."

"As was I," Eleeri confirmed. "But still we stand here."

Mayrin sighed. "I was offered some wonderful things, but nothing that included Romar. And I had to lose too many I love to accept."

Eleeri freed her hands, smiling at the two. "It seems we have all made choices. Let us move on to find out what comes to us from them."

Side by side in the wide corridor, they marched forward. Eleeri knew what she had defeated, but as they walked, she wondered what her friends had faced. What had been the "wonderful choices" Mayrin had been offered? She stole a look at her, then at Jerrany on her other side. What had the Dark offered him to betray them all? That her friends were here showed they had turned away. But curiosity rode her as they walked. She grinned and thrust it away. It was none of her business and there was more to worry about than temptations refused.

Beside her, Mayrin also wondered. Into her mind seeped the memories of that time lost in the mist. One minute Jerrany had walked beside her, the next he was gone. She would have run shrieking his name but that she feared to call attention to herself. She had gripped her dagger and prayed to all those of the Light. Then the visions had begun.

Jerrany also remembered—and shivered in rage. They had threatened, but he had stood firm. But oh, gods, it had been a near thing. One more moment and he might have given up. He tightened his hold on Mayrin's hand.

16

Beside the river the fight roiled back and forth. The mud was tinged with red where the combatants had fallen. Of the ten men-at-arms, only six now lived to fight on. Being swifter, the mares had usually managed to fight free and move back when they were too badly hurt to remain. Of the original eighteen, only half swirled and struck with their human allies. One lay dead with rasti tearing at the bones; the others had fallen away from the battle to reel in the direction of their canyon. Had those who fought on not been too busy to notice, they would have seen that the eyes of all the mares were now the sapphire blue of a creature of Light.

In his clear, carrying voice the master-at-arms shouted an order. The mares obeyed, closing into a circle that faced outward. The men-at-arms were spaced around the group, spears striking out and down as rasti sought to break the defense that bristled at them.

The tower tore at rasti minds to no avail. The scent of

their dead, the stench of blood, had the plains hunters in a frenzy in which the urge to kill and feast predominated. The constant contact with beast minds had gripped the tower also. He would have them obey him. It was all that filled him as he speared into their minds again and again, demanding, ordering them to break off the fight.

He drew on his slave until even in the fury that possessed him he knew that the man was faltering. Yet he would not cease to use the fool. Let the lesser serve the greater. There were others to be had once he had time to turn his mind to them. The two he had seen in that one's heart, for instance. They had more strength than they knew. They would do very well, once this was done.

He attacked his servants anew, striving to force their obedience. His slave, however, had more strength left than he knew. With delicacy, Romar had successfully kept his master from turning to attack the Gray Ones he believed to be the other portion of the fight.

Romar had been able to detach just sufficient strength to open the ancient door his master feared. Within the depths of his mind he yet hoarded himself, his unconquered spirit and the last scraps of power. Help was coming, he knew, and had successfully kept that from his master also. He could feel the touch of the Light as his rescuers neared him. At first he had recognized his twin and fought down terror. Lords of Light, let her not fall into the hands of this one! And what if she fell to the traps along the way? He had not enough of his gift left to reach out against those. His rescuers must fight as they could to reach him.

But a tiny flame of hope was beginning to burn. Little by little he had sensed that they were moving steadily toward him. Now and then he had felt the echoes of some struggle. But always they had moved on again. As they neared him, he could distinguish the spirits of the other two. His sword-brother, ah, gods, who else but Jerrany?

The other spirit, too, was known to him; had he not dreamed her down the long bitter months of captivity? He had seen her in his visions; now he recalled her to mind. She looked almost like one of his race to the eye, but the spirit that burned in her was different, born of another place. Not evil, just different. She was of the Light, that he knew in his innermost heart. He called up her face: his eyes caressed the strong planes, the storm gray of the eyes, the black spider silk of the hair that lifted around her shoulders.

There was a fierce pride and determination in those lines. The mouth was gentle, a mouth to kiss, to love, but below it a determined chin jutted. He smiled tenderly to himself. Such a chin betokened a stubbornness that would carry her onward in the face of any who might strive to halt her. Was this a characteristic of those who found the gates to his world? Others had come now and then; always they had been of a fierce spirit. Perhaps it was the spirit the gates recognized. He did not know. But the more he had seen of this one, the more his own spirit had yearned for her. In the old race desire wakes late, but at first sight of this lady it had woken truly.

Not desire of body alone, but heart's desire. He would walk with her. Learn her thoughts, her fears and delights. Wed her in honor to love all the days of his life—which might not be very long indeed, his mind added bitterly. He could feel the weakness stealing over him.

Still in the core of all that made him human he nursed the vision. His friend and his sister were coming for him, and that other. What she might be to him he knew not, but she, too, fought her way toward him to buy his freedom at the point of a sword. He drew in, hoarding his dying strength.

Eleeri paced slowly along the passage, flanked by her friends. It appeared to stretch on forever. Mayrin halted to ease her sword belt.

"Do we go around in circles in this cursed place? Surely the tower we entered was not so large?"

Jerrany shook his head. "What is within may be greater than what is without; the power has always said this. The tower merely manifests that truth." He stared down the passage before them. "But I do wonder, could it be that we are being led in circles deliberately? Does illusion trick us here?" He reached over to touch Eleeri's cheek. "You marked your face before we entered. Do you still have some of that which you used?"

Her fingers flicked to her belt pouch to reappear with a nubbin of the red chalk that crumbled in cliffside streaks near the canyon. Silently she handed it to him, standing aside to watch with Mayrin as he moved forward. Carefully Jerrany drew a straight line down the center of their road. He paced on, then drew another, a break, then a third. But by now the two behind him could see.

Mayrin hissed softly and waved him back. He came running lightly.

"What is it?"

"The passage curves. It appears straight to our eyes when we stand together, but when you are well ahead, you are moving out of sight around a curve in the walls."

"*Sa!*" His voice was quiet, but there was the triumph of a striking hawk in the hiss. "If illusion holds us, what else have we overlooked? It is a trick to lead us away from he whom we seek, but have we already passed him or does he yet lie ahead?"

Eleeri's fingers went to the pendant in her dagger

sheath. She lifted it free. "Maybe Pehnane can show us the way." But try as she might, there was no answer from the tiny figure.

"Maybe he must wait until we come to the heart of the tower," Jerrany commented. "We are all bound to the one we seek in some way. Let us link and think on him, build him in our minds as we know him in life."

Eleeri was unsure of the wisdom of that. "Could the use of power alert the enemy? This *is* the heart of his place."

"Perhaps, but what does it profit us to be unnoticed if we cannot also find?"

Mayrin reached out to lay a hand on each arm. "Listen, the enemy uses the Dark and power. What if . . ."

They listened, agreement growing as she spoke. Now it was she who stood forward, her hands reaching into her hair to bring forth an ornament. Eleeri studied it as her friend held it up and they clasped hands about it. It had been carved from a pale wood and from it came a faint sweet perfume—one natural to the wood itself, she judged. It was in the shape of a lizard, one whose skull seemed larger than those she had known. The eyes were tiny inset chips of some gold stone, and the tail curled under to hold a lock of hair.

"It was carved for my eighteenth nameday," Mayrin said. In this place she would not name the carver—names had too much power—but Eleeri nodded. Mayrin reached out to bring Jerrany's hands in upon the carving.

"Think on him. Build him in your minds. Set seeking upon this gift, that it hunt him out wherever he may be hidden from us."

Obediently they bent to the task she laid. This was not true power, but a sympathetic magic such as Eleeri was familiar with. So had her own people once hunted. This she could do. She raised the memory of the man she had seen, limned his face in life's colors, sparked spirit in the deep-set eyes. She willed the eyes to meet hers, strained to reach out.

Beside her she was dimly conscious of the effort her friends made. Sweat beaded along her forehead as she strove. It felt as if she were forced back and away from the face she had built. She resisted savagely. She was losing all sense of time or place. It was as if she floated, suspended. Then there came a draining. Dimly she saw that the tiny motes of light that had cloaked her were leaving. They flowed down her arms into the lizard and it turned golden eyes on her. She staggered back weakly as Mayrin released the tiny creature.

It scurried back the way they had come as they turned hastily to follow.

"Concentrate on it. Keep his face in your minds," Mayrin hissed softly.

They loped along, each carrying their dagger in readiness as the lizard sped down the halls. Jerrany halted abruptly.

"This isn't the passage we traveled," he said, his voice certain. "Look." His hand indicated a bright mural. Their eyes veered away from the scene in disgust. "Yes, it's ugly, but which of you has seen it before?"

He watched as both shook their heads. They turned to stare back the way they had come. There was no sign of an archway, no doors or turnings.

"More illusion?" Eleeri queried.

Jerrany glanced at her. "No, I think what we have now is reality. It was illusion we followed before." A chirp from the lizard reminded them. "Best we follow our guide and discuss the nature of illusion later." He trotted after the lizard as it scuttled away again. The women moved up to flank him as they ran. The return journey seemed endless as they wearied, but now they were certain they had never seen these halls or passages before. The guide was slowing as they trotted along. Now they fell back to a swift walk and still it slowed.

"What's wrong with it?" Eleeri whispered.

"Power only lasts so long. None of us is a Great One or even so very strong in the gift," Mayrin muttered quietly as they marched after the slowing carving.

"Could we do what we did again?"

Her friend shrugged. "I don't know. If we can't find what we seek before the power fades, we'll have to try."

They fell silent, concerned eyes on the small guide. The lizard was almost at a standstill, yet it dragged itself along valiantly. Only the smooth marble of the floors allowed it to move; a rougher surface would have brought it to a straining halt. Then it stopped. Mayrin bit back a cry of despair. Her eyes blurred. Through her distress she felt Eleeri's grip tighten.

"No, Mayrin, look!"

Mayrin dashed a hand across her eyes and glanced up. In its last gasp the lizard had turned to rear up against a wall. It was the carven ornament once more, but still it leaned forward as if pressing into the stone.

Jerrany was running his hands over the chill blocks. "I can't find any entrance."

Six hands patted, feeling along the lines of the wall stones. There was no door to be seen or felt. But their guide had not halted in midcorridor as it would have had it simply lost power. There had to be an entrance here. They would not cease to search until it was found.

Finally Eleeri stepped back. Illusions had taken them before. Perhaps now the pendant would consent to aid. She held it against the wall that blocked their path. Again came the draining, but this time the specks outlined an oblong on the stones. A patch of them clustered at shoulder height. Moved by an impulse, Eleeri placed her hand over them. There was a slow shuddering and the stones moved under her fingers. With a gasp of triumph, Jerrany seized the edge revealed and forced it further open.

They slipped through. Behind them the door shut silently and they gulped as they found it would not open again.

It was Mayrin who shook off her fear. "We wanted to go this way. Best we do."

Eleeri lifted her pendant. "Pehnane, please, is there something you can do to help us?"

From the eyes of the figure, light sprang. It touched the walls that imprisoned them, waking runes to light. They were in a cursive script unknown to any of the trio, but they served to show the way.

"Let's hurry. We don't know how long this will last," Eleeri commented as she walked swiftly along the narrow passage. In single file they moved, watching all around as they traveled. Within her Eleeri felt a growing certainty that they neared their goal at last. Sometimes she felt as if they had been within this damned tower forever. If she escaped safely, she'd not be going back in, that was for sure.

The runes ended in another wall, but this time the door was visible. Eleeri slapped her hand against a finger-worn place. That had to be how to open it. Burning pain shot up her arm. She yelped, wrenching her hand away. Blood stained the wall as the door opened silently. Did anyone who opened the dratted thing have to pay like that? she wondered. Not that it mattered. The door was open and it seemed to have caused her no real damage. She sucked the small wound and scowled as her friends joined her on the other side.

Now there was light. Not a great deal, but sufficient to see that they trod a way deep in ancient dust. Jerrany gasped as they rounded a bend and a slitted window appeared. They jostled to gaze out, before Mayrin spoke, amazement in her voice.

"Look at the sun. It's barely moved."

"Time," Jerrany said softly. "Time is different in the tower. I wondered how it was that our fighters still held its attention. But see the sun: less than an hour has passed since we entered. Perhaps only half of that. Our men swore to hold for at least an hour, two if they could. There is time yet for us to seek and find if we be swift. Come." He studied the passage through which they moved, then pointed. "That way leads into the center, surely. This one seems to curve around, but that cuts at right-angles inward. Let us try it?"

The women nodded consent and the three ducked through into the smaller narrowed corridor. Here the light dimmed once more, but with hope they pressed on. Eleeri halted them at the next turning. Her certainty grew.

"This way."

She was hurrying, her feet stirring up to knee level the clouds of dust which still layered the ancient stones. It was certain that no one else had traversed these ways for centuries, she thought. Romar had said she would be guided by ways unknown to the tower inhabitant. How much had he to do with this? Or had it been the aid of the ancient one who had searched her mind in the cavern below? She smiled. What did that matter, so long as she found Mayrin's brother? There was a time to ask questions, and a time to accept without asking and do, not talk. She slowed as a hiss came from Jerrany, who led.

"Another door here, and there's something beyond. I can hear sounds." Eleeri felt an insistent tugging at her waist. She slipped the pendant from her dagger sheath, placing it gently upright on the floor, then stood back.

"What are you doing?"

"I think it's time for him to help," she hissed back. Mist pooled upward from the floor, then fell away again. In its place Pehnane stood. Eleeri stifled a nervous giggle. He looked faintly ridiculous cramped into this narrow corridor. With his gleaming flanks brushing the walls, head lowered so as not to strike the roof, hooves lifting delicately out of the dust, he met her eyes, sharing her amusement.

A lift of his nose signaled them toward the door. Jerrany touched it cautiously, listening. In turn the others came forward to lay an ear to the thin stone. Jerrany waved them back to gather around the bend, heads together.

"Those aren't voices. Not human, anyhow." He turned to look up at the stallion, who loomed over him. "Can you tell us anything?"

The mind-voice rolled like thunder. *It is the last one to serve he who dwells here. It is my ancient enemy. Yours is the task to face he who dwells here, to free his slaves. Mine is the facing of this servant and his final defeat. Long have I waited. Let me go now so that I may rejoin my kin-friends and be at peace.*

Within the corridor they squeezed into position. Jerrany reached around, taking hold of the door and flattening himself against the walls as he did so. The door opened silently and the stallion sprang past him. There was a squeaking as small forms scurried desperately away.

"Thas," Jerrany identified them in disgust. With the arrival of the Keplian, the lights in the room beyond had flared brighter. Now the inhabitants fled to escape that painful light. Eleeri stared at the frantic forms as they ran to and fro. Mayrin had told her of these earth burrowers, but the reality was far stranger than she had imagined. The last of them found sanctuary from the light, vanishing into a wall which had sprung open under their beating. Behind they left a vast, vaulted space.

Only two figures remained. Keplian fronted Keplian, stallion faced stallion. But the eyes of one glowed the blue that was power of Light, the other rolled eyes of crimson fire. Jerrany and Mayrin would have stayed to watch, to encourage Light's champion, but Eleeri seized them in a hard grip.

"Such a fight may attract attention. If the tower turns to see one enemy within, will it not look for others? Let us seek quickly while there is yet time."

Still she was the last to turn away, hearing the voice in her mind. *Seek, far-kin, and may your fortune be all good. Where I go they will remember the daughter of their blood.*

She ran then, to escape the feeling that she deserted a friend.

At the river the master-at-arms gathered his men. None were unwounded, but they were prepared to fight on. He studied the sky and frowned. His lord had hoped some sign would show when the tower was failing. His men and the mares would fight a little longer, but to continue much beyond this time was to die. Still, now might be the time to try a few wiles.

He called orders as the Keplians fell back. They made a running battle of it, with his men spreading out to harass the outliers. Twice they jumped crevices in the earth; each time rasti were lost within.

In the hall within the tower another battle raged. Both power and ordinary strength contended here. Keplian stallion reared high, screaming fury at Keplian stallion. Power blazed and seared in the air between them. They were evenly matched on that level. Well, then, they would fight in the ancient way. They leaped forward, heads snaking out to rend and tear. Hooves hammered in body blows. Pehnane's teeth drew blood as they tore through an ear. In reply his opponent squealed, striking with razored forefeet. Glowing crimson blood trickled from the savaged ear. Blue fire flowed from a hoof-gashed shoulder.

They came together exchanging kicks in turn, then broke apart once more. Now the enemy seized Pehnane's throat, but before he could clamp down, a pawing hoof thrust hurled him back. Like maddened wrestlers, they met in the hall center. Rising, sinking, grabbing for holds only to lose them, leaving bloody fire in the wake of teeth and hooves. Twice the enemy landed blows to the rear flanks of his opponent, high on the kidneys where a sufficient strike could cripple. But each time Pehnane swerved, just a little, and the full power failed to lash home. The enemy's blood pulsed fire as it flowed down the forelegs. He was weakening and he knew it.

Both stallions spun rearing, seeking for the throat grip. They failed and landed back on their hooves again, lashing out viciously. Blue fire laced Pehnane's chest; he, too, was weakening, but there was no fear in his sapphire eyes. It was for this he had remained: to face the one who had chosen Dark power and a Dark master. He feinted, falling back in an illusion of weakness. The Dark stallion shrieked triumph, rising on his hind legs to crash home the death blow. Pehnane shied sideways and as his enemy came down off balance, the blue-laced head shot out. Teeth met in the jugular, crunched down with all the strength left to him.

Convulsively the enemy attempted to rear. He failed as

his legs unlocked. Light faded from the crimson eyes as he sank to the stone. Hatred shone in his dying glare. His choice had been made very long ago; there would be no last-minute repentance.

Pehnane reared, standing almost straight on quivering hind legs. Within his mind a call resounded, to be answered as light flowed about him, silver deepening into gold as the air sliced open onto a sunlit sky. Those he loved best waited for him as he gathered his failing strength to reel forward. Hands greeted him. Behind him the gate slammed shut, light faded from the hall. The body of his enemy drifted up as a coil of blackened smoke and was gone. But in another place friends greeted friends in gladness. A task was completed.

The tower shuddered as the servant died. Blue light ran in power around the rooftop. Even from so far away as the river it could be seen. The master-at-arms reined his horse back from the blood-crazed rasti.

His voice rose up. "Break off, break off."

They fell back, leaving a gap between themselves and the beasts they fought. He waved toward the direction of the tower.

"A sign, our job is done. Let us lead these away from our wounded." He called orders as the injured who could no longer fight started up the slope. The rasti snarled low in many throats. They would not be cheated of their prey.

But far away like a spider spinning its web, the Dark knew danger. It ceased to attack the fools who fought against orders. With that withdrawal the beasts faltered. Part of their madness had been caused by the assault on their minds. With that gone, they gave back a little. Step by step, the master-at-arms withdrew his fighters, making no overquick or clumsy move to spur the rasti into automatic attack. Then the animals began to turn away, hunching their fluid way back to their burrows.

Hapwold moved his warriors more swiftly. The Keplian mares split away from the riders, moving off toward the trail to their home. Two would never return, nor would the four men who had fallen. But they had had blood for their going, a river of it. A warrior asked no more.

They passed over the river high up on the lower hills. There they camped, dressing each other's wounds while water boiled and stew simmered.

The mares climbed their trail painfully. But the canyon welcome them back as did their foals and friends. Only two of the babies stood bereft, whimpering their sorrow and loneliness. Other mares gathered them in. At the entrance, runes shifted into light. Full circle was achieved, and Keplian mares and foals stared at each other, wonder in bright blue eyes.

In the tower, that which dwelled within gathered its power. Enemies were inside. They had murdered its servant. But they should not prevail.

Eleeri ran up a flight of steps to face a great bronze door wrought with many panels. Each held figures which seemed to move slowly, but she had no time for wonders. Her hands leaped out to fling open the last barricade. Her friends stood shoulder to shoulder as she trod boldly in over the stone sill. A circle of chairs filled the far side of the room. Within them lolled six figures. One by one each raised its head to meet the eyes of those who stood in the doorway. Six Romars leaned forward, hope brightening their faces.

17

Eleeri halted, eyes wide in sudden fury. Even now, even at the last, the enemy would test them. She considered. Behind her Jerrany stirred.

"What can we use to show the truth?"

"Me," his wife snapped. "Romar's my brother. I'll know which is the true man."

Eleeri nodded. "But what if they all are?" she questioned slowly. "Would it not be a fine trick to divide his spirit among them?"

That thought held them motionless in the doorway. If Eleeri was right, then to slay any of the Romars would be to lose a portion of all that made him human.

What could help them now? Eleeri listed the possibilities in her mind. The clay presently making an uncomfortable lump at her belt was to be used—but not yet. In the keep she had realized its capabilities. In his solitude Cynan had delved deep into some of the more arcane aids to magic, and passed them along to his eager pupil. But the clay was for later, as was the crystal from the Lady of the Green Silences. But there remained the gift of Light.

She turned to study Mayrin and Jerrany. Could they now use the Light they had been given? She spoke to her friends quietly, their faces brightening as they listened. Then it was Mayrin who marched forward. She put out her hands to clasp those of the first figure in line. Around those clasped hands flared a glow.

The figure keened its agony, dissolving into a heap of thick clay dust. Mayrin moved on to the second as it shrank back. To no avail. She seized its hands in turn so that it shrieked and crumbled, even as the light flamed about them. Then the third—but then Eleeri called her back. With that last the flare of light had been almost gone. To risk a fourth might be dangerous. It was Jerrany's turn and he strode to the fourth figure, hands leaping out to seize as light flamed once more.

The figure crumbled, as did the fifth and sixth. The friends stared at each other over the heaps of clay dust.

"He wasn't any of them," Mayrin wailed. "Why the illusion?"

"To keep us occupied," Jerrany said grimly. "All we've seen so far has been illusion, using power drained from Romar, I suspect. If this Dark lord wastes too much, he may have none of his own. Perhaps he's delaying us, hoping to snare us in illusion or to escape before we reach Romar." His face set hard, lips thinning purposefully. "Let us go!"

They went quickly now, trotting down the passage. Behind them the clay dust stirred into nothingness. Eleeri's guess had been right. Only evil had been affected by the touch of Light. Had Romar's spirit been within any of the bodies, it would simply have been freed to return to his true body. But now the power given them by her far-kin in the tower deeps was exhausted.

Eleeri and Mayrin followed Jerrany. He had had enough of these childish games. Somewhere within this place his shield-brother was being tormented, used, and drained. He would find him, free him, return with him to their home, and that which dwelled here. His teeth showed in a savage grin; whatever the outcome, the dweller in Darkness was going to regret all this.

Behind him Mayrin gasped. "Wait, wait!"

He slowed so she might catch up. "Jerrany, Eleeri thinks we are being drawn again in the wrong direction."

Rage flooded him. That female, always she interfered. If it hadn't been for her example, Mayrin might not have insisted on coming. It was Eleeri who had risked his wife, Eleeri who had tricked them here to where evil might take them. Eleeri . . . His face twisted into terrible lines of hatred and he sprang. But the woman had seen the growing madness in the eyes that watched her as he halted. She sprang back, dagger flicking from the sheath. He stumbled and before he could recover, the blade touched flat across his forehead.

Jerrany groaned as pain slashed through his mind. Then his eyes cleared. "What have I done? Oh, gods, Eleeri, I'm sorry."

She held out the silver dagger. Now it glowed, a soft luminous light that soothed and comforted.

"Take this into your hand and pray to the Light."

He took out his own dagger as she spoke, taking hers in his left hand. Then he raised them to lay along his temples. The points came together to form two sides of a triangle, and as his eyes shut, light leaped from the juncture. Mayrin kept silence until his eyes opened again. Then she waved to where a thin blade of light stretched before them.

"I think you are forgiven."

"A signal?" He glanced shamefacedly at Eleeri. "I beg your forgiveness. I was angry at what this thing has done to my shield-brother. With that anger it seems I gave a foothold to evil. It then twisted my mind so that it seemed it was you I should be angry at."

Eleeri had been angered at his attack, but she had wit enough to understand. This was another attempt by their enemy to divide their strength. If she had no forgiveness, then it would be she who weakened them now.

She stretched out a hand, taking his fingers in a gentle clasp. "I understand that; it was not your fault. We are all here to free one we care about." His eyes searched hers and narrowed in sudden interest. He said nothing, but she could see he wondered. Her head came up a little in pride. If she had begun to care for Romar, what was that to him?

She hid a smile. *Begun to care* was one way to put it. In truth, she would have Romar free of the tower or die in the attempt. That was more than mere caring, but now was not the time to speak of it. Let him be won free first, then let her find he felt the same way. After that, they could speak of a future.

The beam of light showed the way for a short space before it faded. An attempt to revive it failed. They clustered in the center of the passage before Mayrin took out her own weapon. "We didn't use this one. Maybe it can help." She raised it to her forehead, holding the picture of her brother strongly. The light was clear but faint. Still, once more they had a guide.

This time they ran. With the extra speed, faint as the light was, they gained distance. When it finally vanished, they were at a junction in the passages.

"Great, *now* where?" Eleeri muttered to herself.

She peered down both tunnels. "Let's try something

else." She clasped one of their hands in each of her own. "Join your free hands. Now think of Romar. Try to throw out a rope and tie it to him."

They stood there, faces white and stained as they built the picture. At last Romar stood before them. To Eleeri's knowledge this was the true Romar. Not the casual smiling man his sister remembered, nor the warrior Jerrany would have called to mind. This figure was pale of face, lines of pain and weariness showed clear. The clothes were worn and stained and she could feel the disgust that their dirt-thickened feel brought to him.

Hollow eyes turned in shadowed sockets to seek her. Her hands moved in a dance of signs. "Courage. Strength. Wait, help comes." He nodded and was gone, but the feeling of a link remained. They opened eyes on the chill stone of the passage and wordlessly all turned to face the left-hand fork.

"It grows dark down there. How do we see?"

"Wait until we can't; then we'll think of something," Mayrin replied tensely.

Eleeri had walked over to a nearby door. She slid it open sufficiently to peer within. Then she called them quietly.

"There's old furniture in here. If we take as much as we can carry, we'll have light."

They entered cautiously to tear apart the smaller pieces. Legs from some of the chairs would do very well. Mayrin dragged down an ancient tapestry to rip into strips. These she wound about the head of each length of wood. They would catch flame more easily and their fire would in turn set the wood to flaring.

With a bundle of the makeshift torches under their arms, they left the silent room. Ahead the passage darkened, but with fire they could see their way. Pausing only long enough to light the first torch, they tramped on into the dark, hands linked firmly. Jerrany led until the first torch was burning low. Then Mayrin's was lit and she led in turn. At the tail of the small line, Eleeri held out a sword in her free hand. She just hoped there would be enough torches to take them through the dark. It was a gamble. If they went forward until half were gone, then they would either have to turn back or risk being left in lightlessness.

She breathed in deeply. She would not turn back even if she must go on alone. One by one the torches burned until half their number were gone. The stubs were then impaled on a dagger point to be burned, lighting a little farther.

Silently Mayrin took out the next of her torches and moved into the lead. There was no discussion; all had made their decision as they walked. There was to be no retreat. Four torches remained when Eleeri muttered a swift warning.

"Something moves ahead. Mayrin, set your back against the wall and hold the torch aloft so we have light. Jerrany, let you and I flank her with swords and daggers."

They fell into the formation as something huge hulked at the edge of the light. It remained there as they stood facing the sound of its breathing. The torch burned slowly, the dark pressed forward, as the beast loomed in the shadows. Minutes passed, and they waited. A slow conviction grew in Eleeri as they guarded. This, too, was part of a plan, a Dark plan.

She began to speak even as Jerrany, too, made to do so.

"We're being—"

"This is a trick!"

"Yes." Mayrin, too, had seen what was occurring. "That thing is here to make us waste time and our torches." She whirled the torch so that the flame leaped up. "Get out of our way, evil one." She lit a second torch and waved them in her hands, marching confidently forward. The creature slunk back before the searing blaze. Swords flashed out on either side of her as she moved faster. Now she was trotting, the flames streaming back in the wind of her pace. With a final snarl of frustration, the beast loped into a side tunnel and was gone.

They rounded a sharp bend and ahead a faint glow showed. Jerrany reached to take one of the torches, dashing it out against the floor.

"Look, that's light ahead."

Their pace picked up again as the light grew. A second bend, and they came out into a great hall. Within, candles burned while windows were muffled in heavy soft folds of black cloth. Mayrin seized a curtain and flung it backward. Through the window sunlight streamed, touching them all with a golden warmth. The candles smoked into nothingness as a scream of angry pain rang through the hall. Eleeri smiled wickedly.

"I get the feeling that something here doesn't like the sun. Let's let a bit more light in and see how it likes that."

They ran like children from window to window. At each they flung back the heavy cloth, laughing at each shriek of fury that greeted the light. Not until all windows were free of the muffling fabric did they desist.

Jerrany stood panting in the middle of the floor. A thought struck him so that he walked quietly back through the door through which they had entered. He stared down the passage. All was light; the dark had gone. Interesting. It seemed that the great hall here might control other places within this tower. Voices brought him back to where his wife and his friend ran to stare out each window in turn.

"Come and look at this, Jerrany."

He did so. All the views were utterly strange, but a memory stirred. One looked like the place an opened door had shown them earlier. He said so. Eleeri nodded; she, too, recalled the odd desolate scene they had glanced at briefly. These must be some of the gates to other worlds.

Then she stretched. Her muscles felt strained, her legs weary with all this walking, but they had to continue. It could be more dangerous to waste time resting here. They moved on, but not before breaking more chairs into a further supply of torches. Behind them they left the curtains wide open and tied back. If Jerrany's belief was right, it could ensure them light in the passages to come.

It seemed that his guess was right. There was no darkness as they traversed the seemingly endless corridors ahead. And all the time the linkage they had created tightened.

Finally Mayrin halted. "I can feel Romar very close now."

"Spread out," Jerrany ordered softly. "We move up one by one. If there is danger, best it reach only one of us." He unsheathed his sword silently. "I take the lead, then Eleeri, then you." Before there could be any protest, he was in motion, slipping on silent feet toward the door that was appearing in sight around a shallow bend. It was huge, a great double leafing of carved and inlaid wood. On it tiny figures danced, hunted, loved, and jested with each other.

One of them caught Eleeri's eye. The tiny face was alive with curiosity as it watched her. A mad impulse seized her. She grinned, putting a finger to her lips. It smiled and a finger went up in turn as the tiny head nodded.

Jerrany was facing the door. They must open this, but

having laid hands against the wood, he could feel it shut firmly. Perhaps a bar on the inside held it against them? He lifted his sword and Eleeri saw all the tiny figures fall back in alarm. Her hand shot out to clutch at his arm, pulling him backward.

"No. Let me try something."

He nodded, stepping back. Her hands went up to trace runes: the ancient signs of warn and guard that barred her own canyon keep. The miniature people clustered together, then broke apart, eyes watchful, seeming to be waiting as they stared at her friends.

"Make your own hold signs," Eleeri suggested. Mayrin did so, followed by Jerrany. The tiny forms conferred, then the girl who had smiled at Eleeri stepped out to face them. Her hands came up and slowly, deliberately, her fingers wove the signs to match, but she did not cease there. Her hands lifted again. Some of those with her might have stopped her then, but others of their number held them back.

Once, twice, thrice, she drew the ancient runes of opening. At a signal the three before her repeated them. Again and again the repeat. Then a last time—and as Eleeri's hands moved for the ninth time, she felt power gather and break like a wave against the doors. The doors thinned, fading into a glowing blue smoke—and as they vanished, she saw the tiny figure throw up a hand in farewell.

From the actions she had seen, the tiny people had deliberately allowed them passage—and died to do so. Cold with anger at the sacrifice, she hurled herself forward. From a littered desk a form spun, eyes wide with horrified astonishment at her entrance. She wasted no time in staring, but attacked, the knife flashing as it slashed downward. The creature died, croaking horribly as one arm tried to stave off death.

From another door more of them swarmed into the fight. Eleeri shuddered. They were an unholy amalgam of toad and human, but, she reflected as she fought, horrible as they might appear, they were no warriors. They died too easily. Beside her Jerrany and Mayrin fought, swords cleaving the enemy until the last of them had fallen. Without pause, Eleeri made for the door from where these guardians had come. She wrenched it open, hurling herself through and to one side.

Jerrany followed, swinging to the right, sword at the ready. A man confronted them now. A man. But not quite a man, for his eyes glowed red fire in the handsome face, his proportions somehow no longer quite those of humanity. He was well enough looking, Eleeri thought. Short in stature, no more than five and a half feet at most, but well-muscled, and his movements as he leaned forward were supple. His face could have been called handsome, if one ignored the fleshy lips, the bland coldness in the eyes. Already lines of petulance were starting to show, around the mouth. It was the face of one who is usually secure in his own esteem, and self-indulgent to his own whims and appetites.

He was clad in a smooth silken material, designed and cut to show his lithe strength, and open almost to the waist in front. Eleeri could not quite say what was wrong with his shape; perhaps the arms were a little too long, the legs a touch too short. All she knew was that as he stood there summing them up even as they stared back, he reminded her of nothing so much as stepping in something squishy in the dark. She had an urge to make a disgusted sound and step back and away. His over-red lips parted.

"Oh, but you have done so well, come so far—for nothing. Did you think I would give back the one you seek at a mere word?" His face shaped a smug leer. "Yet if one of you would come to me willingly I might be generous. I might be . . . *very* generous." He waited, but none of them spoke. "No? Well, then you are uninvited guests. Leave and perhaps I will not call the Dark against you."

"We have met the Dark. We are here," Mayrin said briefly.

"I could offer you other choices—"

"Those, too, we have seen. We have rejected them," Mayrin returned.

"I could kill the one you seek. Where, then, do you profit?"

"In death he would be free. What then of your own use of him?"

His face twisted in rage. "Then fight and lose, pawns of Light." His hands came together in a single echoing clap that gathered sound to roll like thunder about the room. Abruptly they were elsewhere.

Their hands shot out to grasp. Fingers linked as they swung into battle formation back to back, swords out. Ever afterward Eleeri was unsure if it was their eyes that adapted to the shadowlands or light came to them from some source. But gradually they could see farther and farther although all the land they saw was in the grays of shade and shadow.

"Where are we?" Mayrin's voice trembled a little.

Jerrany shrugged. "I do not know. Maybe someplace of the Dark lord's devising. Perhaps a real world. But I recall once hearing a wise one from Lormt. He told a tale of a shadow world which is half in our world and half in nothingness. Those who are whole can return from it. Those who are not are refused passage. Would that not be a safe place to hold Romar's spirit captive? He would be trapped here, unable to leave, unable to pass the boundary to return to where his body lies."

The two women looked at each other, then nodded. Mayrin spoke angrily. "No wonder he sent us here. But what do we do?"

Eleeri grinned, a smile that was suddenly dangerous. "He thinks it a joke. We're supposed to find Romar, perhaps free him, then try to leave. When Romar can't, that so-called lord will find it very amusing, I've no doubt."

"Then why are you smiling?" Jerrany was puzzled.

Eleeri's fingers went up to touch the lump above her belt. Cynan had taught her spells and all the time she had lived in Escore her gifts had grown in strength. In this trial of her abilities everything she had ever known and all the power she had slowly gained was blending into a whole.

"Let us find Romar," she said quietly. "I may have something which will help us win him free of this shadowland."

She waved aside their queries. "Let us find him first if we can. Free him, then return here. Time enough then to ask questions."

Jerrany nodded. "Let us decide on a direction. Does the mind-rope still bind us to Romar?"

There was a brief silence as they tested. The feel of the link held yet. Jerrany led off, heading for a low range of hills deep in shadow. To either side the women moved out a pace behind him, eyes searching the terrain as they trotted. A soft whimpering caught their attention as they passed a clump of tangled, viciously thorned brambles. Mayrin turned to follow the sound. Then she fell to her knees.

"Look, he's caught." Her hands went out to aid, but Eleeri hauled her abruptly backward.

"Hold on. It may be some kind of trap."

She drew her dagger, the silver shining in the shadow-light. With it she carefully moved the brambles aside until the figure could crawl free. Then she offered the blade.

"If you are not evil, touch this."

It did so, straightening abruptly into a man only a little less tall than they. He bowed low.

"I acknowledge a debt to Light. May I aid you?"

They studied him. With his touch on the silver blade, he had grown. He was male, but not quite human. His eyes were round and his ears long, with what looked like tufts of furry feathers atop them. His hands were three-fingered and stubby.

Jerrany stirred. "Are you born to this land?"

"I am. But neither I nor this place are of the Dark. Here both Dark and Light may abide." He frowned. "Though we are never pleased when those who follow either side strongly intrude. We prefer peace."

Mayrin nodded. "Why were you in the brambles?"

"Because a power is meddling here again." His voice was soft and angry. "I was seized and entangled so that I might entangle you. But I do not choose to do this. You have seen I could touch silver. I am not of the Dark, nor do I choose to be used by it. If you will trust me, I will lead you to the one you seek. The journey on foot would be great, but I can shorten it to a breath." He waited.

Mayrin took a deep breath. Before either could prevent it, she had taken a step forward, laying her hand in his.

"It is my brother who is captive. I trust you to take us to him, aid us to free him or at the least cause us no hindrance."

The male smiled up at her. His hands went out to touch theirs; they gripped his tightly. There was a second of disorientation, a clap of air, and they stood on the shores of a black lake. The inky water rippled toward their feet.

"Which way now?" Jerrany was scanning the lake-shore.

A stubby hand rose to point. They trudged forward through loose black sand to where a small black marble building reared above the low slope.

Jerrany hooked his dagger through the door latch, dragging at the weight of tightly shut wood. It yielded slowly.

Within they could see a figure sitting motionless in a great carven chair. It was bound in heavy loops of chain, but the face as it turned to them was that of Romar. But not the once-elegant, gaily clad sword-brother Jerrany had known. Nor the joyous laughing brother Mayrin remembered. It was to Eleeri he looked the most familiar as she met the exhausted enduring eyes. Resolutely she trod forward, taking his chill hands in hers.

"Well met, Romar. We have come to take you home."

His hands closed on hers and the sudden light in his eyes lit her heart. At first she had pitied him for his slavery. Then she had grown to care for him as a friend. And finally she had known that without this man her life might be incomplete. She breathed in the air of this place. She would have him free of here or die trying. She moved aside as Mayrin and Jerrany thrust past to clasp hands with Romar. Mayrin's face was calm, but slow tears trickled down her cheeks. The first step was accomplished. That which was lost was now found.

18

Mayrin was fumbling at the chains. "I can't see any locks. How are they sealed?

Jerrany had picked up a link and was following it around his friend. He circled, circled again, traced the links over an arm and around the chair. Finally he looked up at them.

"There are no locks. The chain has no end."

"Damn!" Eleeri snarled. "They were put on; there has to be a way to take them off again."

The prisoner smiled bitterly. "You are assuming that my master wanted to take them off. He plans to use me until all I am is gone. Then he will have no need to open the chains. I will no longer be within them."

But Eleeri came of a people to whom there were no impossible problems, only unfound solutions. Touching the chains with the daggers brought reaction. The chains tightened until Romar gasped for breath. Lift the touch of silver and they slackened once more. At length she stood back.

"Romar, if the Dark lord created these, they must be wholly of the Dark. That is why they react to the silver and to anything else we bear that is of the Light. But they are stronger than anything we bear."

She paused, thinking. Perhaps their guide could help them. "What is stronger than the Dark?"

"Love," the creature answered.

"What buys freedom?"

"Sacrifice."

She leaned forward, her eyes holding his, watching for the slightest evasion now. "What breaks chains to free a living captive?"

"That which you hold in common."

Into her mind came the answer then, like curtains raised to show the sun. Her dagger flicked into her hand and with one sweep she opened the skin of her arm. Blood spilled over the chains. For one instant they tightened—she could almost hear the creak of Romar's ribs. Then the black bindings withered, smoking away to nothingness. Her hands went out to lift him up as he took one tottering step forward. Then he was in her arms as his sister and sword-brother crowded about, holding them both.

His face bent to hers. "Tsukup?"

"Indeed." She was half laughing as tears slid down her face. His finger gathered one in.

"Tears for me? No, now is no time to weep." He hugged her savagely. "The three of you have done the impossible. Let us compound this and see if we cannot leave this place."

Their guide cleared his throat. "I can return you to a certain place, should you ask it of me."

It was Jerrany who understood that first. He straightened. "We ask that you take all four of us to a gate from whence we might come to our own lands again." Their guide held out a hand and at a touch they were gone. They stood swaying on short thin grass as their heads cleared. Ahead of them a faint mist alternately obscured and partially revealed a dull gray structure. Weathered stone blocks showed in a lichen-daubed archway.

Mayrin stepped back a pace. Her eyes met those of the guide. "I do thank you, good lord of this land. For your courage and your aid. Is there aught we could do for you in return? Your help has been far beyond any poor debt you might have owed us for releasing you from the brambles."

He hesitated, then nodded. His eyes drifted to the dagger that gleamed softly at her belt. Mayrin freed the sheath, handing it to him, then she drew the dagger.

"This weapon of Light do I freely give to you. Use it with honor. May it serve you as it has served me." She handed it to him, watching as it was sheathed once more. He bowed low to all of them in turn, then he was gone, loping away over the gray moorland. But as he went, it seemed as if his figure changed yet again, so that they stared at each other in silence.

To Eleeri it appeared as if a coyote had turned to study her with amusement as it left. She knew not what the others might have seen, but in her heart she smiled. The trickster came in many guises, as Far Traveler had always said. But they had dealt fairly and so been treated well in turn. That was as it should·be, and as all legends told.

Her friends were studying the gate. It loomed, gray and massive, forbidding above them. Through the ancient arch they could see only mist.

"Well, shall we return?" Romar's voice was almost happy.

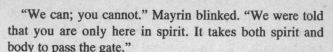

"We can; you cannot." Mayrin blinked. "We were told that you are only here in spirit. It takes both spirit and body to pass the gate."

He stared at them blankly. "Then must I remain here?"

But Eleeri's eyes had opened wide in sudden knowledge. At last there was a purpose for the clay from the canyon keep. Quickly she ran from bush to bush, then dragged out her dagger, cutting free a piece of her tunic. It was Romar who first understood. He nodded, taking the dagger from her to cut a length of his hair and spit upon the clay.

Eleeri twisted grass into thin cord, sewing rapidly. Then she held up the figure modeled from the clay. It bore a tiny dagger rough-carved from a silver wood, and was dressed in leather tunic and breeches.

"And something from all of us," Eleeri said as she dappled her own blood across the clay, then bound her dagger lengthwise along the cut she had given herself to free Romar. Mayrin added a long strand of her hair, Jerrany spat on the clay even as his sword-brother had done. Eleeri nodded.

She beckoned Romar. "Hold this and do not let go, no matter what may happen. Lead us, Jerrany."

He strode through the gate, sword at the ready. Behind him Romar was flanked by the women, each fierce-eyed. Light flamed about them in a blinding aura, heat seared, cold burned. But the women's hands remained clamped to Romar's arms. They were battered, tossed from side to side. Their fingers ached; it was as though they were dragged time and again against their hold.

Then it was over. Three people stood swaying on a stone floor within a great hall. Above, banners stirred. Mayrin shrieked.

"Romar! Romar! He didn't come with us."

Eleeri stooped to take up the clay figure. "He did, you know. Now all we have to do is defeat the Dark lord. Return his spirit, which is contained in this, to his body here, and go home." She sighed elaborately. "All in a day's work."

The giggles that greeted her words were a touch hysterical, but better than outcry. In her hand the clay moved. She placed it on the paving, then watched as it marched forward.

"Where's he going?"

"In search of his body, I should think. He'd have a better tie to that than any of us." They fell in behind at a slow walk. None of the passages they traversed were dark. Runes sparkled from the walls as they paced on. The small figure was tireless, but by now Mayrin was beginning to show her own weariness, and Jerrany and Eleeri were slowing. A glance from a window as they passed told them that time had halted in the shadowlands, but now it moved on again, albeit slower than outside the tower. By the sun they had entered this place no more than two hours ago, although days seemed to have passed. Hunger and thirst plagued them all, so that they passed dry tongues over drier lips as they walked.

The pace quickened until the tiny figure before them was running. It halted the flight at a door. Eleeri groaned.

"Not another door. What do we have to do *this* time?"

Jerrany had opened his mouth to reply when the heavy wood trembled. The door crunched open, as red-tinged light spilled from the room within.

The clay figure darted past Eleeri. She gave a yelp of protest as she followed it in—only to pull up facing a long broad desk. Leaning back in a magnificent chair, the tower's lord glared at them. At his side Romar lolled, body and face slack. In one swift glance Eleeri saw the clay figure lurking under the Lord's desk. She moved to the right, drawing the lord's eyes. The figure scurried forward into hiding behind the chair. Red coals met hers, holding her in their gaze.

"You trespass too greatly on my kindness, woman. It seems I must take stronger action to be rid of you and yours." He spoke a word of binding. Just inside the doorway, Mayrin and Jerrany froze into immobility. Eleeri herself felt as if her body were wrapped in chains.

She must play for time. Time in which Romar might reunite body and spirit. She yawned.

"Why waste strength on one who could be an ally, Lord? I came to this land and it is barren. I have little, who would have more. What could a mighty lord offer one who could be useful?"

His look shifted to a sudden interest. "You are not of this world. Came you through a gate?"

"Yes."

He nodded, leaning back thoughtfully. "That explains why you have been hard to take, woman. Your thoughts do not follow quite the same paths. Your gods are different, your beliefs strange. But I am powerful. Do not think to challenge me."

"I do not. Not yet . . ." she added under her breath. "I merely ask what such a one as I could be worth to you."

He deliberated. From the corner of her eye Eleeri could see the mannequin climbing Romar's chair. A strange feeling distracted her then, something familiar. She kept her face blank. Somewhere within these walls friends came to their aid. The sense of knowing grew until she could recognize it.

By now the Dark lord was deep in his considerations. This woman would be most useful to him. With her power, his plans could leap forward. She could not be trusted, but then it appeared she held some value to these with her. He held them motionless, could slay them if he wished. A promise of their safety might bend her to his will. If not, he had other powers.

Eleeri shifted her head a fraction. Jerrany was held still by the Dark lord's power, but his eyes met hers and swiveled toward the door. So he, too, felt the approach of those they knew. Her eyes shifted back to the chair where Romar lolled. The mannequin came briefly into sight as it reached the top of the chair's back. It slid into hiding behind the body's cloak collar. Good. Now if only they could distract the tower's master for a few vital seconds, they might have something of a chance.

Outside, hooves thudded along paved floors, nearing the doors. Eleeri studied the Dark one. He had made a simple error with her. Even though he himself had said she was different, and although he had seen his powers did not hold her so well, he had still not seen where that might take her.

Her mind focused, tightened into a narrow beam directed straight at her friends. *Hold! Until I give the word.* The sounds outside the door ceased. Sunk deep in greedy thought, the one before her had noticed nothing. Not yet an adept, flawed by pride and vanity, it did not occur to him any could withstand his commands. Finally he lifted his head to stare at her.

She moved her arm, drawing his attention. Blood! She was injured. He could draw on that to bind her now, at once. There was no need to offer her any foolish promises. He swelled in pride as he gathered his strength.

He remembered the day he had stood in the canyon. He had endeavored to use the remnants of power left there and it had backlashed, destroying him. Only his body had died. But it had taken many generations before a wandering hunter had come within reach and he had gained enough strength to take over the man's body as host for his unhoused spirit. But all the time he had waited, he had grown in bitterness and hatred. Once he had been an adept, then a Dark adept. Then no more than a bodiless spirit howling in the wind. With his new body came growing power—and growing viciousness. But he refused to understand the lesson he should have learned from his past. Still more, he refused to see that his power was only a shadow of what it once had been.

He faced Eleeri, and his mind whispered warnings. He flung them off. What! Was he who had dueled other adepts to fear some wandering outworlder from an unknown people? He would take her spirit, break it to his will. Use her power to augment his own. Her friends would be useful to replenish his strength as well. They could have no ability to match his. They'd returned to him empty-handed; his slave remained chained.

He eyed Eleeri thoughtfully. There was something about her. Some vague familiarity. Then he snorted silently. What of it? She was nothing; they were all nothing. He'd regained a body, regained his own tower. Now they would pay. He flung back his head, laughing openly. Pride roared through him. He was master here. Let the insignificant ones bow to him—before he laid his power on them to compel. His eyes met hers and again the odd familiar feeling stirred. He stared angrily at the three.

Jerrany strained to move; Mayrin beside him struggled and failed even as he. From the corner of her eye Eleeri saw and understood. This task was hers. Her far-kin had opened the path to her; perhaps this was why. The Dark lord was not able to hold her entirely. This last act which would seal her heart and spirit to the land she had grown to love. She concentrated. Her foot slid across the floor.

Seated behind the desk, the Dark one noticed nothing at first. It was not until she had advanced several feet that he saw she moved. But even as he would have laid another spell on her, Eleeri, too, acted.

Now!

Hooves crashed against the door as four Keplian heads appeared briefly. The door sprang open a little, then slammed closed in spelled obedience. The Dark one jumped slightly, covering the movement by leaning forward.

"You have friends. They won't help you. They will merely provide me with more power when I take them." Hooves slammed solidly into the heavy wood, distracting him. He frowned, bringing his hands up to weave a spell. He'd make the door impregnable. Then he could deal with these inside first. After that, he would go out in his wrath to show those other fools what it meant to storm the tower of a Dark lord.

Eleeri felt his spell against her fade. Not much, just enough to allow her speech now. Under her breath she began to chant. From somewhere in the depths of memory she recalled the words. A plea to the gods to grant strength to a warrior who confronted the Dark forces.

"Earth Mother, aid your daughter. Sky Father, help a warrior.

"Ka-dih, speed my arrows, let my bow not break in my hands."

She strained to break the power that held her captive. Blood pounded in her head—becoming the drums of starlight. Within that light she could see those who watched. Warriors, black eyes gleaming from where they sat proud horses. Warriors who nodded to her in recognition, war shields and lances upraised to acknowledge another of their blood. Her eyes widened at the salute. The starlight drums rolled louder as deep within she knew pride. Those who were gone returned to account her as child of their blood, true-born Warrior of the Tshoah.

Louder spoke the drums, and louder yet until her head rang, her body swayed to the raging beat of blood and drums. Deeper in her mind than she could ever have recalled consciously, a door slid open. From behind the barrier, words flowed, no ritual chant but one that built on she herself and all she was, and thus its power was greater.

> *"With the thunder I ride,*
> *daughter to Ka-dih, child of Tshoah am I.*
> *Walker on strange roads,*
> *kin to a sister, four-footed, great of heart.*
> *I do not bow to the rule of another.*
> *Let Ka-dih look upon his daughter with favor.*
> *I do not halt at another's bidding."*

Her feet lifted a little as she swayed, stamping lightly to the surging rhythm. She allowed them to carry her forward a fraction with each stamp of a foot. Strength seemed to trickle into her with each tiny movement forward.

The Tower's owner was layering the door with spells against the slamming hooves which threatened to smash the ancient wood. His words bound splinters together, froze hinges, jammed locks. Eleeri's chanting grew louder as she called on the gods of her blood. She felt the answer as power poured into her. For a fleeting moment she knew the fierce pride of those who had ridden the plains, who had been known to all as Tshoah, the enemy people.

Her head came up as her chant grew. The man spelling busily broke off his efforts. His attention slammed back to her as he shouted a word. Eleeri's voice slowed, but she forced herself to speak. It picked up speed. Now she moved forward, sword wavering in her hand. Despite further spells, her grip remained firm. The Dark one flung in all his power to hold her motionless. He failed. She slowed, but still she came on, his death glinting in her storm-gray eyes. Panicked at last, he lashed out at the wound on her arm. He would drain her blood; that would end this farce. She would learn what it was to confront a superior.

But Eleeri had bound her silver dagger over the injury as she left the shadowlands. On that the Dark one inadvertently drew, so that for seconds he convulsed in agony, silver's spirit invading his mind. He cried out, concentration quailing, and as it did so, the clay mannikin leaped out from the chair.

The tiny body powdered against the stone flooring. From it Romar's spirit rose up, entering his body as it lay flaccid against the carved wood. He remained still. He must take all the time he could to become used to it again. To allow strength to flow back into the once-empty shell. His eyes swiveled downward and his lips curved in the shadow of a grim smile.

About him yet he wore his sword belt with scabbarded sword in place. So, the evil one had been amused to allow this empty body to retain the trappings of its warriorhood. Well enough, that carelessness might come to destruction if Romar had his way—and time enough to recover. He relaxed. *If there is nothing you can do, do nothing. Fretting wastes strength,* or so his arms master had always taught him. He would wait. Hooves still struck at the door so that again and again it shuddered, booming hollowly. The very noise was infuriating the tower's master. So, too, was this female who dared to move against him. Nor did all his shouted words of power halt her snail's progress.

He moved back unconsciously, her grimness making him nervous. It was impossible she could reach him, quite impossible. But this silent inching advance was upsetting, as was that thrice-damned noise from the door. He fed power into halting her movements, drawing more from the spell which bound her friends. They appeared frozen in terror. They would keep. It was sufficient to give them back their voices, however, and Jerrany managed to turn his head slightly toward Mayrin.

"Be ready. If they can slay him, remember the gift."

She allowed her gaze to drop down to where the faint bulge in her tunic betrayed Duhaun's crystal.

"Yes."

The increase in power had done nothing. Still chanting softly, Eleeri continued her slow advance. The room was wide, but she had covered more than half the distance. His chair grated against the stone as he shifted it backward once more. The door boomed again and again. He cursed viciously. He would stop that sound if it was the last thing he did. It offended him by its very sound, implying as it did that he was unable to enforce silence. In a fury he drew power from the spell holding Eleeri. He flung it wildly against the door. That would teach those who dared batter at the entrance when he had bade them be quiet. Silence fell at the door, but from where she stood Eleeri's chant rose again.

"I do not halt at another's bidding.
I am Tshoah, kin to Far Traveler.
Let the gods make their choices,
as I have made mine. I do not eat dirt at the hands of
*   another."*

She staggered a whole pace forward as the lord of the Dark Tower gaped at her. The sword length gleamed in her slender hands.

> *"On strange roads have I walked of my own will. I*
> *do not walk with*
> *another's feet.*
> *I do not strike at another's word.*
> *I am myself and my own."*

The sword lashed out.

"Ahe!" The coup cry of her hard-riding line. The sword's point brushed the Dark one, the keen blade slicing through cloth and leather to score across the hairless chest. Blood trickled down. In shock, fury, and a sudden deadly terror, the Dark one stared at his own blood. She had injured him—she had dared! He flung himself back as the sword hummed toward him again.

He fell back still farther, frantically searching for something which might halt her creeping advance. With her gone, he could deal with those others who dared oppose him. It was only this one he feared.

The sword sliced at him once more. Again he shifted back, giving ground. The word of power came to mind then. It was risky. It might take him with it, but he had no choice. At least they'd all die with him; none should survive to count a victory. He opened his mouth to shout it in triumph—and choked. The agonizing pain in his back was more than he could bear. He choked again, his head turning sideways to stare at the figure behind him.

Romar had risen to his full height. In two hands he had taken his unsheathed sword and driven it home. Now he slumped against the seat that had been his for too long.

The Dark one glared at him in hatred and drew in a final breath. He would not die alone; he would take a revenge such as would be remembered down all the years to come. He opened his mouth to shout the word.

But even as Romar had struck, Eleeri had drawn back her blade again. It sang in flight, the tip slicing across his throat, destroying unspoken the word that might have doomed them all.

Drum thunder bellowed in her head. Somewhere beyond the room she saw the stone-headed lances toss high in salute to true-kin. Her voice lowered, deepened with triumph as she chanted the final words.

"I am myself and my own.
I am Tshoah—and thus do we serve our enemies.
I give thanks to the gods above, to Earth and Sky, to
    thunder.
I who am daughter give thanks to Ka-dih."

Before her the body of the Dark one spilled blood. The light of hatred had faded from his eyes, life from his body as it slipped slowly, bonelessly toward the chill floor. Across the table, her eyes met those of Romar. A faint smile moved his lips. Hers curved in answer.

Released from the spells, Mayrin moved first. Her fingers flashed to tear open the lacings of her tunic. From within she lifted the crystal sent her. Raising it above her head, she dashed it against the floor, watching as bright splinters flew. About them the tower began to shudder. All that had been wrought by the one they had slain was failing. Only Romar knew how much that would be. It was he who seized Eleeri and his sister by the hands.

"We must leave, now and swiftly. There is a backlash of power when a master dies. Best we are gone before it builds too high." His own strength was still small, but with the women's aid he could stagger.

Eleeri grabbed at him. "No, look."

Where the body of the Dark one had lain, mist was rising. A growing mist that shaped into the face of the man it had once been. His eyes flamed rage, hatred, vanity challenged and beaten. But from where the bright rainbow splinters lay, another mist arose. It wrapped the face in mist, enveloped it, closed in smaller and smaller until at last it thinned to reveal—nothing.

Romar breathed in deeply. His voice broke then. "That which was here is gone forever. The tower is cleansed. We have still to evade traps that may remain. But my master is no more." His hand tightened on Eleeri's. "I hail a warriorborn. I greet a friend."

Eleeri grinned. "Save the speeches for when we *are* out." Her head jerked around as the door boomed and splintered. Four Keplian heads poked inside.

Sister, are you going to stand and talk forever, or may we leave this accursed place? Tharna sent.

Eleeri grinned again and strode to join her friends. Behind her, Romar gaped. They had spoken of the Keplians. She told him of her belief that they had once been created to stand with humans in friendship. But never had he realized the majesty of the great beasts with their now sapphire eyes. Eleeri was hugging all four at once and checking for injuries. She wasn't sure what that last silencing spell might have done.

Nothing, battle-sister. It simply forbade the door to make sounds when struck.

"And he wasted power for that? It killed him."

Romar chuckled. "Thus does evil often defeat itself—with a foolish indulgence. The noise maddened him so that he used power to silence it. That power used released you somewhat, and your sword in turn drove him back to mine." He reached out to take her hand. "You know my name, but as yet I do not know yours—only that you have called yourself Tsukup. Will you favor me with it?"

His eyes were warm on her so that she felt her spirits rise. This was a warrior, wise in that he gave credit to another. She had not been able to tell him all the story. He knew not as yet that they were far-kin. But for now that was not what he asked. In turn her fingers tightened on his hand.

"I am Eleeri," she said quietly. "Now let's get out of here." Laughing, he leaned on her shoulder as she guided him through the door.

"I shall look forward to a round tale later. Also the Valley of the Green Silences must hear of all that has happened. But"—his face sobered as he gripped her arm—"I know what you risked to save me. Thanks are pitiful in contrast, but they are given."

"And unnecessary."

"But spoken nonetheless," he insisted gently. "But I would share more than gratitude."

She glanced up, to meet a look that sent blood to her face. She smiled up at him then. Well, she'd wondered if she was to be the only barren one in her canyon. It now appeared this might not be so. With a light heart, she shouldered more of his weight as they moved down the passage. There was much still to do, and perhaps in times to come, still more to be. But for now let them concentrate on escaping this trap.

Behind them, Tharna sniffed. *I scent water. Battle-sister, would it not be well to drink? The male you aid is weak from thirst.* Eleeri turned and nodded silently, gesturing the mare to search for the source. Hooves thudded lightly on marble pavement as Tharna moved to seek. Her nose poked out toward a circular spot in the blank wall.

Here.

Eleeri stepped up to lay the dagger against it. The wall seemed to writhe, then opened in a slow twisting motion. A basin protruded with a spout above. Water poured into the basin as the girl swirled her knife through it.

"No change." Her eyes questioned the others. "Safe to drink?" Romar nodded slowly, then bent forward, holding the dagger within the basin as he drank. "It seems so. Let us drink lightly and move on."

They drank one by one as the basin continued to fill. Then all shied back as from overhead came a faint slow creaking. It was as if the roof groaned at the weight of the keep above it. Jerrany glanced up worriedly.

"I think it best we move on. Sometimes when the owner is defeated, the building he commanded falls completely."

Eleeri shivered. "Then let's try to keep marching. I'd prefer not to be under this amount of stone if it does fall." The last of the Keplians had slaked its thirst and Tharna sent agreement. The corridors passed by as they marched. Eleeri had shouldered Romar's weight again; he could continue to walk, but only if he was aided.

Yet although she was growing weary, she continued to support him, trying to share with him her own strength. Hunger grew, both of body and heart. She felt warmth flow through her where his body leaned against her own. She had little to offer him, perhaps. He was son to a wealthy man, even though that one in his folly had scorned him. She was stranger, not of his blood completely. Would that matter to him? She recalled the moment when their eyes had met over a slain enemy.

Nothing had mattered then, nothing but that the enemy was dead and the captive freed.

She prayed silently to the gods now: *Let it continue so. Let us be one as more than far-kin.*

The corridor was slowly opening out into a wider hall with great windows high along one side. Through these, sunlight streamed, making pools of warmth on the chill paving they walked.

19

As they passed one of the great windows, Romar drew Eleeri toward it. He stared hungrily at the landscape. So long, so very long since he had seen grass, felt the breeze or the sun, smelled the scents of his land. His face tilted so he could look at the woman beside him. There were some who would not see the beauty there, but he was a warrior, a hunter; to him, the strength, the lithe grace were beauty, and the clean lines of her face, the proud tilt of her head. She was as lovely as a fine sword, as graceful as a wildcat. He desired her, but more than that; over the nights when only their talking had kept him sane, he had come to love.

He eyed her wistfully as they rested. He had so little to offer. He was brother-in-law to a keep lord, but all that brought him was friendship. Mayrin would give him gifts if he wed, but they would get nothing from the grim old man who'd fathered them. Last word had been that he had wed again, some girl left husbandless by a sword in battle.

She brought to him one child. Rumor had it that another would soon come, and that the old man had promised her the keep as regent if so.

True or not, to claim his birthright he would have to return to his father's hold. Give up the wild lands out here which he had come to love so strongly. No—let this girl and her heir keep what was promised. He'd make a holding out of these lands and name them his.

If only . . . if only this one beside him, her flank warm against his, would accept a penniless hunter. He watched her face; he did not think she would be swayed by greed. She was not of that kind. But all women desired homes, and he had none to offer her. He wondered briefly where it was that she lived. Somehow they had never spoken of that in their dreams. She had probably feared to give a clue to her hiding place, should he break under the Dark one's use. Curiosity claimed him then. Where *did* she dwell out here in the wild lands? Once they were free of the tower, he would ask. If it was big enough for two, maybe she would share. He could bring a hunter's skills, a warrior's training, some little gear and goods. He gathered himself as Jerrany signaled the end of resting. Gods, let them just be free.

They marched with a slow, wary care. But the passages remained light, the traps unsprung, if traps there were. Nor did the distance seem as far. It was only Romar's weakness that slowed them. He had to rest often. Each time was an opportunity to catch up on what their friends had done.

Tharna spoke for the Keplians, as usual. *We waited, but you did not return. The signal came, so that we knew our kin would have ceased to hold that one's attention at the river. When you still came not, we became anxious for you. The door in the outer tower wall was yet open, so we entered. Some of the passages were too small for us, but we could follow others. We could feel our sister, and that tie we followed until we reached the place where you confronted the evil one.*

"You did not pass through a great cave far below?"

The mare looked surprised. *No, we moved upward always. It took little time before we found you.*

The humans blinked at each other with interest. This place was a maze, Eleeri thought. You really *could* get there from here—and anywhere else, too, it seemed. Not that it mattered much; she'd be delighted if she never saw the tower again, let alone tramped its endless corridors. They came to another just as Romar stumbled, dragging her almost to the ground as she sought to hold him up. They rested a little then Tharna poked a sly nose at her. *I could carry your mate for a while, if he would permit?*

She had not mind-sent to Eleeri alone, so that all turned to stare, first at the mare, then at the blushing woman.

Jerrany grinned. "Ha, spring has come early, it seems." His wife flung herself at Romar and Eleeri, almost sending them to the ground again. Jerrany's hand caught them, lending a moment's strength.

"Careful, Mayrin, or he won't be in any shape for a wedding."

Eleeri's blush deepened, "Hoi, I haven't been asked; don't let anyone's mounts run away with them."

"Not been asked, eh? Romar must be getting slow in his old age."

Romar straightened. "Thank you, brother. I can speak for myself." His eyes sought her face and read the answer to his wonderings. Gently, he took her hand and pulled her to front him. "Would you consider a man who has nothing? I can bring no lands, no wealth; I have little of the power, and no one has ever called me handsome. Nor am I any longer so young. I might have some possessions, did I return to my father's keep and bow to him. But that I will not do, even for love."

"Nor would I wish you to!" Eleeri broke in hotly. "Mayrin told me all about it. He's a fool not to see what sort of a son he had."

Romar's eyes lit up. "I have nothing," he warned again.

"You have strength and courage, intelligence and sense. What more do you need?" Her face turned away a little shyly. "I understand you are supposed to wed for lands here. I can bring those, but they are half yours already." She watched as he peered at her in bewilderment.

"Let's take Tharna up on her offer. I'll explain as we move." They marched on, with Eleeri talking, telling of her journey into the mist and the tale as it had been told to her. At the end he drew a deep breath.

"So this canyon and keep are ours by birthright?"

"So our far-kin said."

He reached down for her hand. "I would not wish to live there alone, nor to drive you out." His voice faltered. "I am no great catch, so my father assured me. Yet if you would share my life and all else, I would love you. I—I *do* love you, my most valiant lady." He was forcing his words now. He had spoken lightly to women before, but never seriously. Never opening his heart to one for whom he cared as he did for this slender gray-eyed daughter of another people.

"You're sure you don't just want to have things convenient? The keep is half yours, and—"

His hands shot out to grab her shoulders. His distress gave him sudden strength so that he shook her a little. "No, I do *not* want to have things conveniently arranged. I *love* you! If you don't love me, if you don't want me, then the lands are yours. I'll remain with Mayrin and Jerrany. I know I have so little to offer; I know—" It was his turn to halt as he realized that her eyes were alight with laughter.

"I believe you, I believe you. Just don't shake me to death. It'd be a poor start to a betrothal."

"You will—I mean, you really do—you're sure you—"

Eleeri put a gentle hand over his mouth. "I mean, I love you, I will wed you, and will you stop talking long enough to kiss me?" There was a long silence, broken only by whoops of approval from their friends.

As they broke apart, Tharna pushed her nose curiously toward her kin-sister. *Does this mean you'll foal now?* she queried.

Eleeri started giggling helplessly, joined by Romar and his kin.

"Give me a chance, Keplian," Romar found breath to answer.

I am Tharna.

"Thank you. Then give me a chance, Tharna, and my thanks also for carrying me. As for foals"—he smiled down into Eleeri's eyes—"I think there may be a foal or two in years to come. Just don't rush us."

The mare nodded, starting to walk on. Eleeri walked beside her, her fingers tight within Romar's hand.

All journeys must end, and this one did so into bright sun. Romar shaded his eyes and allowed himself to slip from the broad back onto the sweet-scented grass. He dug his fingers into the earth, studying the brown, crumbling soil in his hand. He'd feared he would never see this again. But beyond hope, on the other shore of despair, one had come to bear him back. No, not one alone; his sister, his sword-brother, and, beyond belief as well, four Keplians. He grinned, laying back on the soft grass.

"I think I'm dreaming all this."

Eleeri dropped down beside him. "Then dream this,

too." She laid her mouth against his, kissing him with love and passion.

He grinned, folding his arms about her and returning the kiss. Then Jerrany cried out, looking upward. As they spun to follow his look, they saw that the tower was slowly crumbling. The top eroded, the door through which they had entered and departed slammed shut. Behind it they could hear stone falling in a long, slow rumble that echoed far into the distance, as if it receded into immeasurable dimensions.

"I think it best we leave here," Jerrany muttered.

There was no disagreement with that as they scrambled onto Keplian backs. At a steady canter, they swept over the plains toward the mountains. There was no hesitation; Romar was not fit to be aught else but abed for a while. They would return to the lake keep until his health and strength returned. This they did, as Mayrin and Jerrany rode on to the Valley of the Green Silences to make report of events and reclaim their children.

They returned with pack ponies and a tail of riders. Eleeri flew out to meet them, Romar at her heels. "It's good to see you back, sister. But what's all this? Have you looted someone's hold?"

Her sister-to-be laughed. "No, but we paid a visit to my father." She giggled as her brother's head came up sharply. "We dropped hints about Romar's wealthy bride and how she had lands and a keep. He said that he would not be shamed before you. So he—ah—sent a few things as bride gifts."

Eleeri surveyed the pack ponies with awe and amusement. "Just how much of this is for us, then?"

Jerrany, too, was smiling widely. "All of it. It isn't as much as it looks, mostly bulk rather than riches, but I think you'll find it all useful. The ponies should go back, both of them, and you could add a few of those furs of yours as a kin-gift in return."

She nodded. The last load she'd brought here had been hides and weapons from the ancient keep armory. There were still many furs safely held in the canyon, well cured and tanned in a variety of sizes and types. Out here they had little value, save to be used. But in the valley, surrounded by more civilized holds and holdings where such furs were no longer obtainable, they were of greater worth. She could make up a pack of the finest, including several of the rasti pelts. That would make eyes open.

Meanwhile, Mayrin had seized her brother's arm. "How are you? Are you completely well? You still look pale. Are you eating enough?"

He hugged her. "I am well, I eat like a snowbear, and I will be brown soon enough." He turned just in time to catch his balance as an avalanche of two children descended upon him. He had been gone almost a year, but neither had forgotten their adored uncle. By the time the excitement had died down a little, they were all within the main courtyard, helping unload the ponies. Eleeri glanced at Mayrin.

"Who are these new people? More to add to your menie?"

"No, to yours. They'll stay here for a few weeks so we can teach them sense about the lands. Then those who wish will come on to your keep. Here they can also meet the canyon Keplian and see they mean no harm."

Eleeri hesitated. She had never considered that they must do more than continue to camp out in the large building. If she would take up the lands, it must be run as a proper holding. She sighed softly. Life was about to change again.

Then she drew back her shoulders. The last change had

been for the good. She had found a land to live in, a mate to love, family, friends, and something to fight for rather than against. She would not fear more change. She turned to look at Romar as he pulled another bundle from the pony. If all changes brought her such joy, then she would run to meet them.

He must have sensed her eyes, for he turned to look at her. Then he handed the package to Jerrany and strolled across. His hands gathered her against his heart. Eleeri looked up as he bent his head to kiss her. She would not fear change. She was a warrior. She would meet it as she had met so many other changes these last few years.

And now she would meet nothing alone. Beside her Romar would stand—swordmate, shieldmate, and beloved. She smiled, relaxing against him. And in her heart she breathed a silent prayer of thanks to the gone-before ones. Their path had in the end brought their daughter home.

Thus this story is recorded in the records of Lormt, where word came many months later. Strange things come out of the ruined lands of Karsten since the turning. This tale is one more. Nor is it likely to be the last. For when powers stir deeply, old secrets rise again.